SULTRY, CARESSING MAGNOLIA-SCENTED BREEZES ...
SUDDEN, FIERCE THUNDERSTORMS ...

Nights of beauty and enchantment
igniting desire as tumultuous and thrilling
as a lightning-split sky,
as warm and enveloping as a late-summer swelter

In these original stories, these three
talented authors of romantic fiction present
the many faces of summer—and unexpected love.

Sandra Chastain
Helen Mittermeyer
Patricia Potter

Sizzle with the summer heat ...
Shiver with the timeless passion of ...

Southern Nights

Southern Nights

Sandra Chastain

•

Helen Mittermeyer

•

Patricia Potter

FANFARE™

BANTAM BOOKS
NEW YORK • TORONTO • LONDON • SYDNEY • AUCKLAND

SOUTHERN NIGHTS

A Bantam Fanfare Book / July 1992

ISBN 0-553-29815-1

Published simultaneously in the United States and Canada

Bantam Books are published by Bantam Books, a division of Bantam Doubleday Dell Publishing Group, Inc. Its trademark, consisting of the words "Bantam Books" and the portrayal of a rooster, is Registered in U.S. Patent and Trademark Office and in other countries. Marca Registrada. Bantam Books, 666 Fifth Avenue, New York, New York 10103.

PRINTED IN THE UNITED STATES OF AMERICA

RAD   0 9 8 7 6 5 4 3 2 1

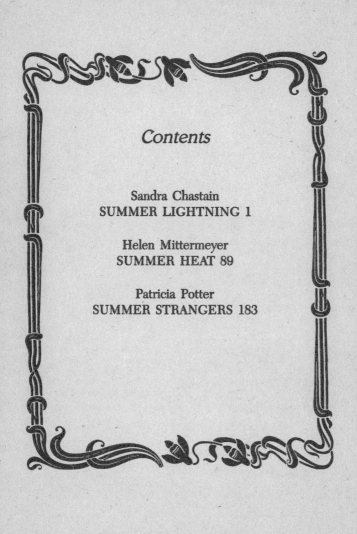

Contents

Summer Lightning

Sandra Chastain

Author's Note

I grew up reading A Streetcar Named Desire and Cat on a Hot Tin Roof. Tennessee Williams, F. Scott Fitzgerald, and William Faulkner were my idols because they wrote of real people with dark secrets and unrestrained passion.

What more could I ask for than an opportunity to re-create those same tempestuous emotions fanned to fire against the primitive elements of a Southern night?

"Summer Lightning" had to tell the story of two volatile, lonely people whose hearts have been hurt, of desire that wouldn't be denied, of a relationship as intense as the summer storm that sweeps across the night, splitting the sky with fire.

Samantha Lorrimar is every woman who wants love, who is desperate to find her own way and determined to change her life. Joe Rydon is every man who has been wounded, who has been to the mountaintop and crashed in the valley of loneliness beyond. This is their story, a story of anguish and love and forever, of souls that reach out and touch, bringing the solace that comes only from hearts made whole.

And so, dear reader, take off your shoes, find a spot where you can be alone and experience the pain of hurting love songs, the joy of eating strawberries with the one you love, the hot intensity of unbound passion, and the sweet dream of fantasy made real.

Come South, dear reader, and experience Southern Nights.

1

She could feel his pain.

For two nights she'd heard him playing his guitar, his fingers testing the chords, adding, changing. He'd reach a certain point and stop. Then he'd curse. Across the garden she could hear his words, words not of defeat but of anger, and she could see his silhouette as he stood in the doorway and stared out into the garden.

Unable to sleep, she'd shared those dark hours with him from afar, the consequences of her own actions flooding her mind as she paced her rented room and listened. The silence seemed to magnify the haunting sounds of his music as it cut through the emptiness like shards of ice piercing a heart.

Who was he, she wondered, this man of pain whose music reached out with the intensity of a physical caress and made her body tingle in response? She didn't know, but as she listened, she longed to tell him that she understood. She too knew loneliness, and she felt every nuance of the pain transformed into sound. Wearing only her chemise, she leaned against the window frame and felt the whisper of night air hot against her skin.

Yes, she understood his music and the frustration of searching for the elusive note that wouldn't come. But more clearly she understood darkness and the comfort it offered to someone who wanted to hide.

For days the doctors had told her that her scars would fade, that her memory would return, either in bits and pieces or all at once without warning. The doctors had reassured her by saying that someone, somewhere would be looking for her. For days the fog of her memory had been impenetrable. And then she'd stopped wondering who she was. She'd realized with growing certainty that she didn't want to be found.

Until that morning three days ago when a man *had* come looking for her. She'd heard him talking to her doctor outside the door of the hospital sunroom, where she was dozing, fighting the half memories that ran elusively through her mind. "Roger," he said, ". . . her manager."

At the sound of that voice her memory had returned with a jolt. And she'd panicked as dread and regret swept over her. She'd escaped from a life she'd grown to hate. She wouldn't go back. Without stopping to consider her action, she sprang to her feet, and a short time later, wearing borrowed clothing, her cache of money hidden in her pocket, she'd slipped out of the hospital and fled into the streets of Nashville.

A taxi driver had told her about Candy Payne, the grande dame of country music who sometimes rented rooms to Music City hopefuls. Candy had agreed to rent a room to her and supply her meals, but other than that she'd left her alone, offering peace without question.

It was the midnight man across the way in Candy's guest house who intruded, whose music ran round the edges of her mind and touched the hidden part of her, the shadowy partitions that for a while had captured her memory and held it hostage.

He began again, playing the same poignant refrain, reaching for a new combination of notes, breaking off when they didn't work.

Like some hypnotic command the melody called to

her, drew her, pulled her with relentless bands of need that touched emotions she was just now discovering.

As she listened, the last breath of air died and the heat fell heavy across the night, intense, stifling. She could have turned on the air conditioner, but she didn't. She'd been cold for so long that she welcomed the heat. Dark clouds billowed up from behind the treetops like plumes of searing smoke blocking out the stars. In the distance she heard the reverberation of thunder. A different kind of wind ruffled the trees and the lace curtains at her windows. Perspiration beaded her forehead. She opened all the windows and doors, letting the air inside to wrap around her.

From across the garden the music caught at her, building in intensity, tugging, forcing her to accept its pull, until she could no longer contain her feelings. Her thoughts whirled in her head. No matter what happened, she'd made the decision to be free, and she'd deal with the consequences. Once she'd loosened the chains of her past, her fear abated and she found herself responding, allowing not her mind but some answering emotion deep inside her to reply.

She pushed open the screen and walked barefoot into the garden, feeling the grass wet and spongy between her toes. The fragrance of a magnolia tree heavy with blossoms filled the Tennessee air and nibbled at the last trace of restraint in her mind. She could see him now. At least she could see the silhouette of the man holding his guitar.

She couldn't see his face clearly, but as she glanced around the shapes and shadows of the room, she recognized a piano, a light-color couch, and a mirror that was reflecting the light spilling from the end of a hallway.

In a low, rich voice the man began to sing, stumbling over the words, changing them as he played. He sang of the end of summer, of the end of love, of letting go. The melody was delivered with such poignant beauty that she felt her heart twist.

Letting go? Endings. The end of summer. No, not the end of summer, the end of Samantha. Summer was only just beginning to come to life. She moved quietly across the patio, through the open glass doors, and into the room. Intent on his music, the singer never heard her bare feet on the polished wood floor. He didn't hear the piano seat sigh as she sat down and waited.

As if she were inside his mind, she felt his frustration, understood the emotion he was searching for. And when he reached the point where his notes stopped, she put her fingers on the piano keys and completed the refrain.

There was a long silence.

The man laid his guitar down on the floor and stood. "Who are you?"

I don't know yet, she could have whispered. But that answer, like the music, remained within some secret part of her, and instead she said softly, "My name is Summer."

"Summer. Summer who appears in the dark of the night, bringing beauty and music to a man who badly needs both?"

Scars forgotten in the shadows, she moved toward him, drawn not only by his need but by hers and the compelling connection that seemed to join them. There was a sensual power to the man, more potent at close range than from a distance. "Yes. You called out to me. I've been listening."

"I know. I don't know how, but I felt your presence. How could you know the end to my song?"

He'd come close enough for the light from behind her to flicker against his face. He was tall and thin, too thin.

His face was hollowed as if he were very tired, and his dark hair was combed back from his face.

There was an eerie understanding between them, a rightness that caught and held her. She had no urge to turn and flee. "I—I don't know," she admitted. "Does it matter?"

"Summer," the man repeated. "No, it doesn't matter. You're part of the music of the night. Come closer." He held out his hand.

She hesitated, drawn to the man by some unexplainable urge, yet unable to step into the light. She didn't flinch when his hand gently encircled her wrist.

"You're trembling," he said. "Don't be afraid of me. Don't ever be afraid of me."

"I'm not," she explained. "I think that I'm afraid of me." He continued to hold her hand, but he remained at arm's length, as if he were allowing her to get used to his presence.

"An earring?" she asked, catching its glitter in the light. A dream, she could have said as she took a step closer to touch his face.

"Barefoot?" he asked, touching her foot with his own. Beautiful, he could have said, for though he couldn't fully see it, he could feel her beauty. In the gray, velvety shadows she stood like a ghostly vision, pale and shimmering in the half-light. Even her skin glowed. Whatever she was wearing caught the light and gave off an aura of silver.

The air was heavy and smothering. Closer now came the loud rumble of sound, followed by a flash of lightning. A quick, brisk wind suddenly swept through the pine trees with the sound of a long whisper, ruffling the magnolia leaves and slamming a door inside the house, plunging the room into darkness.

She took in a quick breath.

He pulled her closer, and when he put his arms around her, she felt comforted. As the rain began to fall in the garden beyond, she leaned her face against his chest. The beat of his heart matched the rhythm of the approaching storm.

She felt as though she were in a dream, as she had when she'd woken in that hospital bed. But that dream was cold, and this dream was alive with warmth. She didn't know who this man was, but she'd stopped asking questions for which there were no answers. Wherever she was, she was supposed to be there. She'd been expected, though neither of them had known. She'd brought him answers to questions he'd voiced through his music. And he was offering her solace.

She smelled the rain. The still, heavy humidity of a Southern storm wrapped them in a sensual heat. She felt his chest hair against her breasts with every breath.

Silk, he thought. She was wearing some little wispy silk thing with thin, nothing straps and a bottom that barely came to her thighs. It was soft and slippery, moving silently between their bodies. Her hair was very long, brushing against the back of his hands as he caressed her bottom.

His left leg twinged, and he shifted his weight to the right one, the movement bringing his knee between her legs. She wasn't wearing anything beneath the silk. The thought stole his breath away.

The thunder rumbled closer. The lightning pierced the darkness, and the rain fell. As if in a dream, he lifted her in his arms.

"What?"

"Shush." He hushed her question with his lips, lips that spoke of loneliness and gentle caring, lips that promised refuge from the storm.

And with his touch her past faded out of her mind.

The lonely pain, the pure frustration of being totally controlled, all disappeared with his touch. In the darkness she gave in to her pent-up longings. She slipped her arms around his neck and parted her lips to taste him. For this night it didn't matter who he was. It didn't matter who she was. It mattered only that they were two people who needed each other.

He carried her down the hallway to his bedroom, finding the bed in the darkness with his knee. He fell across it, pinning her beneath him. The kiss deepened with a hunger fired by fierce need, his lips no longer tasting, exploring, but asking, and receiving promises in return. The hand beneath her knees found its way upward, where it caught her bare bottom and held it, lifting her into the arousal that had managed to find its way through the opening in his briefs.

She was caught up in the feel and taste and touch of the man. Her legs parted automatically, and she felt him throbbing against her. The hand behind her neck caught the straps of her chemise and peeled them down to free her body to his touch. Ridged, calloused fingertips caught her breast and lifted it to reach the mouth that claimed with passionate demand.

Totally starved for the taste of her, this woman of mystery who came to him in the night, he moaned. Flexing fingertips released her breast and moved beneath her once more so that he caught her in the vise of his desire.

She felt as if she were on fire. She would never again be what she had been. She had a new name now. She'd become Summer, and Summer, with no past and no present, was free to do whatever she chose. Long-held emotions ripped loose and swept through her. Need, uncertainty, fear, and joy all merged into a glorious rampage of fire that burned away the last thread of reason. And then he was inside her, and she was welcoming him, wrapping her legs around him, urging him on with undefined whispers of love. What had been a smoldering blaze was now an inferno that crested into savage release, exploding over and over again like the sizzle of hot ash in the icy sea of her thawing emotions.

He groaned and fell atop her, moving one hand from beneath her to gently hold her breast. After a long shuddering moment he rolled over, carrying her with him, arranging her head in the curve of his shoulder and holding her against his heart.

She didn't speak, and neither did he. The moment was too powerful, too stark. Her breathing slowed, and she felt a tightness in her throat. Moisture collected in her eyes. She couldn't believe it, but tears slid down her cheeks.

"Why are you crying?"

"It's being close. I've never been close to anybody like this before."

"I know. Me too," he said, and she understood.

The thunder and lightning ended in a steady rain that closed off the outside world. She wondered briefly how she'd survived without this kind of closeness. Why now, after all these years of being a puppet, trying to please her parents first, then Roger, why had she never tried to please herself? She was beginning to understand that she knew nothing about herself, about the woman she'd been. And she didn't care. She'd left her past behind in a Nashville hospital. The woman being held by this incredible man was Summer. And Summer was safe in his arms.

There were no questions, no explanations. There was only touch and taste and feel. The second time he loved her it was with incredible gentleness. The second time he brought her to the edge of pleasure, it was with joy and such a sense of completeness that she immediately fell into the kind of relaxed sleep that healed and expanded into a quiet peace.

It was sometime before dawn that she woke and heard him playing again. Their song, the song of summer love lost and found. Except this time he completed the refrain. This time her notes were blended into his melody with simplicity and beauty.

Alone in the massive oak bed she lay, the sheet draped across her. The musky smell of lovemaking remained in the air, the scent of him on her body, and the feel of him still inside her. She shifted, feeling desire, yes, but something else. Crashing over her like the thunder from the night before came a sense of dread, not over what they had shared but over its impending loss.

She'd never known love before, but now that she had, how could she ever exist without it? She felt as if she'd been born this night, in this stranger's arms. Her mind had been blank, now the only memory it held was new and precious—one of loving a man in a storm. She trembled. She knew that this was a borrowed moment in time, a moment she couldn't be certain she had the right to claim.

Slipping out of bed, she stood, incredibly weak, and leaned against the bedpost to gather her strength. Beyond the window she could see the daylight throwing watery pastel smears of color across the garden. Draped over the chair was a man's robe. Leaving her ruined chemise behind, she slipped the robe on, tiptoed to the door, and listened. He was still playing, softly now, patterning a different tune, a peaceful sound.

She stepped through the open glass doors and sprinted across the garden and into the room she'd moved into three days earlier.

Only when she was safe inside did she allow herself the luxury of a deep, shuddering breath. She'd gotten away. He hadn't asked questions or discovered that she wasn't the sensual being he'd believed her to be. She didn't know why, but it was important that he knew only the woman Summer.

Somewhere in the twisted wreckage of a crash on the freeway, she'd left her past behind. The hospital, surgery, and pain were part of the painful cleansing process, the ritual of her rebirth, the method by which she'd been made new.

She was Summer now. And Summer had been loved by a midnight man.

2

He couldn't remember whether her eyes were pale blue or gray, he knew only that in the flash of lightning they'd made him think of iridescent pewter. He did remember that her hair was long and straight, silver with a hint of gold.

Joe sat in the morning sunlight and tried to recall the woman who'd appeared like a forerunner of the storm. He'd had visions before. Hell, he'd had his share of hallucinations, but the woman who'd come to him in the night had been real. Because of her he'd finished the song. She'd brought him an ending so strong and vibrant that he'd been compelled to leave her arms and play it through again.

Then, when he'd returned to his bed, she'd been gone. He hadn't been surprised. The women he cared about always left him. This one, though unbelievably beautiful, was no exception.

Joe sighed. After the plane crash his brother Brian, who'd never hurt anybody or anything in his life, had come to him over and over again in his dreams, pleading with Joe not to send the band away without him. But Joe had been invincible, riding on a wave of success that hid his pain and insecurity, blinding him to the needs of others. Where the brothers, Brian and Joe, had once been a team, Joe Rydon had become the star.

He'd flown to Mexico in a private jet, and Brian and the band had flown in a chartered plane, straight into the side of a mountain. He'd killed them. While they'd been dying, he'd been partying on a beach in Cancún with a woman whose name he couldn't even remember. He'd survived, but to what end? Without them he'd lost his drive, his talent, and finally he'd stopped trying. He'd railed against whatever quirk of fate had taken every person he'd cared about and left him with his pain.

And then the previous night a mystery woman had come, bringing a passionate brightness into his life. But fickle fate had been only teasing him once again.

Joe stood and wandered back into the bedroom, rubbing his eyes, trying desperately to bring her back. But she was gone. Only the ripped wisp of silk confirmed that she'd been there at all. That and the finished song, the first song he'd been able to complete since he'd lost his brother.

"A Heart Made Whole," he'd called the tune. The words weren't set yet, but they would come now that he had the melody. Now that she'd brought him the final refrain. He whispered her name, Summer, as he walked back into the garden. The rain had brought a fresh, earthy smell to the air. The flowers were dappled with glistening droplets of water. He stretched, lifting his arms toward the sky as if he were a growing thing reaching for the nourishment of the sun.

She was gone. But the essence of her was still there. He sensed it. He felt it. He breathed, drawing in the scent and taste of her, the woman who called herself Summer. He was smiling, and his heart felt good. She was gone, yes, but she'd return. If not, he'd find her. He had the money to hire the best detectives—the money he'd stashed away for the time when his creative talents would dry up, as he'd always known they would, and the world would know him for what he was, a brash impostor who'd masqueraded as a star.

Inside the house his phone rang. He heard the answering machine switch on, and the voice of his manager pleading, "Joe, this is Sly. Please call me. It's been six months, man. The guys over at Scorpion are demanding a new Joe Rydon album. Talk to me, pal. Write something, even if it's terrible."

There was an expletive, and a beep. Then silence.

Joe walked back inside. He ran his fingers across the piano keyboard as thoughts of Summer slipped back inside his mind. He knew he ought to call Sly, but he couldn't. Calling Sly opened Joe up to the world again, and the world might close Summer out.

Not yet. He'd finished one song, but that wasn't enough. He'd keep working, working and waiting until *she* returned.

Joe walked over to the answering machine and turned it off. Then he picked up his guitar and returned to the garden, where he began to strum, choosing words, discarding them, and replacing ordinary ones with words that came from the heart. In what seemed to be only minutes, but was in fact hours, Brian's song was done. His pain wasn't gone, it would always be there, but he'd acknowledged it.

For the first time he was able to get past what he'd done, and accept not solace but the promise of healing. For Joe knew that in spite of his supreme arrogance in his newfound stardom, his self-centered indifference to the members of his band who had helped him achieve his fame, Brian had followed him willingly, finding a reason for every foolish whim in which Joe had indulged, understanding what it meant to succeed after so many years of trying to keep them both alive. Even at the end, when the band had boarded the plane to leave, as if he'd had a premonition, Brian had given a little salute and quipped, "Thanks for the ride, big brother."

He'd lost Brian. Now Joe had to find a way to forgive himself and learn to face the world again.

Sitting there in the garden, where the dew was still fresh and new, he started a new melody, with new notes ... "Summer's Song." He had the beginning, but there was no middle and no end.

No matter. He'd find them—and her. For now, for the first time in a long time, the warmth of the sun enveloped his body and made him feel good.

3

On one side of the garden Summer slept quietly, a deep, healing sleep without dreams.

On the other side of the small garden as the morning burst into full brilliance, Joe played his guitar, pushing back the questions that tumbled through his mind.

Who was she? Where had she come from? Would she come again? He would talk to Candy, who would have answers to his questions. No one entered Candy's domain except by invitation. But that opened him up to questions in return, questions he didn't want to deal with. Candy had every right to ask him whatever she wanted, but she never had asked anything, not even in the beginning. Even after she'd given him a job playing guitar and singing backup in her band, she hadn't asked for promises or explanations.

Ten years later he'd left to head his own group without a thought of how much he'd come to mean to her failing career. She'd torn up his contract and wished him well, because she cared about him. When he'd returned to Nashville, with no place left to go, she'd taken him in again, because she still cared.

Alone in her little guest house, he'd fought the demons in his past, and gradually, little by little, he'd begun to come back to life. He'd bought a bottle of whiskey and put it on the shelf. More than once he'd been tempted.

He'd walk into the kitchen as far as the pantry and look, but he never opened the bottle. This was the first morning in a long time that he hadn't fought off the urge to have a drink.

After lunch he took a nap, not as an escape but in anticipation, hugging the pillow, which still smelled of Summer's fragrance. When he woke, he heard the sound of the fountain in the garden as it made music in the twilight. Eagerly he rose, and taking the scrap of silk from the bureau where he'd tossed it, he rubbed it against his face, feeling the stubble of his beard catching in its threads.

Her memory lingered in his mind, filling it with excitement and promise. He wondered if she'd come to him again, if she'd stay. Across the room he caught sight of himself in the mirror and cursed. He looked like a wreck, his hair hanging to his shoulders, his face unshaven for two days, or was it three? Maybe longer. His skin looked pale, as though he'd been away for a long time.

Perhaps he had.

Quickly Joe shaved and showered. In the closet he managed to find a pair of clean jeans and a T-shirt that smelled fresh, even if it was wrinkled and faded. Socks escaped him, but he found his shoes under the bed, along with a pair of dirty underwear and a long-empty bottle.

Finally dressed and ready, he wandered through the glassed-in room he used for both his den and his studio, emptying ashtrays, collecting dishes and soft drink cans. He didn't turn on any lights while he waited. There hadn't been any lights the night before when she'd come. Restlessly, he paced, anticipating, wanting, wondering why she'd run away.

His mother had run away too. But he'd found her and had built her a house, where she'd been safe.

"Why, Mama?" he'd asked.

"It was too hard. For a long time I tried, but I couldn't be the kind of mother you needed."

"I just needed you to love me," he'd said, once he had brought her home.

"To do that you first have to love yourself. You're a success, Joe. You don't need my pain."

She'd tried to stay, but in the end she'd found another way to go. And once again Joe was lonely.

Until now. Now Summer had come.

Joe gave up waiting and called for a pizza. He met the delivery boy at the gate, tipped him, and wandered back to the house. Disappointment crushed out his happy mood. He dropped the pizza box on the counter and scowled. Hell, he didn't need some mystery woman. He didn't need a woman at all. If it hadn't been for a woman, Brian and he wouldn't have quarreled. If they hadn't quarreled, Brian wouldn't be dead. He swept the box off the counter and stormed out of the house.

At Candy's Place, the bar she owned in town, he ordered a double bourbon, straight. The bartender, an old friend, frowned, but put the drink in front of Joe. At the other end of the counter a noisy group of musicians discussed the possibilities of a record contract, embellishing the gossip, expounding on the unfairness of the industry.

"Hey." One of them glanced up at the autographed pictures on the wall. "Isn't that Joe Rydon?"

"Yeah. That's him," another commented. "Too bad. A guy like that has it all, and he blows it."

"I heard he lost it when his brother died."

"He hasn't lost it," the bartender corrected with a glance down the bar at Joe. In a stern voice that defied argument, the bartender said, "Joe's just taking some time off to charge his batteries. You guys better hope you don't have to go through what he did, losing his entire band and his brother at one time."

"Maybe," the first speaker said, "but if I ever make it to the top, I won't let the bottle bring me down."

Joe ignored them. They didn't recognize him. He wasn't surprised. He'd changed. There was a time when not being acknowledged would have crushed him. Now he was grateful for the anonymity.

As if fate were mocking him once again, the next song on the jukebox was the first song of his own that he'd recorded, the song that had sent Joe Rydon on his way, the song that he'd collaborated on with Brian. The words had been Joe's, but the music had been Brian's. They'd worked together and stayed at the top for three years.

Joe listened to the musicians as they continued to talk about his disappearance, about how he'd lost control. They were right. He wanted to refute what they'd said. But he couldn't. Dammit, they were too right. He pushed the untouched drink away, stood up, and left the bar. He'd struggled so hard for so long, then he'd become a star and he hadn't known how to be a success.

For hours Joe covered every inch of Music Row before he made his way back to Candy's guest house. It was nearly morning when he finally crashed.

He was half asleep when he felt the whisper of a kiss against his lips. She wasn't here. It was a dream, he told himself, willingly embracing the presence he'd waited for half the night. In his dream he felt the imprint of the mattress and the crumpled up coverlet beneath his back. He heard the sound of the fountain ripple through the windows. Her scent tugged at his consciousness, seducing him into a sensual spell of touch and taste and loving.

Hungrily he responded, parting her lips, sliding his tongue inside the honeyed taste of her, placing his arms around her, drawing her physically into his fantasy. A wave of heat swept over him as he heard the thunder and saw the lightning of the night before. Raindrops pelted the roof, the sound almost concealing the soft moan of the woman in his arms. The dream intensified as her breasts caressed his chest and the center of her warmth met his thigh. Then she slid forward, planting herself firmly over him.

Joe came shockingly awake, shaking with desire.

The strength of his need told him that this was no dream. She was there, sheathing him with her heat, leaning forward so that her hair skimmed his face, shielding her features from his vision.

"Who are you?" he whispered.

"Does it matter?"

A strange answer. But she was right. It didn't. All that mattered was that he needed her, and she'd come to him. She leaned forward and kissed him, her kiss as natural as the beat of his heart. He clasped her buttocks, holding her softness against him, lifting his body so that he could fill her with himself. Higher and higher, they rode the crest of an explosion that began slowly and built to a fiery release, shattering the night as they cried out in ecstasy.

She lay against him, unwilling to pull away, needing to remain connected, to prolong the intimacy of the moment. And through the window, rain drummed on. The night air lost its heat and cooled their bodies with its touch. They slept.

When he woke, the sun was high in the sky and she was gone.

Summer walked to a public phone, called the hospital, and spoke to the doctor who'd become her friend when she'd been so alone.

"Are you all right?" he asked.

"I'm fine."

"The man named Roger came back looking for you. He says your name is Samantha Lorrimar and that he's your manager. Why'd you run away?"

Samantha Lorrimar. Yes, that's who she was. No, that's who she'd been. "I don't know. I just needed to be by myself for a while."

"Your memory?"

"Yes, it's come back. I know who Roger is. Don't tell him—Roger—don't tell him anything except that I'm okay. I'll contact him later. Promise?"

The doctor agreed, eliciting Summer's promise that she'd stay in touch and return to the hospital in a few days to be checked.

She hadn't asked the doctor any questions about where Roger was staying. She didn't need to. Roger never varied his routine. He would be at the finest hotel in Nashville, in a suite on the top floor. He always stayed in the finest accommodations. "You're a star, Samantha, and you must always act the part." As a child she'd been a star, as an adult she wasn't—yet. Roger would make that happen. He had a master plan from which she was never allowed to deviate. What Samantha might have wanted wasn't important.

Adjacent to the phone booth outside the drugstore where she'd made her call was a newspaper box. Her face stared sternly at her from the front page.

At first she hardly recognized herself. The woman in the picture was wearing a basic black gown, with her hair sleekly arranged in a chignon. She had a strained, intense look about her—a haughty, successful look that dared rejection.

SAMANTHA LORRIMAR, the headline read. *CONCERT PIANIST—Missing from local hospital after accident.*

Rising new talent, the story began. Rising new talent? She'd been rising since she was a six-year-old child. Always on the move, always learning, preparing, studying, practicing for the stardom that had forever loomed like a vulture on the horizon. There were no scars on her face in the picture. There was no smile either.

She thought of her midnight lover and felt her heart quicken. In the drugstore window above the newspaper box she could see herself, and the face she was looking at, while pale and thin, was wearing a smile big enough for the world to see. No black dress now. Instead she was wearing bright new clothes she'd bought in a thrift shop, sandals and a sundress with a long skirt, a skirt that felt wonderfully free.

Reluctantly she fed coins into the box, pulled a paper from the rack, and stuck it under her arm. She'd read it later, when she was out of sight of someone who might recognize her.

Recognize her.

What about Candy Payne, her landlady? Would she have seen the picture? The story was bound to be on the television news. Would Candy report her to the authorities? Summer groaned and hurried back to the graceful old mansion.

The cab driver who'd taken her there had explained that Candy was one of the first girl singers to appear on the Grand Ole Opry, following in the footsteps of Kitty Wells and Loretta Lynn. Her house, surrounded by a high hedge-engorged fence and spacious grounds, was downtown, near the heart of the country music industry and the hundreds of people she'd given a hand to along the way. Candy, with her big heart, was everybody's friend, the driver had said.

Back at the estate, Summer knocked on Candy's door,

hoping the driver was right, that Candy would be her friend.

"Mrs. Payne?"

"Come in, child," was Candy's bright reply. "How are you today?"

Summer entered a room that was overflowing with pictures and mementos. Candy laid down the book she'd been reading and turned inquisitive eyes toward her guest. Summer stalled by walking over to the piano, studying the framed pictures that stood like a troop of marching soldiers across the top of the baby grand. "I'm fine."

She lifted a silver-framed snapshot of Candy and a tall, thin man with dark hair and a brash, devil-may-care smile. "Oh, that's—" but she didn't know his name.

"Joe," Candy supplied. "You've met Joe?"

"Yes—I mean, he lives across the garden in your guest house."

"Yes, he does."

Summer waited for Candy to offer more. She didn't. She too seemed to be waiting.

"I wanted to thank you," Summer began, "for taking me in. This is the first time I've ever—I mean, I know that it must have seemed odd for me to appear out of the blue without a suitcase or . . ."

"No need to explain, child. You needed safe haven—not questions. By the way, I've hung some clothes in your closet. I think they will fit. Feel free to use whatever you like. While you're here, my home is yours. One thing, though. Joe is . . . vulnerable right now. Be careful. I wouldn't want to see him hurt."

"Oh—you know that I—we—?"

"I know that many guests have occupied the room you are staying in, but you're the first to . . . *know* Joe. He's very special. And, I think, so are you, Samantha Lorrimar."

"You know who I am?"

"I know, and I know that you've lost your memory, or so the paper says. Is that true?"

"For a time, but not any longer. The only memories I've lost are those I want to lose."

"Take care, Samantha. We may not like who we are, but we're the sum of all the people we've met. And when we wipe the slate clean, we're like a newborn child who has to learn all over again."

"Perhaps we can then become what we choose, not what is chosen for us."

"Perhaps, like Joe, you are vulnerable too. Take care that you don't hurt yourself as well."

After his long nap Joe worked through the rest of the afternoon. By evening he'd drawn together the essence of a new song. Where "A Heart Made Whole," Brian's song, had been sad and haunting, the new tune, "Summer's Song," spoke of sheer beauty.

The sun had slipped behind the trees when he finally laid the guitar down and flexed his tense shoulders. He was hungry, really hungry for the first time in a very long time. A quick check of his pantry produced two more cans of soup, and the half empty bottle of bourbon that had mocked him for the last three months. Quickly he dressed, donned the perennial dark glasses, and drove to the market. By the time he'd finished filling his basket, he'd bought enough food to feed two people for a month.

Joe had been forced to learn to cook. His mother, when she'd been home, had usually been entertaining a man, or had been so far gone from reality that food was the last thing she'd thought about. When Brian was born, it was Joe who cared for him, saw that he went to school, lifted money from his mother or her latest friend to buy essentials. By the time they were teenagers, his mother had disappeared and Joe had started working as a dishwasher in the daytime and a guitar player in Candy's backup band at night. Brian had spent his days in school and his nights under the cook's table at Candy's Place.

But tonight Joe was cooking for Summer. This time he knew she'd return. He'd needed her to come before, and she had. He wanted to give something back to her. She'd been too thin and too tense. He recognized all the signs of someone who was in trouble, a woman whose control has been stretched to the breaking point. He'd been in her place, and now he wanted to pay back all the helping hands that had been held out to him.

Joe placed the rolls on a plastic tray to be warmed in the microwave. A chicken was roasting in the oven, and the salad greens were ready to be assembled. He smiled and began to whistle. He hadn't whistled in a long time. The tune he whistled was "Summer's Song."

As Summer looked into her closet, her resolve wavered. Roger would be angry, but if he'd listened to her pleas, she wouldn't have become desperate and this might never have happened. He'd have to learn that she was no longer a puppet to be manipulated. Sooner or later she'd have to face him—but not yet, she decided.

She found her own way to have some time alone, time to consider the direction her life was taking. Rebellion was a trait that Samantha had never thought herself capable of, but there with Joe it was easy to believe that she could leave her old life behind.

The garden, the guesthouse, Joe—it all seemed like a dream. On her worst nights, after she'd traveled all day, spent hours practicing, and finally conquered her fear of the stage so that she could perform, she'd wander, drained and spent, through her hotel suite, and dream about being with a man who wanted only to love her. Never in her wildest imagination had she ever believed there could be such a man.

She thought sadly of Roger, the pain and the disappointment. She and Roger had never made love. They'd simply had sex. Once.

Then she thought of Joe again, and her guilt and pain vanished in the memory of wild kisses and bare feet. Only with Joe had she made love. Joe . . . Joe was just across the garden, and she knew that she couldn't stay away.

The clothes Candy had left were soft, flowing garments, period pieces. Summer ran her fingertips down one of the dresses, a cream-color lace that suggested fields of wildflowers, parasols, picnics by the sea—and a lover.

Lover. Even the word brought a picture of Joe to mind, of him touching her, his expression reckless, desperate, almost as if he expected her to disappear if he let her go. She leaned against the door frame for a minute and let herself relive being loved by this reclusive, intense man.

And then she saw it, a note propped against the mirror on her dressing table. The dark, bold handwriting said simply, *Dinner at eight? Please come early so that I can see you in the light.* It was signed with a J and a squiggle that trailed off into nothing. He'd left it while she was phoning the doctor. That thought took her breath away.

She didn't need his invitation to draw her back.

Quickly she took a shower and dressed, brushing her hair, letting it fall where it would. Shoes? No, she'd go without. Somehow the absence of shoes was a symbol, an expression of her freedom. Across the thick grass carpet in the garden she glided, her heart pounding, her mind resolutely closing off any questions about the future. It was as if she'd folded Samantha Lorrimar inside the newspaper and left her on the bed back in her rented room.

Across the lawn, beyond the glass doors, Joe waited, coming to meet her as she slipped silently inside.

"You came," he said, and held out his hand, clasping hers and pulling her into the room.

"Yes."

She was more beautiful than he'd remembered. Her

eyes seemed blue in the light, veiled and distant, sending mysterious messages that he couldn't read.

"Tonight I shall feed you. Then we will talk."

"Perhaps," she murmured softly.

He smiled and led her to the table he'd prepared.

A white cloth covered its surface. In the center, fat pink roses drooped over the edge of a cut glass bowl. The flames from two white candles kissed the glass bowl, which refracted the light into a rainbow of colors across the room.

They sat, knees touching, feeding each other bites of chicken, mushrooms, and tiny pieces of bread. He said something amusing. She laughed, a light, contagious laugh that might have been out of place once. He hummed, singing little phrases of endearment and funny little rhymes that made no sense, yet seemed perfect in their nonsense.

Finally he filled their glasses with a liquid he called punch. It was pale pink and flecked with tiny segments of strawberries. He handed the drinks to her, removed from the refrigerator a bow of berries dipped in white chocolate, and sat on the floor. "Come, talk to me," he said. "I want to hear your voice and learn all about you. I'm Joe. Joe Rydon. Who is Summer?"

She followed him, dropping down beside him on the rug, leaning back against a white overstuffed couch. "Who is Summer?" she repeated, unwilling to allow any negative thoughts to spoil the moment. "Who do you want her to be?"

"I think that I want her to be mine."

He took their drinks and placed them on the bare floor at the end of the couch. Taking a large red berry, he held it to her lips, watching her take the end inside, touch it with her pink tongue, nibble daintily. With his other hand, he caught her face, then he leaned forward and captured a drop of the escaping juice with his mouth.

She closed her eyes, giving in to the touch and taste of him, sharing the sweetness of strawberry between them.

"No. Open your eyes, Summer. I am real, and so are you. No more midnight dreams. No more imaginings. No more merging with the shadows."

But for Summer the words were lost in sensation. He offered her a sip of her drink, then returned it to the floor, to be shared later to quench a different kind of thirst. His fingertips left her face and slid down her neck, skimming the swell of breasts, now exposed and straining with the need to be kissed. He opened her gown wide, pushed it to her shoulders, then slid it away, leaving her body bare to his sight.

"You are so very beautiful," he whispered.

"No," she murmured. "I'm too thin—my scars."

"Mine are deeper. You can't see them, but they're etched in my soul. Yours are almost gone." He kissed her gently. "Why did you come back to me?"

"Because for now I am Summer, and Summer needs to be with you."

He looked away, sighing for a second. "My world is chaotic. My life is filled with demons. Are you sure you want to take a chance on me?"

She opened her eyes, allowing herself to gaze at his face. Darkness was there, yes, and intensity too. But almost hidden from himself, perhaps, was hope. He needed the dream as much as she. Joe Rydon was a tortured being, holding himself too tight, waiting while she looked deep into that mass of conflicting emotions reflected in his eyes.

"Yes," she said simply, and lifted her hands to touch his face. As if memorizing his features, she examined every part of him; his brows, the fringe of velvety black lashes that fanned eyes as dark as the night he'd pushed aside to welcome her in, the tiny lines at the corners of his eyes, the frown that narrowed his lips.

"I may hurt you," he said. "I do that to those I care about, though I don't mean to."

"We may hurt each other. But will the hurt be any greater than that we've already known?"

"No. And the joy will be worth the risk."

He planted feathery little kisses across every scar on her face, as if by his very touch he could erase them. Then his lips found hers, and there were no more coherent thoughts.

"Promise me you won't leave me again," he said as he pushed his silver maiden back against the rug and moved over her.

"I promise I won't go."

He started to remove her clothes slowly, as if he were unwrapping a gift. Unfastening the remaining buttons, he opened the dress to its hem, carefully pushing it back so that she was a sculpture encircled by a lacy frame of white.

Then he stood, willing her to look at him as he removed his clothes. Kneeling beside her, he played his fingertips through her hair, arranging it across her body so that it covered her nipples. He loved her breasts. They were surprisingly lush and earthy for such a slim figure. Her nipples were pert and firm, surrounded by large, dusky circles of color.

"This is the way it should always be," he shivered, lowering himself over her, pausing for a moment as if waiting for her permission before he entered her.

She gave a soft moan and lifted herself to meet him. But in that second when he'd pulled back and waited, she'd understood that if she'd wanted him to stop, he would have. Then the pleasure she felt drowned out the last lingering reservations about what she was doing, and she took him inside her.

She was tight, moist, and hot. Joe realized, as he unconsciously had the first time, that she was inexperienced, almost shy in her movements. His virginal vision had known a man, but not recently and not with the total intimacy they'd shared. Joe felt a great sense of commitment steal over him, and he pledged to give to this woman, give her as much as her presence was giving to him.

There was no storm this night, no lightning, no pounding reverberation of the elements to feed the fury of their passion. It was real and powerful, and all he'd ever dreamed loving a woman could be. He could feel the rapid pulse at the base of her throat, the pounding of her heart against his chest. Her body writhing beneath him, searching for, pleading for the ultimate pleasure.

"Not so fast, darling," he said, lifting himself so that he could feast on her breasts, circling one nipple with his fingertips as he captured the other with his mouth, pulling at the tightly knotted bead. As she began to moan, he pulled away, sliding out of the tight sheath of her heat, moving his lips lower and lower. But when he came to the soft down that cradled her secret parts, he felt her suddenly go still.

"Joe?"

"Ah, yes, my love. Let me hear you call my name as I love you." And his lips nibbled their way lower, centering on the apex of her desire.

"What are you doing?"

"I'm loving you, darling, where no man has touched you before."

"Yes." If she'd been in control of her senses, she might have questioned how he knew, but she didn't. The hot pleasure that was already rippling through her on stormy waves was something she'd never known before, and she gave herself freely over to him.

His mouth found the spot he was seeking, applying light teasing flicks of his tongue with results that sent Summer into new spirals of delight so intense, she could hold back no longer.

And then he caught her body with his hands and lifted her, thrusting inside her, catching the eruption of her climax just as he reached the zenith of his own explosion.

As the last lingering sensation died away, he rolled over, bringing her with him, holding her close as the candles on the table beyond burned down and the night dropped its curtain of darkness over them.

"Such music we make together, darling," he finally said. "There are no mere words to express what we just said to each other."

"Now," he said, after allowing her to sleep for a bit, "it's time we talk." He lifted himself to one elbow so that he loomed over her. "Who is Summer?"

Samantha lay very still, listening to her heart pounding. What could she say? How could she tell him that she didn't know? How could she not tell the truth? She'd been with this man in the most intimate way possible. What difference could it make who she was, or who she wasn't? No more fantasies, she was forced to resign. This was only temporary. Sooner or later, no matter what she wanted, Summer would disappear and Samantha would return.

"For a while I didn't know who I was," she finally said.

"We all reach that point," he agreed.

"No. You don't understand. I lost my memory. But it came back to me. I think that I liked it better when I didn't know."

Awareness seeped into him. "You mean you really lost your memory?"

"Yes. I was on a bus. The bus was caught in a rainstorm and skidded off the side of a mountain. When I came to, I had a concussion and my face was badly scratched."

"The scars," he whispered, touching his lips to them again. *An accident. She'd crashed, and she'd survived the accident.* He couldn't explain the impact of that revelation. It was as if fate had stopped laughing and said, "Maybe, Joe Rydon, maybe I'll offer you another chance."

"Yes. For a while I had no memory of the person I once was. That's why when you asked me who I was, I said Summer. I don't much like the person I was before."

"There was a time when I tried to lose my memory. I tried in every bar and every bottle in half this country. But it didn't work. Every time I woke, I was still Joe Rydon."

"I know," she said simply. "I was still the same woman I tried to run away from—until I met you and became Summer."

"Maybe that was my problem. I never met anybody like you. But how did you come to be here, in Candy's house, in my arms?"

"Once my memory returned, I—I ran away from the hospital. A taxi driver recommended this place. He said Candy often took in young hopefuls. I think he thought I was a destitute would-be singer."

"And are you destitute?"

"No, of course not. I have enough money—" But she didn't. The small amount of money she'd found in her skirt pocket was almost gone. To claim her money, she'd have to go back, and she couldn't—not yet.

"So if you're not Summer, who are you?"

"You haven't watched the news or read a paper, or you'd know."

"No. I don't pay much attention to the outside world," he admitted, cupping her face with his hand. The last of the candlelight disappeared, and the only light left was from the moon shining in the garden.

"Tell me." He'd just made love to her, just taken her with the same intensity they'd shared the first two times, and already he felt himself stirring to life again.

"My name is Samantha Lorrimar."

"Samantha Lorrimar," he repeated, the name settling on him with familiarity. "Why do I know that name? Are you a movie star?"

"No." She could feel him hardening against her hip. Lifting her face, she sought his mouth with her lips, swallowing his words and his questions. He didn't refuse, kissing red, swollen lips long and hard, then pulling back.

"And you're not a singer, or I'd know you." Joe's gaze caught the consternation his questions were causing, and he hushed. "You really don't want to be Samantha Lorrimar, do you?"

Still shaken from the power of his kiss, she strained to answer. She could have said that she didn't want to be *what* Samantha was, not *who*. "No. Samantha was a creation, a shadow person who went through life doing what she was told to do. One day she didn't know herself anymore, and her mind just erased itself. I saw her picture on the front page of the newspaper. She didn't even look like Summer."

"Then Summer is the woman you will be, my darling. Nobody else will know but me."

"Candy knows. She—she warned me about you."

"Warned you about me?" Joe didn't mean for his voice to be so abrupt. But it was unlike Candy to talk about people. Why would she warn this woman about him?

"Warned me not to hurt you."

He looked at her for a long time in the darkness, drinking in the essence of her, the protective way he felt, the need he had to possess her completely. "I think, my darling, that it might be the other way around."

"She warned me about that too."

Tree frogs talked to each other in the garden while Joe and Summer ate the rest of their strawberries and drank the frothy drinks. At one point Joe poured the last of his across her stomach and licked away every drop of the sweet liquid. Summer returned the gesture, finding that tasting his body was much more intriguing than drinking from the glass.

It was very late when Joe lifted her and carried her into the bathroom. He turned on the shower and stepped inside, adjusting the shower head so that they were sprinkled with a fine mist of cool water.

Afterward, when he'd dried her and laid her on his bed, he sat beside her and took her hand. "Summer, I've been responsible for most of the pain in my life, but I just want you to know that you don't have to be afraid to love me—I'll take care of you."

"I don't want you to take care of me, Joe. I want to take care of myself. I've never done that before."

"But, Summer, my darling, you need me. You're so innocent, you let me love you without a thought of the consequence. You need to know that I've been pretty wild, but until now, I've never taken any chances."

She didn't understand what he was saying.

"Darling, we didn't use anything when we made love, and I just thought you ought not to worry." Almost as an afterthought he asked, "Are you on the pill?"

"No, not anymore." Suddenly it was as if Roger had come crashing unwanted into the room with them. He'd bought the pills before he'd ever tried to make love to her. She'd taken them for a week, and then she'd refused. She wanted no part of Roger's body, or the pills, ever again. When he'd understood, he hadn't even yelled at her. He'd simply nodded and left her, his anger totally in control.

"Roger," she said, and flinched.

"Who's Roger?"

Joe didn't have to be told that Roger was somehow responsible for hurting Summer. He could feel it in her sudden tension.

"He's my manager. I wanted him to do something. He didn't even consider my wishes. I ran away from him. Finally he came to the hospital looking for me. I didn't want to go back with him."

"Did he hurt you?"

"No. At least not physically."

"Are you sure?"

"Roger has looked after me since my parents died. He cares about me. He has for a long time."

"Your manager? Well, it's pretty obvious that you're into music."

"Yes. I play the piano. All the news media know that I've disappeared. Roger must be frantic to find me."

"Do you want to call him?" Joe felt a dread as he asked the question. He liked being there, alone with Summer. He liked it that nobody knew about them, about their pasts or what they had found together, but he knew what Roger must be going through, losing someone he cared about.

"No!" She caught his arm and held him close. "I don't want him to know yet. Once he knows, he'll insist that I go, and I don't want to leave."

"And I don't want you to go. But it's very hard to hide.

You can disappear from the world but not from yourself, not forever, Summer," he said, then added, "Samantha."

"Why not? You have. Please, Joe, call me Summer and don't make me think about who I really am. Let me stay with you. I need to be Summer, just for a while."

And he wanted her to stay, to belong to him. He didn't want any other man touching her. If she wasn't on birth control, she might already be carrying his child. That thought stunned him, so much so that he lay back and reclaimed her, drawing her into the space beneath his heart. He understood about finding a place to hide. He could give her refuge, maybe not forever but for now. They would be safe there for as long as he could keep the world closed out.

The loneliness he'd lived with for so long was breaking into tiny bits and disappearing into the night. Each time they came together, their secrets seemed less important and they became more secure. Each time they were joined, it seemed more right. Now, in the moonlight he studied her.

Samantha Lorrimar. He'd heard that name, but he couldn't bring an identity to it. No matter. Samantha was tied to a man named Roger. Samantha was locked in her past, just as he'd kept the memory of Brian locked in his. They'd keep the memories frozen back there where they could be controlled. The truth was an unwelcome intrusion, and he'd put it off as long as he could.

They'd face reality when they had to. Behind these walls they had each other, and that was enough.

5

They were sitting in bed, propped against their pillows. Joe was feeding her strawberry ice cream with an antique silver spoon. The tantalizing smell of perking coffee wafted in from the kitchen.

Summer felt as if she'd created a fantasy and stepped into the middle of it. She glanced over at Joe, who was staring off into space with a silly, relaxed grin on the face she'd called too thin only a short time before. In only two days her life had completely changed from a controlled schedule to what her parents would have considered a shameless life of decadence. They would have been wrong. She couldn't see her face, but she was pretty sure it looked as satisfied as Joe's.

"The note you left on my pillow, how'd you know I was renting Candy's room?"

"Candy told me."

"Oh." Though she wasn't surprised at the disclosure, Summer was disappointed. Candy had made it plain that she had Joe's interests at heart. Still, Summer had hoped her landlady would keep her presence a secret. But of course her loyalty to Joe would come first. Summer took another secret look at Joe, who was digging a strawberry out of the chunk of ice cream left in the paper carton. He looked wonderfully sexy, but what kind of basis was that on which to judge someone? The best, she finally decided, pushing aside the possibility that her judgment of people might be a bit faulty. Forming opinions was a new experience for her, and she was determined not to be timid.

"Candy told you?" Summer asked, not so much as a question as a means to hear his voice. It was a slow Southern voice that belied the velvety richness she'd heard when he sang. She decided that he didn't talk much, and when he did, he was uncomfortable about expressing himself, so he talked with wonderful similes, grand physical examples, and food.

Joe held out the spoon, twirling it back and forth as he considered his words. "She didn't exactly tell me. If you're worried about her letting anybody know about you, don't be. Candy is very loyal. It was more what she didn't say. When I asked her if she knew a night spirit named Summer with silver hair and gray eyes, she said that she knew many spirits that came in the night, and that every man must deal with his own."

"So how did you figure that her spirit was me?"

"It took a while, but I finally figured out that outsiders don't get inside these walls unless Candy invites them." He scooped another spoonful of the pink concoction and teased her lips with its sweetness. "Open up, Summer. Let me sweeten your morning."

"You have a thing about strawberries, don't you?" Summer opened her mouth, accepting the frozen confection that was threatening to fall into her lap if she didn't. Where the ice cream might end up and what would happen to it when it did, was a thought that took her breath away. Since he'd christened her with her drink last night, she'd learned that Joe handled clean-up chores in the most interesting ways.

"Yes, I like strawberries. When I was a child, they represented everything I didn't have. I made up my mind that one day I'd have all the strawberries I wanted."

"And do you?"

"Yes. But they aren't so special without someone to share them. What about you? Is there something special that you've always wanted to do but couldn't?"

"Other than finding you?" she said, "and spending all my time in bed making love to a fantasy? Yes, going barefoot, I think. My mother and father would never let me go without socks and shoes. I always had to be spotless, perfectly dressed, and silent."

"How awful! What were they, child abusers?"

"No, I don't think so. They just didn't know what to do with a child. They were scholars, wrapped up in the world of Plato and Aristotle. They never wanted me, you see."

"Then they were not simply cruel and inhuman, they were fools." He stood up, brandishing his spoon like a sword. "As king, I could never stand a fool."

A plop of melted ice cream landed on Summer's chin, and all jousting came to a stop while the king turned into a willing slave and licked the cream from its resting place before reluctantly turning back to his dripping carton.

"Thank you, Joe, for sharing this with me. I've never before had a nude man ply with me with fruit and nectar. You make me feel like a queen." She reached across and shyly touched his chest, drawing little circles around his bare nipples, watching as they seemed to swell beneath her fingertips.

There was a long, breathless moment while he watched her fingers play about his chest. "And I feel like your slave. Command me, my queen."

"All right, I command—no I'd never do that. I'm asking you to tell me about yourself." She had turned to face him, clutching the sheet to her breasts in an effort to still the sudden rapid beat of her heart.

"What would you like to know?

"Everything. Starting with Brian. Who's Brian?"

Joe blanched and went still as a statue. The ice cream he'd just plopped into his mouth slid down his throat and fell like an icy cube in the pit of his stomach. "How do you know about Brian?"

"You talked about him in your sleep. Over and over again you kept saying that you were sorry."

Joe took a slow, deep breath. He couldn't blame her for her curiosity. Candy, and the few outsiders who refused to be driven away, had learned never to mention Brian. They tiptoed around the subject, waiting for Joe to say something. Until now he'd refused, both grateful for their compassion and angry that by their very silence, they too seemed to condemn him for what had happened.

And yet, looking into Summer's eyes, Joe felt the pressure lighten. He let out a shuddering breath as though some great weight had lifted from his shoulders. Summer, in all her innocence, was asking about Brian, and by her asking, she was making herself a part of the pain. Joe was surprised to realize that he wanted to tell her. Perhaps it was simply that she was temporary, a stranger, and it was safe to talk to a stranger. Two ships passing in the night. Perhaps it was time he talked about what had happened.

"Brian was my brother. He's dead."

"Oh, Joe, I'm sorry. I didn't mean to pry."

"It's okay. No, it isn't, but I'll tell you, or at least I'll try. Brian was the youngest Rider. You might have heard of the Outriders?" His voice lifted in question. He wanted her to have heard of him, but was glad when she shook her head.

Summer's hand still rested gently on his chest. She knew that her question was painful. She could tell from the halting way he searched for words. She hadn't intended to bring hurt to this man who'd given her such joy.

"No. I'm sorry, I don't seem to know the Outriders. Or maybe I have heard of you, and I just can't remember."

She never had time to listen to modern music. Frivolous, Roger had called it. She was acquainted with musicians all dressed in black formal wear, cold, alien as they waited for her. Nobody had ever known the icy fear that paralyzed her as she stood in the wings viewing them spread out in a circle around her piano.

"I've wished," Joe said slowly, "I've wished a thousand times that I *couldn't* remember. It would have been so much easier. I guess you don't even know who Joe Rydon is either."

"No," she admitted, "I'm sorry. Is that a problem?"

He gave a wry laugh and slapped his thigh, his move pulling away the sheet, exposing his nakedness. He crossed his legs, assuming the lotus position, then pulled the sheet back over himself.

"A problem that you don't recognize me? No. I like knowing that you're in my bed because you want to be, not because you know who I am."

"I guess this means you're a star?"

A brief look of pain sliced across his face and vanished just as quickly. "I was—once. I—we ... we all were. Joe Rydon and the Outriders had four straight number-one songs, five gold albums, and one platinum."

"Brian was an Outrider too."

"Oh, yes. Brian was the heart of the Outriders. He kept us together, even when I tried to tear us apart." Joe sprang to his feet, leaving the sheet bunched behind him on the bed. He walked toward the kitchen, carrying the empty carton of ice cream in one hand and his spoon in the other.

Summer waited for a moment. When he didn't return, she followed, wrapping the sheet around her like a sarong as she walked. In the kitchen Joe had filled his coffee cup and was swallowing the liquid as if he were unaware of its heat.

"A country singer by the name of Hank Williams did a song called, Cold, Cold Heart. It was one of Brian's favorite songs. I didn't want to record it. I thought it was too old and out of date. It turned out to be my—our first hit."

"You're a country music singer?" She couldn't keep the surprise from her voice. She should have known. She was in Nashville. Candy had been a country music star. But if she'd been forced to choose, she'd have made Joe some sardonic, message-driven folk singer.

"I *was* a country music singer. I haven't recorded a song in over a year."

"Why not? Because your brother died?"

There was another long silence.

"No. Because I killed him."

The shrill sound of a telephone ringing cut through the room. "Thank you, Lord," Summer whispered, still frightened by the intensity of Joe's words. But Joe made no move to answer the phone. Repeatedly it rang, until finally the answering machine came on, and Summer could hear the aggravated response of the caller.

"Joe, you turkey, this is your agent, Sly Woody. You remember me, don't you? The people at Scorpion are giving you two weeks to rejoin the world, or you can forget ever making a record in this town again. No more fun and games, dude. You've got to fish or cut bait. Where's my new song?"

Summer stumbled on the sheet. She reached down,

grabbed the corner, pulled it up between her legs, and tucked it in above her breast. Perched on a stool beneath the kitchen counter, she watched Joe's stiff back. She'd severed all connection to her past willingly, and she'd spent the night with a man who'd just confessed to murder. She should feel shock. She should feel fear. All she felt was his pain.

"You'd better go," he said quietly, not turning around.

"Go? Where?" Summer could return to the hospital and allow the doctors to contact Roger. She could retreat to her room at Candy's. Or she could stay with a man about whom she knew nothing, a man who'd made love to her and created a beautiful fantasy in which she was the queen and he was her slave.

But after all the loose, disjointed thoughts ran through her mind, she knew. Returning to her old world didn't even rate a second thought. Joe had taken her in and given her a lovely dream. Now he was suffering because of her question about Brian. She couldn't leave him in such a state. She had to repair the damage she'd done.

Summer couldn't be certain about her powers of observation, but her instinct told her that no matter what he said, Joe Rydon was no murderer.

"Why are you trying to get rid of me, Joe?"

He turned and moved to the counter opposite where she was sitting. "Because I'm not good for you, Summer. Candy was right. We'll hurt each other."

"Joe, what do you know about me? *I* might be a terrible person. *I* might be wanted by the law, or I *might* have a jealous husband out there somewhere."

He turned a sad, tender smile on her. "Wanted by the law, maybe, but a husband? No. Of that I'm certain."

"How can you be sure?"

"Three very good reasons. You're special, Summer. The way you move, the way you talk, everything about you speaks of wealth and breeding. A rich, good-looking woman like you would be wrapped in diamonds if she were married. You aren't, and your finger doesn't look as if you've ever worn a wedding ring."

"So, I'm not wearing a wedding ring. What else?"

"The other two things are a bit more personal, darling. A man can tell if a woman has sex on a regular basis. Over time her body makes certain adjustments for a man. Yours is practically untouched. More than that, you're wonderfully inexperienced."

Summer blushed. Knowing that he could tell how inexperienced she was hurt. Everything had felt so natural to her that she hadn't realized how awkward she must appear to an experienced man like Joe Rydon. He must have had women flinging themselves on him. He probably had laughed at her ignorance.

"I—I don't know what to say."

"Don't be embarrassed, Summer. I like being your teacher. I like being with you. It's like having—" he almost said like having someone to love and care for again. But that wouldn't have been true. He might have cared for Brian when he was growing up, but it had been Brian who'd become the caretaker in the end.

"Like having what?" she echoed. "No, don't answer. I think I'll feel better if I don't know. And I don't believe for one minute that you killed your brother. Tell me about your caller. Who's Sly?"

"Sly is my manager. He's convinced that Scorpion, that's my record company, will produce a new album for me. He thinks that I'll put together a new group, and the Outriders will be on top again."

"And you're not?"

"The Outriders died in a plane crash in Mexico almost a year ago, the plane I should have been on and wasn't.

Even if I did put together another group, it wouldn't be the Outriders. Besides, I don't have any music."

"What about the song you were playing the other night?"

"I can't—not that song. That song belongs to Brian. He'd started working on the melody when—just before he died."

"Okay, if not that one, another. You can do it. I heard you, remember? I don't know much about country music. But I do know you're very good."

"I manage. But the real talent in the family belonged to Brian—in spite of all I did to keep him out of the entertainment business."

"Why did you want to keep him out?"

"He was too good for that kind of life. I tried to get him to study law, or become a doctor. But because I wanted to be another Hank Williams, he studied music."

"Why Hank Williams? Why not Mick Jagger, or even Neil Diamond?"

"Because Hank Williams knew how to sing about the bad times. And that's all I knew how to write about. Brian understood. He studied music to help me. We were a team. I supplied the words and pretended to play the guitar, but it was Brian who was the real star."

"You're wrong, you know. I heard you. If those are your lyrics, you're very talented." And it isn't always bad times that give emotion to your music, she could have said. She knew that well, it was the one thing lacking in her performance—emotion. Bad times could kill the emotion as well as foster it.

Joe took a long time to answer. "I'm very determined, or at least I once was. I learned how to fake it, how to surround myself with people who made me look good. I'm a fraud, Summer. I was trying to finish that song for almost a year, and I couldn't, until you did it for me."

"I did?"

"You did." Joe studied her carefully. "And the ending you gave me was pretty complicated. I think you could be a composer, my spirit of the night."

"No. I don't write music. Sometimes I think I might have something to say, but there is never time. Roger doesn't allow me to waste myself."

"Waste yourself? I heard you. Remember? And that was no one-finger rendition. Play something for me, Summer. Play something now."

"No. I'd rather not."

"You'd rather not? You see, you don't say that you can't, just that you'd rather not." Joe leaned across, capturing her chin in his hand. "Please, Summer, play—for me."

His dark eyes caught at something deep inside her. He'd asked, and she couldn't refuse. Suddenly she was sitting on the piano bench, her hands poised on the keys. But nothing came. She trilled her fingertips across once, then again, then rested them. "I don't know what to play."

Joe sat on the end of the bench beside her, took his guitar in hand, and began to strum. The haunting refrain, "Shenandoah," a ballad used in many fifties movies, came from his fingertips. From there he led into "The Green, Green Grass of Home."

And then she was playing too, not just following, but embellishing and enriching his simple cords. He stopped, allowing her to play on, changing from the simple ballads to a complicated concerto that only an expert could have mastered. When the last stanza had been completed and the last note had died away, Joe began to clap.

"I knew you were special, but I didn't know that you were a genius, a real honest to goodness genius."

"Genius?"

"Yes, genius. A real talent. You don't belong here, with a washed-up guitar bum. You belong on the concert stage. I might know some people who could help you."

"No! I'm not a genius. I don't belong on the concert stage. I won't go on the stage again. You can't force me—not anymore!" She cried out sharply and stood, fear irrationally clouding her mind. Frantically she glanced around, located her dress, and wriggled into it, buttoning it as she strode out the glass doors and across the garden. "I'm not a genius," she yelled. "I'm not! I won't ever be that again."

"Wait!" Joe called out, laying his guitar down and chasing after her. Halfway across the garden he felt a limb rake his bare leg, looked down, and realized he wasn't wearing any clothes. Whirling around, he fled back into the bedroom and pulled on the shirt and the pair of jeans he'd stepped out of the night before. Stumbling through the cottage, he finally found and crammed his feet into his shoes. Satisfied that Candy wouldn't have him arrested for indecent exposure, he started back across the garden.

Just as he reached the main house, Candy exited the kitchen, letters in hand as she headed to the mailbox.

"Morning, Joe. Glad to see you're up and at 'em, finally."

"You don't know the half of it, Candy, my love." Though he wasn't up now, he had been for a good portion of the night. He reached Summer's door and pushed against it. It swung open. "Summer, we need to talk." He moved inside. But the room was empty. She was already gone, leaving only an open newspaper on her bed.

Joe started past the bed, stopped, and went back. The woman on the front of the paper bore a strong resemblance to Summer. *CONCERT PIANIST—Missing* . . . He picked up the paper and began to read. He'd been right. Summer was a musician, she was one of the world's up-and-coming artists. His Summer was really Samantha Lorrimar, child prodigy, who was just coming into her own as an adult and had disappeared from the hospital where she'd been recovering from an accident.

Joe tried to make sense of what he was reading. According to Samantha's manager, Roger Weston, the authorities believed that Ms. Lorrimar could be suffering from amnesia and not understand the seriousness of her situation.

Samantha Lorrimar? The sleek young woman with the upswept hairstyle was his Summer? No! He dashed back to the garden just as Candy reentered the gate. She gave a jerk of her head and a broad smile as she stood back for him to pass through.

He jogged out the gate and stopped. Just ahead he could see Summer, head down, striding along as though she had a strong wind at her back. "Wait, Summer. Don't run away!" She turned the corner and started toward the horde of shops and tourist attractions owned by the country stars who lent their names to the establishments. He caught up just as she reached one of many music stores for which Nashville was famous.

"Summer, please, whatever I did, I'm sorry."

Summer glanced around frantically and fled inside the record shop, hurrying down the aisle between the long bins of old records, past the newer sections of CDs, coming to a stop in front of a wall of posters that formed a background for a small stage.

It was the poster in the corner that stopped her short. It showed a band, dressed in long coats and rough western clothing, dusty boots, six-guns, and sweat-stained cowboy hats. The lead singer, standing in front, wearing a challenge-me-if-you-dare expression on his dark face, was Joe. The name of the group was spelled out in leather letters across the bottom of the picture: *The Outriders*.

"Joe—" she said with a start, "it's you."

"I'm afraid so," he replied, unable to pull his eyes away from the poster. All he could see was Brian's concerned expression and the more restrained resolve of the others. It had been their last album. It had taken them days to shoot the cover because of him, because he'd been drinking and argumentative. Lord, he'd been cocky. He'd been a star. He'd been on a roll that he had every reason to expect would last forever. The album cover he was looking at should have been done in half the time, but he'd challenged every decision that Brian had made.

Even now, he still couldn't believe what he'd done. After years of poverty and being a nobody, suddenly Joe Rydon was somebody. He was recognized and catered to by what seemed like the world. But each time he sang, he lived with the fear that he'd lose everything just as quickly as it had come. The fear accelerated, and the only way he could relax was with a beer. Soon the beer had turned into something stronger.

The higher he climbed, the harder it became, until he couldn't function without plying himself with alcohol. He'd become a carbon copy of Hank Williams, the man he'd hoped to emulate. Except it hadn't been Joe who'd died, it had been Brian.

When the new album was finished, they'd finally shot that cover in a dusty town in the middle of the mountains of Mexico. Afterward they were scheduled to play two gigs and then wait for the record's release. But Joe had rebelled. He'd announced that he was taking some time off, on his own. He was tired. He told the band to go back to Nashville and wait until he got there.

Ever since, he'd lived with the knowledge that if he

hadn't decided to take off with Jeri, or Monica, or whatever her name had been, Brian would still be alive.

"I didn't know this poster was still here," he muttered.

"Sure thing, Joe," the bearded, bespectacled shop owner said as he joined them at the edge of the stage. "Good to see you, man. It's been a long time. Who's the lady?" He took a long look at Summer, before the light of understanding clicked on in his eyes.

"Say, I know you. You're Samantha Lorrimar. You're famous. I heard you play once. Everybody this side of the Mason-Dixon line is looking for you, ma'am. Don't you want to call someone and tell them you're all right?"

"No." Samantha said in a pleading voice.

"No!" Joe snapped.

The record shop owner stopped, looking from Joe to Samantha and back. "Sure, okay, ma'am. So what's happening? You and old Joe here having some kind of secret romance?"

"No," she said softly.

"Yes," Joe answered at the same time with some idea of shielding her.

But there was no shielding him. Joe Rydon's past had suddenly become the present. Here, in the music store, he was still country music's Entertainer of the Year. And all the guilt and insecurity came back. If he could just get Samantha out of the store before some fan recognized and cornered him.

Summer felt as if she'd been shot with a stun gun. Samantha Lorrimar. *You're famous.* A rush of cold swept over her. *I heard you play once.* Ever since Joe had called her a genius, she'd felt as if she were being crushed by one sensation of dread and fear after another. And she couldn't stop the anxiety attack. It had never been so bad before.

Glancing around, she caught sight of Joe staring at her.

If she could just get away from him long enough to deal with the myriad sensations that were assaulting her mind. But once the floodgate opened, the fear rushed in.

"Don't suppose you'd like to drop by and do a show tonight?" the record shop owner asked Joe, all the while continuing to study Summer curiously.

"No, but thanks, Justin. I'm still not quite ready for that."

"Anytime you want to try, Joe, I'll clear the stage for you. No harm done if you can't do it, or if you're rusty."

"Thanks, Justin. Maybe soon." Joe caught Summer's arm and propelled her toward the door.

"Joe," she protested. "Let me go. I need—I'd like to be alone for a while. I—I . . ."

"No, not alone. You're with me. You were upset with something I said back at the house, and I want to know why. I won't hurt you, but I have to know what I did."

He wasn't going to let it drop. She'd have to tell him the truth, share with him as much as he'd shared with her. She owed him that. "All right, it was being called a genius that upset me. Samantha is the genius, not Summer."

They reached the sidewalk and were walking back toward the house when Summer caught sight of them in a shop window. The picture of the two of them so intrigued her that she stopped and stared at their reflection. He was tall and angry-looking. In her lace dress she might have stepped straight out of a gothic novel. All they needed were the English moors and a foreboding mansion with a light in the upstairs window.

"I don't think I'm going to like Roger," Joe said, coming to a stop beside her. "I get the feeling that he would never be with a barefoot girl in a lace dress."

"That's true. Roger would die if he saw me. I look like some . . . some . . ."

"Like a beautiful fantasy. Unless Roger is deaf, dumb, and blind, he'd be as caught in your spell as I. I don't suppose Roger has some kind of blind spot, does he?"

She laughed. "Roger? No way. Roger has twenty-twenty vision. He hears perfectly too, though there are times when he chooses not to."

"So forget Roger, the perfect. How's your vision. Do you have eyes in the back of your head?" He caught her arm and turned her away from the glass.

"No. Do I need them?"

"Not unless you want to watch yourself kissing me."

"Joe, we're on a public street. Suppose someone sees you?"

"Suppose someone does? Suddenly I don't think that I care. Do you?"

She didn't. After he'd thoroughly kissed her, a smattering of applause broke out from a gathering of onlookers.

"Hey, isn't she that missing woman?" one of them whispered. "The one on TV?"

"Nah. That woman was real sophisticated. But that's Joe Rydon she's with, I'm sure of it," another person added.

"Can't be," the first one argued. "He's become a recluse, never comes out of hiding anymore."

"Yeah. I heard he's drying out in some clinic, under lock and key."

"Right," Joe said. "That's where he is all right. My eyes are hazel. Joe's eyes are brown. I'm a look-alike, guys. I play Joe at the Hall of Stars show at Opryland." He gave an exaggerated bow. "Come see the show. Tell the barker that Joe and Summer sent you."

The visitors studied Joe and Summer for a long minute before they decided that the man was just what he'd said he was, a fake.

"Yeah, two fakes," one said. The others agreed and turned away in disappointment.

Once the tourists were out of sight, both Summer and Joe began to laugh. "You're some crazy magician, Joe Rydon." With a kiss he'd moved Roger out of her mind and back into the past.

"Crazy about you," he agreed, taking her hand in his. After all the months of avoiding the outside world, one kiss had made him forget his fear of facing his fans.

"Let's hurry," Summer said, dancing down the sidewalk. "This concrete is hot."

"I left my white horse at home, so I guess I'll have to carry you."

"Never mind. I'll walk. I'm too big," Summer protested.

"I thought that was my line," Joe protested, and reached out to pull her against him.

"Not a line, Joe," she whispered wickedly. "As you would say, anybody who isn't deaf, dumb, and blind would know the difference between big and small. And I'm a fast learner. I'll race you back."

She took off at a run.

He took off after her.

It wasn't even a match. He caught her at the corner. But then she wasn't trying to get away.

They walked back to Candy's holding hands and stealing kisses, delaying any further discussion of why Summer had barreled out of the house.

"What did the man at the record store mean, do a show?" she finally asked.

"On Saturday night some shops have live entertainment. It's a good way for newcomers to get rid of their butterflies, and for the old-timers to fool around. It's like jamming. Fans come to the shop, get a free show, and buy records."

"But you refused. Why?"

"I haven't made a personal appearance in a long time."

"Not since your brother died."

"I made a few after the crash, but it wasn't the same. It was too hard without Brian and the guys. I just couldn't. I . . . I finally stopped doing it."

He wasn't telling her everything. But she sensed that she'd pressed enough. "Candy is very fond of you," she said, changing the subject.

"Candy is a special lady. She gave me my first job."

"In her band?"

"No, in her bar. It served food back then, and I was the busboy and dishwasher. Later she let me sit in with her band until I was good enough to go on the road. She's been the closest thing to a real mother I've ever had. Now, my night spirit, it's your turn. Tell me about Roger, with the perfect vision."

Joe gave her hand an encouraging squeeze. How would he compare with this Roger? He couldn't think of a single reason why a reasonable woman would want him. He had no education. Hell, he'd been washing dishes since he was sixteen. Now, at thirty-two, he didn't even have a job. And his reputation as a wild-living, hard-drinking rogue was all wrong for a lady who played concerts and wore her hair "up."

It puzzled Joe that Summer had been on a bus when the accident occurred. He'd bet his platinum record that she'd never ridden a bus before in her life. Ms. Samantha Lorrimar was more accustomed to limos than to public transportation. And judging from the way she was walking, going barefoot was a new experience as well.

But Summer didn't feel the concrete beneath her feet. Joe's question was more painful than the heat. What could she tell Joe about Roger? Anything she said would make her appear to be some kind of ungrateful person, either that or a fool. Never before had she refused to do what she'd been told. But she'd finally reached the point where she wouldn't be dictated to any longer. The conversation with Roger came back, so clearly that it might have been happening all over again.

"I told you that I wanted a vacation, Roger," she'd said. "Why would you do this without asking me?"

"Now, Samantha. I'm your manager. Your mother and father trusted me to know what's best for you. This is too good an opportunity for you to turn down," he'd said. "You haven't played Carnegie Hall since you were sixteen. This is what I've been waiting for."

It had been the *I* that had done it. "You've been waiting, Roger? What about what I want? Have you ever asked me what I want? Well, I'll tell you what I want. I want that vacation. I want to walk on the beach, sleep until noon in a house that doesn't even have a piano."

But Roger had only patted her on the hand and told her to get some rest—just as her parents had done during all the years when she'd wanted to go to Camp Tonnawanda like the other girls in her school, and they'd sent her to music camp instead. Roger left her to rehearse while he'd made the travel arrangements. By the time she'd got back to her room, he'd defied her wishes by packing all her clothes and sending them to the airport, leaving her with only the skirt and blouse she'd been wearing.

She might have made a scene, except that she already had and had gotten nowhere. He'd ignored her as always. Instead, while Roger was on the phone, she'd emptied his billfold of their travel money and left the hotel, not clear of what she intended to do until she saw the bus station sign.

"Roger scheduled another performance for me instead of the vacation he'd promised," she told Joe. "I was tired, very tired, and I didn't want to go. I told him, but he wouldn't listen. He never listened. This time I left."

They reached the gate to the property. Joe opened it and locked it behind them. "So you're hiding out because you don't want to perform, and I'm hiding out because I can't. What a fine pair of misfits we are."

"I think we're a very fine pair. And I don't consider us hiding. We're simply not involved with the outside world."

"So now are you going to tell me why the word *genius* upset you?"

"I don't want to be a genius. I don't want to be a child prodigy. I don't want to be the foremost concert pianist in the world. I just want to be a normal, everyday nobody."

"A nobody, huh? Well, stick with me and you just might make it."

There it was again, the barely concealed pain in his voice. She'd listened to him unravel his story, one tiny piece at a time, and nowhere had she gotten even a hint that he was capable of hurting anybody but himself. She'd seen the poster and heard him admit to his success: the number-one hits, the platinum records, his star status. What was he trying to do by constantly putting himself down?

"All right, Joe Rydon, what does a normal, everyday person on vacation in the city of Nashville, Tennessee, do? I don't want to hide. I want to be a tourist. Will you be my guide?"

Joe frowned. He'd been lucky. He'd been to the corner grocery store, to the record shop, and on the street without any major catastrophe. Of course the locals were accustomed to stars, and they pretty much left them alone. But tourist attractions meant fans, large numbers of fans. Could he chance another venture into the real world?

He took one look at Summer and swore. Why did she have to look so trusting, so angelic, so spiritual? Why had she crashed into his safe little haven with needs that reached out and made him forget pain and loneliness? He'd never trusted women, except for Candy.

And now there was Summer with the silver hair. Summer, who cried when they made love and seemed to see something in him that nobody other than Brian ever had. She was a star in her own right, or she would be someday if she went back to her career instead of staying with him. What could he give her? All he had to share was his pain.

And then it came to him. It was so simple that he almost missed it. All she was asking for was a normal life, not forever, just for a time. He could do that for her in return for the unselfish happiness she'd brought to him.

"You're on, spirit woman. You want a vacation. Let's get you into some normal clothes, and I'll show you my town."

"Would you really do that for me?"

"I'd be delighted."

"And what can I do for you in return?"

"Just stay with me, Summer, for as long as you will. Forget Roger and the rest of the world. Love me, and we'll make special music together, you and I. This is our moment in time."

This moment. Did she dare? What Joe was saying was, "Have an affair with me." Affairs were brief, torrid, intense, and temporary. Could she do that, have an affair to remember?

She could.

The one thing she hadn't told Joe was that Roger was more than her manager. He was her fiancé. Getting married had been his idea, not hers. But long ago, when she'd been very lonely and afraid, he'd been there. She'd thought that she'd loved him, and when he'd kissed her, she'd let him. When he'd taken her to bed, she'd let him do that too. But it hadn't been what she expected, and the second time she'd pushed him away.

Roger had agreed to the nonsexual relationship, almost too willingly. There'd been other women for Roger. She'd known that and hadn't objected.

She smiled and thought of Joe. He would never have agreed to such a relationship. Even before she knew Joe, his music had spoken to her emotionally, drawn her to his side, probed her inner soul for shared strength that both had badly needed. She'd given herself to him willingly, over and over again. Now he was offering to give her what Roger had refused: time, space, and freedom.

Still she knew that Joe wasn't her future. He was temporary. But for this one brief moment she wanted whatever time she could have with Joe. She wanted to love somebody and be loved in return. She wanted to stay there with him, for as long as she was allowed.

"This moment in time," she whispered. "Yes, let's go for it. What does a tourist wear, Joe Rydon?"

"Jeans, shorts. What do you have?"

"A skirt and blouse and some lovely old dresses that Candy loaned me."

"The skirt and blouse should do, and shoes. As much as I love your bare feet, Summer, darling, where we're going, you'll need shoes."

She might have argued, said that she'd always worn shoes, that this time she wanted to do something absolutely wild and out of control. Instead she simply asked, "Where are we going, Joe?"

"To the top of the world, my love, the top of the world," he answered.

And Summer knew that he understood.

It wasn't the top of the world, but to Summer it was close enough. They were stopped at the pinnacle of the Opryland Ferris wheel. The sky was a soft blue, sprinkled with popcorn-shaped clouds being scooped up and moved about by a breeze that tousled Summer's hair wildly.

"Oh, it's wonderful, Joe. Look at all the people. They look like dolls. I've never seen anything so—so grand."

Her joy was contagious. She'd been like a little girl, eager to try everything. They'd had cotton candy, candy apples, and hot dogs. They'd ridden the carousel, the roller coaster, and now the big wheel.

"I'm glad you're having fun."

"I've never had such fun in my life, Joe. Thank you. Thank you. Thank you for bringing sunshine into my life."

She gave him a kiss with every thank you, and Joe felt his heart jangle in response. "You're very welcome, Summer. I'm so glad you came into my life. I want to give you the sun and the moon and—"

What was he about to say? His heart? He'd stopped. But the thought was there, the knowledge too. He was in love with his spirit woman. He'd promised to protect her for a while, to let her be a normal nobody. But she could never be less than she was, even though, for Joe, she was the piece of his heart that had been missing.

"And now you're going to take me to see the Joe Rydon look-alike perform, aren't you?"

The Ferris wheel started to move again. They'd been on top of the world for a moment. Now they were on their way back down to the real world.

"Aren't you, Joe, darling?" *Darling*. She'd never called anyone darling before. The only time she'd ever heard the word with any affection had been from her mother, and that had been before her parents had determined that their child prodigy was to become a concert pianist, before Mommy and Daddy had engaged the first of the tutors who'd eventually turned into Roger, before Mommy and Daddy had been killed and she'd found out that they'd handed her future over to a stranger—permanently.

But Roger had never called her darling. Darling was personal, and their personal relationship was a lie. "Creative people can't afford to divert their emotions," he explained. "As your husband, I'll be better able to take care of you, Samantha. You must channel all your energies into your music." And she had.

Until now.

"Joe, do you believe that having a relationship drains creativity?"

"If you mean you and me, darling, I'd have to say that you make me feel very creative. As a matter of fact, I feel a sudden inspiration coming on."

In the darkness of the fun house, she had to agree. When they'd completed several trips by boat through the darkness, Joe's creativity peeked. On the third trip Joe bribed the attendant into a temporary shutdown that gave him just enough time to introduce Summer to an innovative approach to rapid solutions. There was no hesitancy in Summer's response, nor her willingness to follow wherever he led. As their little boat moved through the dark waters, she squeezed the muscles in the part of her body that sheathed him and rode out the stormy waves of heated response.

Exiting the fun house moments later, Summer knew she was blushing. For Joe, being recognized by a dozen fans didn't take away from the glow of the aftermath of their lovemaking.

As they walked through the crowds, Joe remained oblivious to the fans who recognized him, who caught sight of his expression and backed away to give him privacy. Summer felt as if she and Joe were protected by some bubble. Beyond its invisible boundaries the world went on.

The sun reached the tip of the trees, casting shadows across the park. Lights came on suddenly, twinkling like fireflies in the dusk. By now the crowds had thinned, except for the line gathering outside the Opryland Auditorium.

"Joe, you asked me to play for you, and I did. Now I'm asking you to sing for me. Will you?"

He had been singing that first night, selecting words

and phrases and discarding them, but singing nonetheless. What she wanted was a real song, a show on a stage.

But he couldn't do that. He'd told Summer that he couldn't perform after Brian's death, but he hadn't told her the whole truth. He hadn't told her that his drinking had lost him engagements, his voice, and finally his will to perform. She didn't know what she was asking. Or perhaps she did. He looked into her trusting eyes and knew that he wanted to give her what she asked.

On impulse, drawing Summer behind him, Joe ducked behind the auditorium and knocked on the performers' special entrance.

The tall man wearing the rhinestone-embroidered jacket took one look at Joe and gave him a back-slapping welcome. "Rydon, you mangy dog, where've you been? Get in here and let me look at you."

"Hello, Porter, good to see you. This is Summer. Summer, Porter Waggoner, an old friend."

"Summer, huh? Are you responsible for getting this fellow back on the straight and narrow?"

"Oh, no. I'm just a friend."

"Uh-huh, and I'm Prince Charles. Come on in. Are you in the show tonight?"

"No, I just wondered if I could borrow the stage for a minute. I'd like to show it to Summer."

"You can borrow the stage, the musicians, and if you need it, I'll even lend you my jacket."

Joe looked at the purple coat with the sequined roses and shook his head. Porter was a legend, not just for his voice and his western suits, but for his generosity of spirit. Joe knew that the Opry would welcome him back with open arms, but he didn't want that. He just wanted to share a part of his past with Summer.

Together they walked on stage. Joe dropped her hand and walked past the microphones to the edge. He took a deep breath and looked out into the darkness. How often had he stood in this very spot, studying the auditorium crowds, winking at the prettiest girl in the front row, while mentally positioning her so that one of the gofers could be instructed to issue her a special invitation to join him after the last show.

Summer watched this man who still remained such a mystery to her. For a moment he'd forgotten she was there. For a moment he was in the past. For a moment she was certain that his brother and the rest of the Outriders were there beside him. She too felt some ghosts. The stage was new, but the ambience was the same. She closed her eyes, and she could hear clapping hands and see the sparkle of jewels twinkling in the ghostly glow of chandeliers overhead.

Behind them, electricians were laying lines and checking microphones. Performers were tuning their instruments. Beyond the floodlights she could see the concession stand employees loading the shelves with what Porter identified as the famous Goo Goo Clusters candy bars. There was an air of constrained excitement that reached beyond the apron of the stage and touched everyone.

"What about it, Rydon, want to tune up and go a few bars with me?" One performer had plugged in his guitar and was testing his strings.

"Eh, what?"

" 'Night Music.' I always thought it was your best song."

The musician played a few chords.

The electrician handed Joe a mike. "Here, try it. I need to adjust the bass anyway."

Joe took the mike. He stared at it for a long time, glanced out at the audience, then back at Summer, a strange, uncertain expression on his face.

"Please?" Summer whispered, then walked down the side steps and took a seat in the front row so that she could look up at Joe. "Sing to me, midnight man."

But he couldn't. He simply stood, staring into the audience while the doors opened and the patrons filed inside. As they caught sight of Joe, they stopped, waiting quietly, then began a rhythmic applause.

Joe blinked, realizing what had happened. Then he gave a strained nod and backed away from the front of the stage. Summer stood and moved around the apron, climbing the steps so that she could intercept Joe beyond the curtain. She too was aware of the audience, but more, she knew how vulnerable Joe was at this moment. She felt his fear and sensed him closing off his emotions. The fans had gotten through his shield, and Joe wasn't ready to face what she'd asked him of him.

"Rydon, you've still got it." Porter was standing by the back door. "Come back, man. You're a part of us."

But Joe didn't answer. He didn't even wait for Summer. She had to hurry to catch him at the tram that carried the visitors back to their cars. This time, when a fan spoke to him, Joe scowled and pushed by, ignoring the elderly man who only wanted to wish him well. Summer gathered up her skirt and broke into a run. She swung onto the tram at the last minute, finding a seat at the rear.

At the parking area where he'd left his car, Joe stepped from the tram and came to a sudden stop. He turned back. "Summer?"

"I'm here, Joe, right here."

He took her into his arms, and she felt him trembling as he held her so tightly that she could hardly breathe. "Let's get out of here," he said with a growl. "I need a drink."

"A drink?" She'd seen him drink coffee, fruit juice, and punch—but liquor?

He helped her to the car, closed the door, and strode to the driver's side. Moments later they were racing out of the parking area and down the highway. She watched the last sliver of sunlight fade from the sky, leaving a velvety blue-black surface pin-cushioned with stars as Joe's car ate up mile after mile. He seemed almost to have forgotten where he was going, or that she was there.

Joe was once more traveling alone.

Joe finally left the freeway, turning on a curvy, narrow mountain road that ended at the remains of a burned-out log house hanging onto the side of the mountain. He cut off the engine and leaned his head against the wheel.

"I'm sorry, Summer. I could have killed you too."

"Too? You didn't kill Brian, Joe. An airplane crash killed your brother. Stop thinking that." She wanted to shake him. Why couldn't he see the truth? Finally in exasperation she said, "Would he be any less dead if you'd died with him?"

"No. But if it weren't for me, the accident might never have happened."

"I doubt that. Was the plane chartered?"

"Yes. We chartered it in Nashville."

"So you would have traveled on that plane no matter when you returned."

"Yes, I suppose. But—"

"Was there a storm?"

"No. The FAA said there was some kind of malfunction."

Summer touched Joe on the arm. He was like steel, holding muscles and nerves as tight as coiled springs. "Then what could you have done to save Brian? Die in his place?"

He didn't answer. Anger, guilt, and remorse choked off

his defense. He could have told her that his father had died—and his mother too—in the very house outside which they were parked. Words still came hard, as did the remembering. He'd searched for his mother and had found her and brought her back to this place. He'd thought that she'd be happy, that she'd never have to worry anymore. But he couldn't take away her demons, and no matter how hard he'd tried, she'd never been happy there. Then the house had burned. She'd finally found a way out.

When Brian's plane crashed, Joe added more guilt to what he was already carrying around. Like his mother, Joe finally found a reason to self-destruct. Until Summer had come into his life. Then in three short days, laugh by laugh, kiss by kiss, he'd felt his protective shell crack and widen. Nothing he'd told Summer had put her off. She stayed with him, believing in her quiet, positive way, forcing him to begin to believe in himself.

"I've lost people I loved too," she said. "My parents. In an automobile accident. There was a time when I wished that I'd been with them."

"But you went on without them, Summer, darling. You're a success. You have the world on a string."

"No. The world has me on a string. Or it did. Until I cut it. That's what I did, you know. When I left that hospital, I was smothering under the weight of my past, as you were. We escaped. We just found different ways to do it. Let's go home, Joe. It's time both of us let go of our pain."

Joe raised his head and turned to look at her. His dark eyes glistened with unreleased moisture, his lips began to relax, and he let out a ragged breath without realizing that he'd been holding it.

"I've failed everybody I've cared about in my life, Summer, even Candy."

"Not me. Trust me, Joe, please. I'm not like the others. I'm not asking anything of you. I know what it means to be used. We'll never do that to each other."

"People use each other, even those who care. Everybody wants a little piece of you. They exaggerate, even lie. They use you until they don't need you anymore, then they say it was all a mistake. But, Summer, I was as guilty as the rest of them. I learned how to use people too."

"Not us, Joe. Promise me."

"Yes. Let's go home."

Joe started the engine and turned the car around, pulling Summer into the curve of his arm as he drove back to Nashville. The hot summer air whipped through the open car windows, bringing a promise of a new storm. The star-studded sky seemed to pale, as if a net curtain were drawn across it, closing out the world.

And as he drove Joe began to sing—hesitantly at first, then louder and with more certainty. Beginning with "Cold, Cold Heart," he sang all his songs for Summer, ending with the one he'd been finishing that first night, "A Heart Made Whole," Brian's song.

Later, inside the guest house, he undressed her slowly, prolonging the sweet agony with his loving gaze. Under his touch her body remained in a constant state of readiness. A look, a caress, a released breath touched her mind, and the sweet agitation began once more.

Dark eyes, turbulent, heady with passion, devoured. Gray eyes once as still as deep water now became as volatile as waves in a storm at sea.

"I—I—want you," Joe said in a low, tight voice as he laid her back on the bed and stared down at her, his fierce expression raging with his need to be gentle. He could have said that he loved her, for he knew that he did. But it was too new, too powerful, too fragile.

"Me too," Summer whispered, holding out her arms to welcome him into that place where he felt so secure.

Their lips met, and the night seemed to explode. The elements, as though ordained to comply, matched the explosion of their lovemaking with the fury of the storm.

Joe filled her body with himself, and her heart with love. They soared through the night until they'd passed the far reaches of their universe and began to fall back to reality, spent, sated, and together.

He slid to the side, still claiming her with one leg across her thighs and one arm beneath her neck. When he opened his eyes and caught sight of the emotion reflected in hers, he began to tremble. "I may be falling in love with you," he said, and watched her eyes fill with tears.

"I know," she said. "Me too." Her mouth formed the words, but her throat closed off, and the sound didn't come.

His fingertip caught the tear that spilled over and ran down her cheek. He seemed to be studying her as if he were storing her memory forever. He skimmed his lips across her breasts, marveling at the way they instantly responded to his touch. His fingertips danced across the length of her long, shapely legs. "You're like one of those women who stood on the rocks and called out to the sailors on passing ships. You make me crazy."

"You're not crazy, you're wonderful," she answered. "If you weren't holding me, I'd still be bouncing across the sky."

"If you went flying tonight, you'd get wet," he whispered. "It's raining."

"Good. I like the rain. It makes the world clean again."

Joe continued to caress her body, slowly, with the kind of lazy attention that said he understood her needs. "Ah, my spirit woman, what do you know about the dirt in the world?"

"Not much. But I know what it is to be emotionally cold and physically tired. I've gotten up before the sun, not to work in the fields or watch the sunrise, but to practice, alone, sealed away from any kind of real life. I've flown all over the world, trying to sleep on a plane, eating food that was overcooked or cold and tasteless. I know that must sound terribly shallow of me, Joe, darling, but I got so weary of being wound up like some toy and shoved onto a stage to perform.

"I understand that," he agreed. "But didn't the surge of adrenaline, the high you get from playing, make it all worthwhile?"

"Not for me. All I ever really wanted was home and someone to hold me, someone to tell me that I was special—not my music, not my performance—that Samantha *the person* was important."

"Samantha is important. Summer is important. They are both important in my life," he said, and she knew that for Joe, at this moment, the statement was true.

Thunder rolled in the distance. Far away, jagged little squiggles of lightning etched the sky as the storm moved nearer. They'd left the windows over the head of the bed open so that Summer could hear the rain on the tile roof.

"It rained the first night you came to me," Joe said. "Lord, that seems like yesterday, and yet I can't imagine life without you."

"Day before yesterday," she corrected, squirming closer, unwilling to allow even a space of air to come between them.

Joe accommodated his body to her move. Summer might have been inexperienced, but she was as creative and as artistic in her sexual response as she was at the piano.

A gust of air swept into the bedroom, catching the gauze curtain and ruffling it over them like some canopy. Summer took a deep breath, laughed, and shimmied away, springing to her feet. "Joe, let's go into the garden. I want to make love there, in the rain, beneath the stars."

"Summer, darling, there are no stars." He stripped the coverlet from the bed and followed eagerly, ready to go with this woman who, as if she'd been conjured up, had come to him and illuminated his darkness.

"For us there are." She took his hand and led him out into the garden. Joe laid the coverlet on the thick carpet of grass beside the fountain. A light rain continued to fall as they made sweet love. Afterward, when the rain stopped, Joe pulled Summer back inside and dried her with towels as soft as velvet and a touch as heated as the fires that simmered constantly beneath her skin.

For the next week they stayed in the little guest house, talking, sharing their dreams and their music. Joe began to write again in earnest. Though Summer had never thought of herself as a composer, she found that together they could find the notes and chords to reflect the emotion of Joe's words. They finished one song, then a second, and a third.

Summer prepared their meals, reveling in the simple task of learning to read a recipe and presenting Joe with a soufflé or a casserole. She made strawberry pie, strawberry shortcake, and finally a frothy concoction of strawberries, bananas, nuts, and whipped cream.

They talked about Samantha's mother and father, about how stiff and formal they'd been with their only child. It was as if they'd never been children and had had no thought that this tiny reproduction of themselves was not an adult. Nannies, tutors, governesses, and instructors in all the arts had appeared dutifully at the proper time, and had all reached the same brilliant conclusion—

Samantha Lorrimar was a remarkable child, advanced beyond her years in both her mental and her artistic abilities.

When Samantha was five, she'd learned that performing for her parents brought the only genuine response from them she'd ever known. They'd pushed away her sticky kisses and bright attempts at conversation. But when she'd played the piano, they'd sat, rapt, giving her their undivided attention. At that moment the direction of her life was set. And for the next ten years she'd closed out everything but her music.

Roger had become her personal manager when Samantha was sixteen. When her parents were killed in an accident the next year, Samantha had grieved briefly, but in truth she'd hardly missed them. She'd continued playing with the major symphonies of the world, until she'd honed her skills to the point where she was ready to leave the child genius category and join the masters. Her world had become Roger and her music.

But each performance had become harder as her stage fright had intensified. The doctor Roger sent her to had diagnosed simple stress, understandable under the circumstances. He'd prescribed tranquilizers. She'd thrown them away, and the anxiety had grown—until now—with Joe.

In Joe's little house the days passed much too swiftly. One morning after sleeping late, they were feasting on a breakfast of fruit and popovers. Barefoot, Summer was dressed in another of Candy's loose, flowing dresses. Joe, wearing only his jeans, stretched his legs out and took a bite of the pastry, chewing slowly as he stared into the garden.

"About Roger," Joe began. "I don't like the guy, and I don't even know him. But don't you think you ought to call him? I'd be going crazy if I didn't know where you were."

"No. I can't. You don't understand. If I call him, I might have to go back."

"He can't make you do anything you don't want to, Summer. He doesn't have any claim on you, does he?"

"He's my manager," she said. He expects to marry me, she could have added. But Roger and the kind of marriage he represented were in the past that she'd left behind. She refused to think about him, or her commitment to a man she knew beyond question she had never loved.

Joe stared out into the garden for a long minute, then turned back to Summer. Knowing his own need for anonymity, he didn't know why he was pressing Summer, but he was. Maybe it was because he didn't want her to become a recluse like him. He knew how easy it was to make seclusion into a way of life. "But eventually you will have to face him and your other self, won't you?"

Summer didn't know how to answer. Roger wasn't a bad man. He'd protected her, guided her career, and in his own way he thought he was making life easier for her. But it had all been on his terms. She knew Roger must be out of his mind with worry. But she didn't want to think about what Joe was saying. She simply stared at him in denial.

"I mean that's what you've been telling me, isn't it? 'Write again, Joe. Make music. You can do it. I'll help you.' And you've made me believe it. Now I need to do as much for you."

"You already have, Joe. You've given me the one thing I've never had, someplace to belong, someone who needed me just for myself."

But as she looked at him, she knew. He was right. By helping him with his music, she was pushing him out into the world, where he needed to go. He needed the sunshine to bring him back to life. She was hiding away because she needed the security of this place, and this man. She needed the shadows.

Joe caught her hand and held it tightly.

Beyond the glass doors he saw the gate open. He saw Candy arguing with a familiar figure. Sly was forcing his way in. He was being followed by a second man, who looked as out of place in his double-breasted suit as Sly did in his cowboy hat and boots.

Joe felt his heart contract. He'd just told Summer that it was time for them both to face their pasts, and now his was about to stare him in the face. Their enchanted hiding place was being penetrated, and all he wanted to do was take her hand and run.

The men were at the door, knocking, the stranger pushing himself in front, opening the door. "Samantha, I've come to get you. I'm prepared to press charges against this hillbilly."

"Roger?" Summer's face turned white. "How'd you get here?"

"Sly, what the hell? Why did you bring him here?"

"Joe, I'm sorry, man. He's her manager. Some fans saw you together and called the police. They came to me. I stalled them as long as I could. But, man, he's as spooked as a hound dog with a burr stuck under his tail. I finally convinced him that we could settle this quietly—between us—without the law."

Summer stared at the man from whom she'd run away. He was angry, more angry than she'd ever seen him. But along with the anger there was confusion and fear. Joe was right. Roger had been worried about her. She did owe him an explanation.

"Roger, I'm all right. None of this is Joe's fault."

"Your face! The doctor said there might be scars."

"She's beautiful," Joe said vehemently. "Don't make her think she isn't."

Roger ignored Joe. "And your memory? Your memory has returned?"

"Yes. It came back."

"Thank God. Your musical memory is still intact."

"So is the rest of me, Roger. I guess I owe you an apology for running away. I should have stood my ground and insisted that you give me some time off."

"Don't worry, darling. I'll set you up with as much time off as you need, as soon as we fulfill the contract at Carnegie Hall. I was able to get your appearance rescheduled because of the accident." Roger took a step toward her.

Joe, seeing the look of panic on Summer's face, quickly stepped between them. "Hold on just a minute. Seems to me that you're being a bit presumptuous. Hadn't you better ask your *client* if she *wants* to make that appearance?"

"My client?" Roger said stiffly. "Not just my client, you hooligan. Samantha Lorrimar is my fiancée. I've decided to forgive her ... infatuation with you. After all, she was injured and not in complete control. Your little fling is over. Samantha and I will be getting married."

"Fiancée? Is this true, Summer? Are you engaged to this man?"

Summer wanted the earth to open up and swallow her, the skies to split and wash away the intruders. She closed her eyes, hoping that she'd wake up and find this was all a nightmare. But it wasn't.

"It's true," she finally admitted. "We were to be married. But that was before—"

"Before you let me fall in love with you."

It wasn't anger that washed over Joe, but fear. She belonged to another man. She'd run away from the man she had promised to marry, straight into his arms, his bed. She'd even said she loved him, a down-and-out country music singer. They'd shared their dreams and promised never to hurt each other. It had all been a lie.

Suddenly he was a small boy again, listening to his father scream accusations at his mother, charges of lying, of cheating, of using him. He'd seen his father storm out of the house, never seeing the speeding truck that had barreled down the narrow street and killed him. Even at Joe's young age, he'd known that his father had been right.

His mother had gone on lying and cheating, turning her back on the two small boys who'd needed her love, reaching out to strangers who could provide some elusive something that Joe could never understand.

It was happening again. He'd been Summer's stranger. And she'd been his summer love.

"Why?" he asked, his voice tight with pain. "In the beginning we both accepted that this was just a moment in time, but I thought that had changed. Was I wrong?"

"Yes—no, Joe. Please . . . listen. Let me explain."

But his eyes were filled with anger and contempt, maybe even hate. Summer knew that she should have told him she was promised to another man. But she'd been afraid. Even when they'd been as close as any two people could be. She'd asked him to trust her, then she'd lied. They were hurting each other now, he through lack of faith and she through lack of courage.

Summer read the truth in his face. She'd thought that she'd closed out reality, but life had intruded on her fantasy. She'd thought loving somebody took away all the pain. She was learning that loving somebody made the pain greater. As a child she'd reached out for love and been rejected by people who'd had no time for her. As an adult she'd reached out to a man who had time but no faith. She could restore Joe's confidence in his music, but not his heart. From now on she'd learn to find her own way, by herself.

She started through the door, across the garden toward the room where she hadn't slept in days. "All right, Roger. I'm ready to leave."

As she reached the man Joe called Sly, she stopped. "Joe has finished that song for you, Mr. Woody. He's ready to come back. Make him record it—for Brian."

But it wasn't Brian's song that he did. The first song that Joe Rydon recorded in over a year was a ballad about love lost and found, a song he called "Promises." It quickly made the country charts and zipped to the top. It was followed by "Summer's Song," and finally "A Heart Made Whole."

When fans attended the Grand Ole Opry, they saw a new star, a man who called himself simply Joe. On the road he used only a guitar. At the Opry he used the house band.

"When are you going to get another group together?" Porter Waggoner asked him after he'd appeared at the Opry for the second time.

"Never. If I make it, it'll be on my own. If I fall, there's only me who will lose."

He sang only hurting songs now, and his popularity soared at the same rate his heart broke. He'd been a fool to let Summer go. He'd managed to keep up with her schedule. He'd been in the audience when she'd played Carnegie Hall to standing ovations. Her pictures were on the front page of the entertainment sections and the music magazines. But she no longer wore her hair up. It fell across her shoulders like a silver web. Her black dresses gave way to gowns of lace that flowed gracefully around her too-thin body. Pictures showed her to be almost spiritual, ethereal, and very sad.

For Samantha there was no vacation following Carnegie Hall. She hadn't expected there would be. She heard Roger's raving about the change in her appearance and promptly forgot it. When her music style began to change, she ignored Roger's frantic pleas to forget that country singer and marry him instead.

There was no wedding. And finally the tour she'd been obligated to make ended. It was in Boston that she was asked to judge a music competition. She and Roger listened to all the entrants, until a young boy came to center stage and began to play the violin. At the end of his piece Samantha knew that they were watching a true child musical genius.

The boy played not because of hours of instructions, but from the heart. One look at Roger's face and the face of the proud parents in the audience, and Samantha knew that Roger could give this boy what she no longer wanted from him.

Roger argued when she told him she was retiring. He protested when she set up a meeting between the young violinist's parents and Roger. But in the end even Roger admitted that her decision was not unexpected. He let her go because he cared about her, and he recognized that her heart was no longer in her music but back in a Nashville honky-tonk with a cowboy who sang hurting songs.

Two days later she was in Nashville in Candy's living room.

"I've come back, Candy. I don't know if he'll want me, but I know that I want him."

"He wants you. He was just afraid that something bad would happen if he loved you." Candy told her about Joe's mother and how he and Brian had been abandoned by her. Then, when success had come, Joe had managed to locate his mother and built her a fine house in the mountains.

"The house, did it burn?"

"Yes. She got drunk and set it on fire. Killed herself finally. She'd been trying for years."

"Then Joe started to drink."

"Yes. Never did understand that. I would have thought that after he saw what happened to his mother, that was the last thing he'd do. Joe is a strong man. He always had to be—for Brian. But deep inside he never believed that his mother loved him."

"And," Samantha added, remembering how little faith he had in women, "he was afraid that he'd lose me. As long as he didn't care, losing wouldn't hurt."

"You may be right," Candy agreed, "but how do you explain what's happened to him since you left? He lost his mother, and he lost Brian, and he lost his way. He loves you, and you left him, and he's gone straight to the top."

Candy was right. When she'd left Boston for Nashville, she hadn't known what would happen when she faced Joe again. She'd left Roger because she had to decide what she wanted to do with her life. There were contracts that she'd been obligated to fulfill, and she had. But each time she went on stage, she knew that she was playing for the audience, or for Roger, or for her parents.

Not for Summer. Or Samantha. Or Joe.

Summer's heart was back in a little guest house in a Tennessee garden where lightning pierced the sky and rain left diamonds on the magnolia tree. When she'd played there, it was from the heart.

And that day at the competition she'd known that great music didn't come from pure skill, but from love. She'd thanked Roger for what he'd done for her and had left enough money to pay for the young violinist's lessons. Then she'd let the invisible music in her heart lead her home.

"That's simple, Candy. Joe knew that I had to leave so I could come back. And he's waiting for me. He knew that I'd come. Where is he?"

"At the Opry House. This is Awards Night. With any luck he'll be named Country Music Entertainer of the Year again."

"Thanks, Candy. By the way, was there a Joe in your life?"

"Yes. And he let me go. But I didn't come back, not soon enough. You were smarter than me. You did. Now go after him. I've been thinking of letting someone else have my guest house. I don't think Joe will be needing it anymore."

Summer didn't have a ticket to the awards ceremony. She couldn't have gotten one if she'd begged for it. Every seat in the house was sold out. After entering Opryland Park, she skirted the building and found the entertainers' door at the rear. She gave a silent prayer and knocked.

After Summer insisted, the man who opened the door sent for Porter Waggoner, who identified Summer and brought her backstage. He pointed out the area where Joe was sitting and conspired to keep Summer's presence a secret by hiding her when Joe came onstage to perform the song for which he was nominated: "A Heart Made Whole."

Wearing a black western suit, Joe looked every bit the sardonic star he'd once been. His midnight eyes were as fathomless as ever. His mouth was narrowed into a familiar scowl. His dark hair was slicked back.

When he stepped onto the stage, the audience stood,

cheering and clapping wildly. When the applause died down, Joe began to speak.

"Thank you. Thank you for letting me come back home, for listening to my music and sharing what I try to say. Tonight I want to do a song that's dedicated to the two people I loved most, my brother, who gave me the beginning, and Summer, who helped me find the end."

He began to sing with no backup, no band.

Summer, who helped me find the end. Summer felt her heart swell. He was wrong. This wasn't the end. This was the beginning. She listened to the music that had drawn her to this man who'd been so filled with pain. She heard his words and knew that they'd filled her life with meaning. And then, just as he reached the point where he'd always stopped, she stepped onto the stage behind him and sat at the empty piano. As Joe's voice rose to the finale and paused, she began to play, finding the same notes she had that night so many months ago.

Joe whirled around, caught sight of her, unhooked the strap of his guitar, and placed the instrument on the floor as he held out his hand.

"Are you real?" he asked, as she came slowly forward and took his hand.

"I'm very real, Joe Rydon. I love you, and I've come home—to stay."

"I don't know if we can sustain the illusion, Summer," he said softly. "We've let the world inside."

"The world is the illusion, Joe. We, you and I, our love is the reality. We don't need dreams, just each other."

He kissed her on the stage of the new Opry House, and it didn't matter a bit if the entire world was watching. For Joe, they were together, and that was all that counted.

That night Joe made three trips to the stage. Once for Song of the Year, once for Album of the Year, and finally for Entertainer of the Year. And every time he climbed the steps, Summer was by his side.

Later that night they went back to the guest house where they'd first fallen in love. Joe opened the door and carried Summer inside.

"Are you certain this is what you want, Summer?"

"I was certain the first time. I just had to face the past before I could live in the future. And you?"

"Me? I'm going to smother you with flowers, and strawberries, and—me."

"Better hurry, midnight man, you're already late."

Joe turned on the light and looked around in amazement. The room was filled with flowers and baskets of strawberries, and Summer, who brought moonlight to the darkness.

He smiled. "All we need now, my night spirit, is a storm."

As if on cue the thunder rumbled and lightning crisscrossed the sky. In minutes the power was gone. Joe didn't need the light to undress her. He did so by touch, tenderly, shyly, as if they'd never loved before. Summer, wrapped in the heat of the night and their need for each other, reached up and took his face in her hands.

"I thought once that we'd never hurt each other, and we did," she said. She let her fingertips slide down his cheeks and play across his mouth. "But I understand now that love holds no guarantees. There is no magic in its power. When we love somebody, we give that person the power to hurt us."

He kissed her mouth, capturing her words and forcing them inside as he heard her soft moan and felt her collapse against him. Outside the storm raged. Inside they were swept up in the glory of renewal.

Summer flung back her head, and the lightning illuminated her face. Joe tangled his fingertips in her silver hair and buried his face in it. Then their clothes were gone and they were touching. She caught her breath with the wonder of it all. For weeks she'd waited, longing to feel him against her, inside her.

With great reverence he knelt on the floor, drawing her with him. Long weeks of desire set fire to his loins and heated his skin. With agony so great that he could barely contain himself, he pressed her back on the soft carpet, leaning over her, feeling his hardness against her moisture, forcing himself to hold back so that he could prolong the moment.

Summer was beautiful. She was still the ethereal spirit of the night who came to him in his loneliness and filled his heart with joy. He'd meant to wait, but when she reached up and pulled him down to meet her, he forgot all his good intentions. He plunged inside her, reveling in the eager way her body welcomed him.

Beneath him Summer thought surely her heart would burst with happiness. Outside the rain beat across the garden and the rooftop like a racing heartbeat, harder and harder. But it was the explosion within that quelled the storm and quenched the fire.

Afterward they held each other, complete, satisfied, safe. Summer sighed. The past was gone, they were each other's future.

"Where will we live, Joe?"

"I have a piece of land on top of a mountain. How would you feel about living on top of the world?"

"I'll go anywhere you go. It isn't the place, it's you that I need."

"I love you," he said.

"I love you," she said.

And as quickly as it had come, the storm ended. A sudden beam of moonlight pierced the darkness and cast a silver sheen over the two people entwined inside.

"Just think about all the storms we'll watch together," Joe said.

"And think of all the music we'll make."

Joe pulled her over him and kissed her. "I hear it now, don't you? Let's see where the melody carries us."

And they gave themselves over to the music of the night, and all the nights for all their lives to come.

Summer Heat

Helen Mittermeyer

Author's Note

Summer is pleasure. I found my love one July evening in the middle of a hot week. He was a blind date, and I was doing a favor for a friend, since I was on the verge of accepting a proposal from another. But I never looked back, and two weeks later I became engaged to the man who became the father of my children.

Summer is pain. Several years later I gave birth to a daughter on the anniversary of the day I met her father. She died eight months later, but she lives on in our hearts.

Summer has always been special to me. The heat, the rain, the intimacy with heaven and earth, the lushness, growth, birth, and death of summer. I was born under the sign of Venus, goddess of love. Surely her children are connected with summer in a most special way.

Perhaps because summer means so much, it seems so short. But each year it comes back and embraces me with heat, and I feel well and growing. Summer is truly life.

I hope all my readers will feel the torrid pull of earth's greatest promise when they read "Summer Heat." Bless you all.

This is for Sue Graham, Ph.D., and Deb Dooley, Ph.D. More than friends, more than professors, they are special people who will save the planet because they care. This is for them.

Prologue

"You found her." Shaken, Jake held the phone to his ear with great effort. His muscles had turned to water. At last! It had been so long, he'd begun to expect failure with every phone call. Not any more. "Go on."

"Well, sir, I know you're a busy man, and this is long-distance—"

"Forget that. Tell me everything."

The private investigator cleared his throat. It wasn't his nickel. If Jason Colby wanted the entire report over the phone, it was fine with him. Colby was rich enough to buy the phone company anyway. Maybe he owned it already. He headed up one of the largest communciations firms in the hemisphere. Funny that he had to search for a woman. Seems as though the women would be tripping over themselves to get to him.

"Ah, pardon me, sir," he said when Colby sharply asked what was taking so long. "Just getting my papers together."

He began to read, and got most of the way through, until Colby asked, "Children?"

"Yes, sir. Two of them. Might be the housekeeper's or somebody else's. It's a big place with a good piece of land around it."

So, Jake thought, his wife had set up a new household, complete with children. She'd run from him almost four years ago. He'd loved her, given her everything. Yes, they'd fought sometimes, but he'd thought their marriage was solid. Damn her! Now he had her, and he'd confront her. No more hide and seek. He'd get some answers . . . and then begin divorce proceedings.

1

Fate and some damned good detective work had found Zane Arnot Colby in Isabella, Louisiana. A backwater town of some five hundred souls, less than thirty miles from New Orleans, Isabella was an old jewel with little luster. Quiet and contained, almost hidden from the modern world, it pattered on kitten's paws on the outer fringe of modernism.

The day Jake drove toward Isabella, rain poured down in silver sheets, muddying the road and filling the ditches that edged it. Tree limbs, flowers, and vines drooped dispiritedly, drowning in the relentless downpour. No rational person would be about in such weather—but Zane was.

Yes, fate and detectives had found her, but only fate could have led him to her the first minutes of his arrival.

Jason Stark Colby, called Jake since childhood, might have laughed if he hadn't been so stunned. There she was, standing in the rain, thoroughly soaked and alone. He'd been heading toward the place where the detective said she lived, and never would have expected to find her standing alongside the road on the outskirts of the small town.

He would have known her anywhere, even in the mawkish disguise weather had given her. Her auburn hair was flattened down on her head and the sides of her face, but nothing could have disguised from him her elfin features, the golden eyes rayed with green, the naturally arched brows, the full lower lip that quivered when she laughed. Tall, slender, softly muscled with beautifully sloping shoulders, she was one of the loveliest women he knew.

She swiped soaked strands of hair back from her cheeks as she waved for him to stop. She was standing near a vehicle that had skewed off the road, its back end mired in mud. A tow truck was needed.

He stopped too quickly, and his rented car fishtailed slightly. She was walking toward him already, as though she wasn't about to let him get away.

Bedraggled and soaked, her clothes matted to her body, she looked like a lost puppy. Looks were deceiving. Zane Arnot Colby had never acted lost, nor puppyish. She was a sharp, intuitive twenty-nine-year-old woman of varying talents, with the deep intelligence and feeling to expand them. And four years ago she'd torn up his life. Now he was going to put an end to the everlasting nightmare of wondering where she was and how she was doing. It was time for him to get on with his life. She had, it would seem.

His car slid to a stop, and she slogged toward it, mud up to her ankles. He cut the motor, and saw that she was carrying a tire iron. Smart lady.

It wouldn't suit him if she recognized him too soon. He wouldn't let her disappear from him again. The last time had been shortly after another argument about her trying to begin a career as a cartoonist. He hadn't been bothered by her career, but by her choice of art schools. There were fine places in Chicago where she could have studied, but she'd been insistent on a school in Minnesota. They'd argued back and forth for weeks over why they could move and why they couldn't, neither wanting to back down. The disagreement had gained momentum, assuming gigantic proportions, so that any slight deviation of opinion would set them back to the same theme.

Two days after another disagreement she informed him she was going to go visit a school friend in southern Illinois for a few days. When she hadn't returned or contacted him in a week, he figured she was simply having such a good time. He ached to call her ... and finally did. He hunted up the friend, who said she hadn't seen Zane in more than a year. Shock, rage, and betrayal blasted through him. Then he waited, sure she'd contact him about a divorce. That didn't happen. After nearly three years of silence, three years in which he was certain he would forget her and yet never did, he contacted the private detective agency.

Now they would meet again. He was through waking up in the night, believing her next to him. And he was damned sure, after the divorce, he would be able to force her from his mind completely.

Hunching over, relying on the rain-streaked side window as cover, he waited until the last second before pressing the button to lower the window. "Hello, Zane."

Luckily he had quick reflexes and ducked when she swung the tire iron. The force of her swing brought her hand in the open window, and he grabbed her wrist.

"Do I pull you in through the window?" he asked. "Or would you like to enter by the door?"

Rain pelted them steadily, soaking his one arm and dampening the rest of him.

Shock sent Zane reeling. Even when she'd struck out at him, it had been a reflex action. She hadn't really believed it was Jake. He'd walked in her mind so much, he could have been a wraith, a figment of her imagination. No such luck. He was there, inches from her, her nemesis, her onetime boss, her erstwhile husband, and father of her two children . . . but he didn't know that. She'd always had the feeling this day would come. Time to contact her lawyer and fight any claim he could make. And she'd battle him too.

But fighting Jake was a tenuous position at best. He knew all the moves. She'd need more armor than she had.

Staying hidden from him had seemed her most viable alternative, though she'd often questioned the rightness of it. Many times she'd longed for him so deeply, it was a physical pain. As the days pushed into weeks, though, as she learned about her pregnancy, her reluctance to contact him deepened and hardened. After a while, too much time had passed. She knew she couldn't return, even if she wished. She'd come to think of herself as safe. Now he was here. She swallowed, her body trembling with all the fears she'd lived with for almost four years.

"I'll come in the door," she said tautly.

"Fine." Jake kept hold of her wrist as he opened the door and stepped out into the rain. He took her other hand, intending to pull her into the car with him, but stopped. Touching her was an unexpected stunner. She still had the power to melt his intentions and his knees. Fiercely reminding himself why he was there, he urged her into the car. She tried to pull free of his hold.

"Wouldn't it be easier for me to go around instead of crawling over the seat?"

"You're getting wetter as we argue."

"So are you," she shot back, feeling childish.

"C'mon, Zane," he said, amusement overriding his irritation. She'd always been able to do that to him too. She could make him laugh as no one else could.

"Don't drag me." She finally managed to free her hands and clambered over the driver's seat and the console, settling into the passenger seat. He slid back into the car and slammed the door shut. Enclosed in the small space with him, Zane couldn't get her breath. He'd always had that effect on her—and probably every other woman he met. But all that was behind her now. She didn't want anything to do with him. Why was he in Louisiana? And why now? She'd begun to wash him from her life. Whole days went by when she didn't think of him. She was happy. Her life was full. What unhappy Fate had brought him here?

Few outsiders appeared in Isabella. Her business was through the mail, and she used a pen name. She'd kept a low profile all these years, so how had he found her?

"What are you doing in Isabella?" she asked.

Jake didn't answer. He barely heard her as he stared at her. He hadn't expected her to still be so beautiful. No, more beautiful. Even without makeup, her clothing and hair dripping wet, she was even lovelier. There was a full-ness to her now, a deepening, ripening to her lissome beauty. She should have been a model, not a business major with an art minor; a movie star, not a talented sketcher. He could recall the many times she'd done him in charcoal. She was good. Had she burned those sketches? Acid twisted his guts.

He'd expected his fury, but the surge of passion rocked him. Just glancing at her had his body hardening, the want swelling like a flood. Damn her! It was over. Maybe it had even been over before she left. So why the hell should he still want her? Their marriage had been great at the start, then she'd grown increasingly restless. He'd understood her need to be her own person, but he hadn't wanted a long-distance marriage.

Did she care that he'd looked for her after she'd run?

"It's been a long time," he said at last.

"Yes," she said dully.

"Almost four years," he added. And not a word from her. Did she care that he'd prowled their home in Chicago, room after room, night after night, sometimes not sleeping? Hell! She obviously hadn't wasted a minute thinking about him. She looked better than ever.

Zane bit her lip to keep from moaning. Four years of fighting her way out of fear, of having no one to share her pain, of being so downhearted she'd cried for hours at a time. How many times had she questioned whether she'd been right or wrong? Could she have handled her problems with his cousin and uncle better? Could she have received the education she wanted in Chicago? She'd gotten along without it in New Orleans. Alone, so damned alone, when she'd given birth, when she'd called out for him during the long and difficult labor. Yet when she'd seen the twins, a wellspring of love had erupted in her, and had not abated since. They'd saved her sanity, becoming her focus, the center of her struggle to survive.

Forcing Jake Colby to the back of her mind, she honed her skills as an artist so she might find work she could do at home. Political cartooning had been her first choice, and she'd sent out many. All had been returned, but she'd begun to know the people. One had suggested she try strip cartooning. At first she'd had no success, then a small opening. Now she had a daily strip, not in the famous national papers but in several local ones. She was getting paid, not huge stipends, but she was meeting most of her bills on time. She had a life; she was making it. She didn't need Jake Colby.

"What do you want?" she asked him.

"That's my girl," he said acerbically. "Succinct and to the point. Some things don't change." He steered cautiously down the narrow, steep grade that led into town. With all the rain, it had turned into a mud slide. The car sloughed and fishtailed through the mire. "Did you find what you were seeking?"

"I didn't leave to find something, Jake," she said hurriedly. Anger and a need to tell him had the words bursting from her. "I had to salvage what little there was left of myself, after a year and a half of that special Colby treatment that reduces all mankind to jelly. You and your family—"

"My family was good to you." Her words were like painful lasers, slicing into him.

"Ha! Your uncle offered to pay me off so often, it became a monthly ritual."

"He's an old man. He didn't handle everything well, but he cared for you.

"And your cousin? What did he want? A piece of the action?" She shook her head. "I don't think I want to know the answer to that." He hadn't believed her when she said Cal had made a sexual advance toward her.

Fury burned Jake, not just from her words. Too easily he could conjure up an intimate scene of her with another man. That was painful enough. It was agonizing if the other man was his cousin.

"Don't give me that," he said, more harshly than he'd intended. "You handled my family well, and easily. You laughed at both my uncle and my cousin. You wanted out of our marriage, and you used my family and that Minnesota art school as excuses. Don't blame your defection on them."

"What was I supposed to do? Throw a temper tantrum because my husband didn't believe me, yet would accept anything bad his relatives said about me." She couldn't bring herself to add that he hadn't supported her desire to be an artist. He had offered to pay her tuition, but only if she chose a school close to home. Her reasons for balking at his strictures seemed thin on reflection. At the time she'd considered them viable.

"That's not true, Zane. I talked to both Uncle Lionel and Cal. Neither had approached you in a threatening manner as you'd claimed. Dammit, my cousin was up north on the night you said—"

"We're just going around again," she cut him off. She couldn't recall that night without shuddering. She'd been a fool. She should have punched Cal in the nose. That might have ended it.

"Be honest enough to admit our problems were our own doing," Jake said.

"It might be easier all around," she muttered.

"What does that mean?"

"Nothing."

"What are you talking about? Tell me."

His angry question brought her up short. Did he really not know? She was so sure he would have discovered Cal's perfidy in some of the business dealings, and would make the connection with his personal life. His cousin was smarter than she thought. Obviously he'd convinced Jake he'd never tried to undermine his marriage.

"Nothing," she said. She had no intention of rehashing her marriage. It wasn't part of her life anymore. "Let me off in the center of town. I can—"

"I'll take you right to Spanish Moss. That's the colorful name of your home, isn't it?" Her abrupt nod almost made him smile. She hadn't expected he'd know where she lived. "Sounds very grand."

"It's plain. I'd rather you didn't drive me there. I need to talk to Sain'Cyr at the filling station about towing my van."

"Where did you pick up the vintage bus you're driving? An antique car show?"

"Very funny, Jake, but I don't give a cotton damn what

you think of my vehicle. I just know I don't want you at my home, nor do I need your input in anything in my life. So drop me off and leave."

She stared out the side window, clenching her fists, wondering if he'd do what she asked. She'd loved him so much. He'd been all of life to her, until she'd found out that she couldn't reach him, that an insurmountable distrust had built between them. When she'd confronted him about it, her soul had screamed for him to deny it. He hadn't. Slowly their closeness had eroded, their togetherness fragmented, until she knew it was time to go. She hadn't realized she was pregnant then, but she must have had an instinct about protecting what was to become the most important facet of her life.

"I understand you're an illustrator," he said, ignoring her request.

"A cartoonist. I do a daily strip called 'The Little Rabbit Who Could.' Several local papers carry it, and there's a chance I'll be syndicated in about six months." She crossed her fingers at the white lie. She hadn't actually been offered a contract yet.

Jake glanced at her, his eyebrows elevated. "I saw your cartoon when I picked up a paper at the airport. Liberal as hell. It's amazing you've lasted this long."

"It's not the conservative stuff your friends would use in their periodicals, but I try to be fair," she said huffily.

"You were never fair about your politics, Zane. You used to light into all my uncle's friends until they were almost ready to agree with you to keep you from breathing down their necks." Unexpected amusement bubbled in him as he recalled the evening she'd told Malcolm Breaker that his narrow view of the world had caused unemployment and the wretched existence of homeless people. The wealthy, pompous real estate developer had stomped from the house, vowing never to return while

Zane was in residence. "I'm sure Malcolm Breaker would be impressed."

She snorted. "How is the old curmudgeon?"

"He and my uncle still meet at their club once a week."

"And how is Uncle Lionel?" Despite their differences, she'd missed the older man. She hadn't, however, missed his son one iota.

"Good. Anxious about you."

She smiled wryly. "I can't see your family being too bent out of shape about me."

Jake shrugged, fighting the simmering anger. What had happened to her in the past four years? There was a compelling strength and maturity about her that hadn't been there before. Was that the result of a new man in her life? "Tell me about your work," he said, forcing aside that painful thought.

"It doesn't show up in the *Wall Street Journal*, but I've had very positive response to it. Unbelievable, isn't it?"

"You always had a quick tongue. Judging from the strip I read today, you've become caustic." He didn't mean it, but was striking out at her in an effort to counter the potent emotions she was arousing in him.

"Caustic?" she exclaimed. "You're a fine one to talk. Get out of my life." She had to force back her tears as he pulled into Isabella's one gas station. Tears? She hadn't cried since the birth of the twins.

"No." He reached for her arm as she started to open her door. "I'll go and talk to the man."

"In Cajun? I don't think so."

She shoved open the door and got out, and a few moments later she felt him at her side as she jogged to the relative shelter of the garage. It was made of tin, rusted and sagging, and the noise of the rain hitting the metal sounded like bursts from a gun.

"Sain'cyr?" she called. "Where are you?" It hadn't taken her long to relearn Cajun. Her grandmother had been Cajun, and she'd talked to Zane in the wonderful patois of archaic French mixed with idioms from other languages common in the New Orleans area. Though Zane was Northern born and bred, she'd also felt a tie to the South, forged by her wonderful, dark-eyed grandmother. Unfortunately, her grandmother had died in the same fire that had claimed the rest of Zane's family, her mother, father, brother, and aunt, while they'd been dining at a bistro in New Orleans. Zane hadn't gone on the family visit to Louisiana, because she'd been in the middle of midterm exams at the University of Chicago.

Sain'cyr, dark-haired and dark-eyed, stepped out of the small shop adjacent to the garage. "Hein? Zane?"

Jake followed Zane across the garage, watching and listening, but understanding little of what they said. He did comprehend that much of the conversation was about her van and some was about him.

At last Sain'Cyr nodded, said something else in Cajun, then added deliberately in English: "Will you be all right?" He jerked his head at Jake.

Zane glanced at Jake, jolted anew by the sight of him. "Merci. Yes," she said to Sain'Cyr, then turned to Jake. "I'm all set. Look, why don't you settle in at the Bayou House. The rooms are clean, the food is excellent ..." Her voice trailed off as he slowly shook his head. Her chin lifted. "I'm not extending an invitation to you."

He shrugged. "You never signed a legal separation agreement. You never filed for a divorce. I have every right to be with you."

"Not if I don't want you." Was that why he had sought her out? she wondered. To get a divorce? But what else had she expected? Jake was a powerfully sexy man, tall, broad-shouldered with sleek looks, and a steel-trap mind.

His deep gray eyes were just as compelling as always, and she saw a few streaks of silver in his dark brown hair. Building a small news agency into a national and then a world-class communications outfit took brains and savvy. He had plenty of both. "Thinking of remarrying?" she asked, hating her curt tone.

"Maybe. I thought you'd be interested in being free to make a few choices yourself."

She looked away. "There is that."

"Shall we go?"

They stepped back into the rain as a sense of doom, more penetrating than the tropical storm, invaded Zane's soul. Shivering, she got into the car.

2

During the drive to Spanish Moss, Zane felt she were suffering an attack of food poisoning. Everything twisted into knots inside her. Fear rose like nausea. She clenched her teeth to keep from giving anything away to Jake. He was too sharp. She swallowed and took several deep breaths, trying to stay calm.

She was her own person now, she reminded herself, handling her life, dealing with problems. The rationales didn't work. Trepidation laced her every breath. What would he do when he found out about the twins? If he sued for custody, she'd fight him every step of the way. She closed her eyes against the fright hanging over her, feeling as though she'd frozen solid as they approached the access road to Spanish Moss. Perspiration dotted her upper lip.

"Turn here," she told him.

Jake stared at the rutted lane that could have used several loads of crushed stone, then eyed his passenger. What was driving her? Had he ever known? And why did she look so frightened? She acted as though he'd come to repossess her house. Hell! She'd threaded her hands so tightly, it was a wonder she didn't break her fingers. Abruptly he realized what was wrong. She hated having him there. That knowledge lanced through him. He knew now that over the past four years she'd never thought of him, never missed what they'd shared. Damn her!

His hands tightened around the wheel as he concentrated on the rutted road. He almost skidded into the deep drainage ditch that ran along either side of the lane, and he was tempted just to drop her off, turn around, and fly back to Chicago. But he wouldn't leave until she'd answered some of his questions.

Zane glanced covertly at him. He was still as handsome as ever, still bigger than life. It was hard to believe he'd been her husband; that they'd made passionate love over and over again, unable to get enough of each other; that they'd planned a "forever" life with each other. Fantasy. Unreal. Yet sometimes those hot memories woke her in the night, her body bathed in perspiration. She'd force the memories away and, dry-eyed, attempt to get back to sleep.

She looked at him again. He was here, beside her! He had more presence than a king. Even when she'd lived with him she'd had a hard time accepting that. Now it was another world.

Through the trees she saw the beautiful outlines of her antebellum home, Spanish Moss. Courage dropped to her shoes. She tried to look at the house as Jake would view it.

From a distance one could see the graceful Greek lines, the Doric columns, the graceful sweep of fan-shaped steps. Only from much closer could the worm-eaten wood he discerned, the sagging pilasters, the damp rot that helped to tilt the gracious two-story portico. The structure cried for reconstruction, for paint, for roofing, for tender, loving care.

Bushes, shrubs, and climbers grew wildly, blooming erratically and meagerly because they were in dire need of pruning. Once a month Sain'cyr ran his hayer over the lawn, but its once emerald beauty was pockmarked with brown and bare spots. Spanish Moss needed money to be restored. Maybe someday.

Jake stopped the car, or rather he went lax at the wheel, and the vehicle dribbled to a stop. "Quite a place," he murmured. "In the grand manner."

Myriad feelings spilled through him as he accelerated slowly and steered along the curving drive, parking in front of the portico. As if on cue the heavy rain had tapered off to a gentle drizzle that misted the house, making it appear both more romantic and more decrepit. He'd expected anything but an antebellum mansion. The place needed overhauling, but it was a beautiful specimen of pre–Civil War architecture, and it exuded all the elegance and power of that period. Seeing it was like gazing at Queen Victoria in her last days. None could deny the royal lines, but the better times were past. "It could use some work," he said mildly.

Zane stiffened, pushing at the door. "I know that." Anger and fear rode her, and she could hardly gather her thoughts, let alone verbalize them. Jake was danger, and the peril of his presence closed around her throat like giant hands. "Thanks for the ride. I'm sure you'll be able to get a room at the hotel in town. I'll be in touch, about when will be a good time to meet and talk."

She knew she was being abrupt, but she had to get away from him.

She got out of the car, not looking back, and walked toward the high, wide double doors of Spanish Moss, which stood open to catch the cool breeze coming from the bayou, a mile away. Praying hard that nothing would prevent Jake's retreat down the driveway, she quickened her pace.

"Maman. Mamannnnnn!"

Zane groaned, winced, and ran.

Her son Brill's voice preceded him only by seconds. He raced out the massive double doors and onto the front porch. "You're back," he exclaimed. "I'm glad. Melda said you musta drove into the bayou—"

"Must have driven," Zane said while she tried to corral the three-year-old bundle of energy and screen him from the car. Behind her she heard a car door slam, and her heart sank. It had been too much to hope that Jake would have left.

"That's what Melda said." Brill peered around her. "Who's that? I like his car."

Jake lightly leapt up the porch steps. "Hello," he said cautiously, his narrowed gaze going from the child to Zane and back again. "I'm Jason Stark Colby."

"Yeah? Me too. My name's Brill Stark Arnot. Funny, huh?"

"Very." Jake inhaled deeply as he stared at Zane's averted face, then he hunkered down in front of the boy. "I'm going to be visiting in the area for a while. I hope we get to be friends."

"Okay." Brill whirled around and called into the house, "Bett! Come quick."

Zane's daughter stepped out of the house to stand beside Brill.

"Bett, that man has the same middle name as me," Brill said. "Great, huh? I like his car."

Babette, a shy girl with the same dark hair as her brother and father and the same golden eyes as her mother, took her thumb out of her mouth, smiled, and returned the digit between her lips.

"This is my sister, Bett. We're twins," Brill said proudly, urging her forward.

"They're mine," Jake said through his teeth.

Zane swung around. "No. They're mine."

"You knew," he went on as if he hadn't heard her, his

voice a thunderous whisper. "When you left me you knew."

His eyes were like silver daggers. She shook her head. "I didn't know I was pregnant when I left." She took a deep breath. "At first I thought the bouts of nausea were simply due to stress. When I found out I was pregnant, I'd been gone two months. It—it seemed better to let sleeping dogs lie." The excuse was weak, ludicrous, but it was the best she could do at the moment.

"You should have gotten in touch with me. At once." She'd been alone and pregnant in a rickety old house with no modern hospital and probably no first-rate physicians nearby. Cold perspiration trickled down his spine, despite the ninety-degree heat.

Zane shook her head mutely, turned away, and walked into the house.

Brill's smile faltered as he stared after his mother, then he beamed at the man. "C'mon in, sir. Melda's baking." He gestured Jake into the house, then grabbed his sister's hand and ran inside.

Zane had paused just beyond the doors, and looked back at him. She didn't want him there, but a part of her reeled with joy at just looking at him. Tall, handsome, electric, sophisticated . . . and she had once loved him wildly.

"Tell them who I am," he said tightly, "or I will."

She stared at his contorted features, at his hands, flexing and unflexing as though he could barely contain the rage within him. "Do what you must, Jake. You always have."

Despite her brave words, her insides were jelly. Shock had turned her to liquid. Why hadn't she known he wouldn't give up? Jake was indomitable. For years she'd feared he would show up, yet he hadn't. It was almost as if he'd purposefully waited until she'd lost her fear of being discovered. Not that she'd ever stopped missing him. He was too much a part of her soul for her to eradicate him.

Now he was here. Fear drove her into the house.

Jake watched her disappear inside the dim interior of the mansion. He waited a few minutes before following, taking deep breaths and feeling weak as a kitten. Hell! He could barely stay upright.

All his preconceived notions about settling a sum of money on her and obtaining a quick, uncontested divorce had gone out the window the minute he'd seen her. He'd wanted her at once, completely, with an intensity that had shaken him. But this second shock had really taken him down to the ground. He had children. Twins. Zane had a fight on her hands if she thought he'd just walk away now. She wasn't going to dump him.

He stepped into the foyer, blinking in the sudden dimness. Two stories above him soared a coved ceiling in carved plaster. Artisans had designed the rococo animals and creatures that decorated the ceiling, and artists had fashioned the cloth that covered the walls from trim to wainscoting. But all of the cloth was spotted and torn. The ceiling had water spots and broken cornices. Staring around the foyer, Jake saw that someone had loved the house once. Only a lover could have added such tasteful accoutrements in the gracious entry. Years of neglect had taken their toll though. The wood floor had once been smooth and shiny, but now the cypress boards were stained and slivering.

"This will take money," he murmured, when he spotted Zane at the far end of the foyer, watching him. He wasn't surprised when she clenched her fists.

"I know that," she said. "And Spanish Moss will have it. Things are looking up for us. With judicious saving, we'll be able to start renovating in three years." With a jerk of her head, she whirled away from him and marched down the center hall to the back of the house.

"And your job pays that much?"

She halted and glanced back at him. "It will. As you can see, we're managing." Her challenging look silently added, "without your help." She continued down the hall, disappearing through a doorway.

"I might have a few different ideas about how you're managing," Jake muttered to himself. He ambled after her, pausing on the threshold of the largest kitchen he'd seen outside of a restaurant. Along one whole wall was a black antique stove, rusting in spots and spouting heat like a furnace into the already heavy, moist air. Every window was open.

The woman who turned from the stove was large, not tall, but full-figured, as though she sampled all the goodies from her kitchen. She had rolls of fat under her chin, and her eyes looked like raisins in dough. She wiped her hands on her apron as she crossed the room to him.

"I'm Melda. Have some bread. It's fresh. So's the butter." She shook his hand once and turned back to the stove. "This is my kitchen. You will not mess it."

"I understand," Jake murmured.

Nervously Zane picked up a peach.

"Wash it," Melda said without turning.

Zane went to the sink and did.

Jake moved up behind her. "What's her secret? I could never make you jump like that."

Zane stiffened. "Common sense. You don't have any."

"I have enough to know that I'm staying right here." When she whirled around, he stared down at her. "Believe me, nothing will get me to leave, Zane. Now go and take a shower. You're still soaked. And show me to the bathroom I can use."

"We only have one in operation," she said weakly. "You use it."

"Don't be an idiot. You're the one who's wet. I'll talk to the children." He walked away from her, then glanced back. "But I'm staying. Remember that."

3

The guest from hell!

That was how Zane thought of Jake. She gritted her teeth and taped her strip sheet to the drawing board. Bayou Ben, The Little Rabbit Who Could's best friend and owner, wasn't being very cooperative. He was an independent rascal most times, but this morning he was way out of line. Too angry. Too belligerent. Too Jake. Damn him! She kept drawing his face on the board.

"Hell," she muttered, "he's only been here two days. Mr. Takeover. He acts like the superintendent of earth. Roast his hide." She glared down at the pen-and-ink sketch of the boy with bare feet, torn cutoffs, and a fishing pole, the rabbit by his side.

"Talking to yourself?"

She stiffened, staring out the open French doors to the kitchen garden. Sultry, heavy air hung over the ripening vegetables, seeping into the room, into her being. She could see Jake in the reflection of the glass. She could feel him in her soul. Someday she'd be rid of him, inside and out. "I'm working." She coughed to clear her voice of its huskiness.

"This is a great work area."

"It needs refurbishing too," she said, trying not to sound too defensive. Jake brought out the worst in her.

"Yes, it does." Jake noted her stiffness and smiled.

117

She'd always been sensitive. One evening not long after they'd met, they'd been walking back to her apartment after dinner. They'd come upon two teenagers who were maliciously teasing a kitten, and she'd wrested it from them.

"Shiloh misses you," he said suddenly. Of course she'd adopted the kitten and brought it with her when they'd married. She looked up at him, and the glint of tears in her eyes wrenched his heart.

"I've missed him," she said. "He's well and happy?"

"I'd describe him as fat and sassy. He runs the joint." Her ability to empathize and protect had endeared her to him from the start.

He frowned, pushing that thought from his mind, and looked around him. She'd taken over what he assumed had been the library. Built on the end of one wing of the house, it was an open room, two stories high. A staircase in one corner led to a second-floor balcony, which edged the room on three sides and provided access to floor-to-ceiling bookcases. The balcony was rickety and hanging askew, and the bookshelves were all but empty, the wood warped and bowed. The few remaining books were in questionable shape.

On the lower floor, light poured into the room on three sides. The French doors and chancel windows had been handcrafted with rich stained glass in the top panes; the lower ones were leaded and glistening. Their graceful Palladian tops let in the maximum amount of sunlight. It was a shabby but grand and wonderful room.

Zane followed his gaze around the room, wincing at the signs of decay, noting the frayed drapes pockmarked with moth holes. Generally she closed the drapes in the afternoon, keeping in the relative coolness. She was used to their threadbare condition. One day they'd be replaced . . .

"Beautiful architecture," Jake said.

"Yes, it is," Zane answered, turning back to her work. "I'm busy at the moment."

He pushed away from the wall. "So am I. But Melda asked me to call you to lunch."

"No, thanks. I'll just grab a sandwich . . ." Her voice trailed off as he walked up behind her and looked at the board.

"Very talented," he said. "And don't bite your lip. It wasn't a patronizing remark." Heat shot through him as he thought about how he once would have caught that lip with his own teeth, nibbling on it, worrying it. The loveplay would have ended in bed.

Lifting her chin, she stared at him. "I don't try to analyze your meanings anymore, Jake. Nor do I get a kick out of the verbal jousting you love." She put her hand protectively over the strip. "And I don't need you to validate my work." Still, she had to struggle against wanting his approval. She'd come so far, she didn't think she needed it. Yet she wanted it . . . and him.

His eyes narrowed. "As I said the other day, you didn't used to be so caustic, or defensive."

"Everybody changes," she said abruptly, hurt by his words. "And I don't consider myself caustic or defensive."

He shrugged, apparently deciding to back off. "The children showed me your work. Not just in the dailies but in the Sunday paper too."

She nodded. "Papers in Louisiana and Tennessee carry me so far."

He leaned over again to study what she'd done that morning. "It's good, Zane. It's deep, but also childlike. I like that."

She didn't know why she felt so rosily happy about his remarks, so giddy. "Thank you."

"You're welcome. Now come and join us for lunch. Brill and Bett leave for play camp in less than an hour. Surely you want to eat with them."

Zane was startled. She had a hard time getting the twins to the table at any time. Usually they ate with their assortment of pets. "All right." She cleaned her pens, topped the ink bottles, whirled around on the stool, then gasped. He hadn't moved but was standing only inches from her. She stared up at him, praying he couldn't sense her body's turbulent reaction to his proximity.

"Allow me." His hands at her waist, he lifted her off the stool. "Still as slim as ever." He squeezed lightly, feeling a rush of blood through him. She'd always been exciting. "Did you have a good pregnancy?"

"Not too bad," she said cautiously.

"Don't look so suspicious. I'm concerned, Zane." He laughed harshly. "Why wouldn't I be? You're my wife."

Her heart jolted. "Not anymore," she said, looking away from him.

"Still," he said softly. "Tell me about your pregnancy."

"I suffered through the usual nausea and tiredness." And hopelessness, and fear, and, wretched loneliness. There'd been nights when she wept uncontrollably. Finally, slowly, her focus had swung to the unborn children, saving her sanity. She still looked away from him, but she could feel his breath on her face, his intent gaze, as though he could see into her mind. She couldn't move, for he'd all but pinned her to the drawing table.

"How about the birth?" he asked.

"Rough. Twelve hours. But I made it. Ouch!" His grip had tightened on her. She looked up at him, frowning. "Jake, let me go."

"Damn you for not telling me." She could have died, he thought, anguished. Alone!

She pushed against his chest. He was immovable, staring down at her with an odd expression on his face, as though he was in pain. She doubted it. Jake had always been unflappable. Yet some strong emotion had gripped him. His mouth had twisted, and his complexion was a strange putty color. "I . . . I was all right," she whispered.

"Were you?" For long moments he gazed into her eyes. Then he stepped back and dropped his hands. "I want to know everything. I'll keep asking until I do."

"Maybe I won't answer." She stalked across the room and yanked open the door, then her mouth dropped open. The thick walls of Spanish Moss rendered each room nearly soundproof. Now myriad noises assaulted her as she gaped at the strangers trouping through her foyer. Jake had said something about wanting to repair some of the basic damage to the house. She'd pictured a carpenter, maybe a plumber, not . . . "What on earth— How many people—?"

"They're the architect's workmen," Jake said laconically.

"But we agreed—"

"The workmen are necessary for the initial estimate and some of the immediate repairs. My children live in this house. I'm going to make damn sure it's structurally sound. Don't bother arguing. We do it this way or I find another place for you to live."

"Another place! This is my home. Spanish Moss is—"

"Fine. Then we'll go ahead with the renovating—"

"Renovating?"

"Will you stop repeating everything I say. And duck your head or you'll smack it on the scaffolding."

Zane stopped dead in the foyer, looking upward at the skeletal metal structures that had mushroomed since she'd gone into her workroom that morning. She'd heard the clanging and banging, but had assumed a plumber was working on one of the nonfunctioning bathrooms.

She hadn't envisioned this. "See here, this is my home. And when I have the money, I will restore it to its original beauty. I don't want any modernist changing one inch of Spanish Moss—"

"I agree. Philo Headen is one of the best resources of information about the—"

"Philo Headen! The classic restorer from Vicksburg? You can't get him. He's booked for a thousand years. And I won't have him because I can't afford him. So you just take this army of—"

"If they go, so do you all," Jake said brusquely. "I mean it. If I have to, I'll drag you out of here and burn the place to the ground. You and the children are not staying in an unsafe house."

"Unsafe! Spanish Moss? Burn it? Never! Interloper. Vandal." Zane was sputtering, anger flaming through her. "Get out of here. I'll have you know ..." Her voice trailed off as he grinned at her, his grin that meant he had the upper hand. In the sudden silence she realized she'd been shouting at him, that Melda and the children had come from the kitchen to stare at them, and that the workers had stopped what they were doing to watch. Zane looked back at Jake, inhaling deep breaths, slowly calming herself. "I'll talk to you later, Colby, you—you assassin," she said through her teeth. She wanted to smack his chuckle right back down his throat. Instead she marched down the hall, zigzagging among the ladders and scaffolding.

"Maman, isn't it great?" Brill shouted to her, waving his arms. "I like it. Bett and I are going to help. Are you going to shout at Jake some more, or are we going to eat?"

"Tell him I'm his father or I will," Jake whispered from behind her. He stepped back instinctively when she swung around, fists clenched. "My, we are angry," he

Passion awaits you...
Step into the magical world of

Loveswept

E N J O Y . . .

A Magical World of Enchantment Awaits You When You're Loveswept!

Your heart will be swept away with Loveswept Romances when you meet exciting heroes you'll fall in love with...beautiful heroines you'll identify with. Share the laughter, tears and the passion of unforgettable couples as love works its magic spell. These romances will lift you into the exciting world of love, charm and enchantment!

You'll enjoy award-winning authors such as Iris Johansen, Sandra Brown, Kay Hooper and others who top the best-seller lists. Each offers a kaleidoscope of adventure and passion that will enthrall, excite and exhilarate you with the magic of being Loveswept!

- ♥ *We'd like to send you 6 new novels to enjoy–<u>risk free!</u>*
- ♥ *There's no obligation to buy.*
- ♥ *6 exciting romances–plus your <u>free gift</u>–brought right to your door!*
- ♥ *Convenient money-saving, time-saving home delivery!*

Join the Loveswept at-home reader service and we'll send you 6 new romances about once a month– <u>before they appear in the bookstore!</u> You always get 15 days to preview them before you decide. Keep only those you want. Each book is yours for only $2.25* That's a total savings of $3.00 off the retail price for each 6 book shipment.

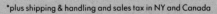

*plus shipping & handling and sales tax in NY and Canada

Enjoy 6 Romances–Risk Free! Plus...
An Exclusive Romance Novel Free!

Detach and mail card today!

Loveswept

Yes! Please send my 6 Loveswept novels RISK FREE along with the exclusive romance novel "Larger Than Life" as my *free gift* to keep.

RE123 41228

NAME

ADDRESS   APT.

CITY

STATE   ZIP

MY ''NO RISK''

Guarantee

I understand when I accept your offer for Loveswept Romances I'll receive the 6 newest Loveswept novels right at home about once a month (before they're in bookstores!). I'll have 15 days to look them over. If I don't like the books, I'll simply return them and owe nothing. You even pay the return postage. Otherwise, I'll pay just $2.25 per book (plus shipping & handling & sales tax in NY and Canada). I *save* $3.00 off the retail price of the 6 books! I understand there's no obligation to buy and I can cancel anytime. No matter what, the gift is mine to keep–*free!*

SEND NO MONEY NOW.
Prices subject to change. Orders subject to approval. Prices shown are U.S. prices.

FREE BOOK OFFER

RUSH!

BUSINESS REPLY MAIL

FIRST CLASS MAIL   PERMIT NO. 2456   HICKSVILLE, NY

POSTAGE WILL BE PAID BY ADDRESSEE

LOVESWEPT
BANTAM DOUBLEDAY DELL DIRECT
PO BOX 985
HICKSVILLE NY 11802-9827

NO POSTAGE
NECESSARY
IF MAILED
IN THE
UNITED STATES

said, wisely holding back his smile. She was more beautiful than he'd remembered. Oh, he'd recalled her fire, the way she would reach for him, how her limbs would coil around his wantonly, desiring as he did to be spun through the hot paradise of sexual delights. His frustration with her eased as the memories coursed through him. He'd welcome any physical contact with her, for he needed to touch her, hold her, feel that torrid desire once more.

Zane's lips had tightened to a thin line at his threat. She knew she would have to tell the children who Jake was, but she was fearful of their reaction and wanted to give them more time to get to know him.

"Stuff it, Colby," she said. "You don't tell me what to do or not to do with my own children."

She saw the leaping fire in his eyes, and recalled the verbal jousting they used to fall into so easily. Often it ended with them in bed, caught in that unforgettable passion . . . with nothing resolved. That monumental standoff was one reason why she'd run. She'd looked down the years into a long, empty tunnel of nothing resolved. She'd left that same week.

"Of course," she went on incautiously, "I don't have to worry about your saying anything to the children. You prefer to avoid emotional confrontation, don't you?" Hardly were the words out of her mouth than she wished she could recall them. It was the sort of attack she hated, and she tried not to be small in her dealings with people. Jake made her so crazy though.

A familiar glacial mask slipped over his face. She sighed. His eyes were bellicose, glittering. "I had no intention of trying to hurt you," she said. "Believe it or not."

"Really? I thought you were just continuing with

something you'd become quite proficient at," he said through stiff lips.

She felt slapped, kicked by his words and tone. "Then leave. It should be as obvious to you as it is to me that we mix as well as oil and water."

"We used to be glue, from chin to toe, darling," he said smoothly. "And the proof of that is the children we made."

Zane wasn't fooled by the satin in his voice. There was murder in his eyes. Lifting her chin, she swung away from him and stalked to the kitchen, her footsteps echoing off the parquet floor. She knew full well he was at her heels.

"Come and have your lunch," Melda said, jerking her head at Jake. "I only serve meals once. We don't have dozens of servants marching around here like tin soldiers, waiting to feed you whenever you want."

"I'm sure you'll have me waiting on you before long, Melda." Jake grinned as the Cajun woman eyed him suspiciously. The children giggled, and he turned his attention to them. "What will you do this afternoon when you come back from camp?"

"Help the workers," Brill said promptly.

Bett smiled shyly and looked down at her sandwich, which had been cut with cookie cutters into diamonds and circles.

Jake leaned forward on his elbows, studying the little girl. "You're a lovely lady, Babette."

"We call her Bett," Brill said. "I talk good. Maman says so."

"I agree," Jake said, and laughed.

When Zane heard Bett laugh too, she stared. So did Melda. Bett seldom talked. Her brother did that for her. It was good to see her exert herself to laugh. Zane knelt beside her daughter's chair and hugged her. "I like to hear you laugh, cherie."

Jake watched as the child reached up and kissed her mother on the mouth. The childish openness, the easily seen love between mother and daughter had the breath catching in his throat. All at once he was miserably jealous that his wife was kissed by someone else, even his daughter, and that the same child could show such beautiful affection ... but not to him. His appetite fled. He quaffed his iced tea and stood. "I think I'll forgo the food, Melda. Thank you, anyway." He left the room quickly, leaving behind four staring people.

"What is this?" Melda asked Zane.

"I don't know, Melda."

"He's mad," Bett said suddenly, bringing all eyes her way. "I like Jake."

"Me too," Brill said, grinning at his sister as though they shared a new joke.

"How nice," Zane muttered.

"I like him," Melda said.

"Great." Zane was ready to kill him. He'd swung her family over to his side without firing a shot. Damn him. Taking sides? What was the matter with her?

"I'm finished," Brill said from his chair. "I'll help Jake until the bus comes." He jumped down before his mother could stop him.

"Me too." Bett grinned at the two women, then she was off, scrambling after her brother.

"He is the father," Melda pronounced solemnly.

"So?" It didn't surprise Zane that Melda knew. She had the Cajun's mystical ways.

"He belongs here."

"Over my dead body."

"So be it," Melda said heavily.

Zane glared at her, then hurriedly finished her sandwich.

"I'm going back to work."

"Good. I want to clean my kitchen before they fix it."

"What?"

Melda shrugged. "You should listen when I talk to you, petite. In a day or two we must move into the old overseer's cottage at the back."

"But ... but ..."

"Do not stammer, petite. It—"

"Melda!" Zane stamped her foot, earning herself a frown from the other woman. Taking deep breaths, she lowered her voice. "Are you saying this kitchen is being renovated and that's why we have to move?"

"Yes."

"Why wasn't I told?"

"The workers told Mr. Jake. I thought he told you."

"He didn't." Zane whirled around and stomped from the kitchen. Zigzagging her way through the ladders and scaffolding again, she saw Jake up on one of them. "Get down here," she called to him.

"Ah, the dulcet tones of a sweet wife—"

"Don't call me that."

"But you are. My wife. We aren't divorced." He swung his leg over the scaffolding stanchion, then easily made his way down the ladder.

He'd always been too limber, too conditioned, for his own good. Macho man. He'd been a track and field star in college and tried out for the Olympic team, not missing by much. She'd been fooled by the suave athlete once too often though, and was no longer enamored of his sophisticated sexiness, his smooth earthiness that had made her body vibrate with need. She was beyond that. She was a different woman now, and she wouldn't go back to being the person she had been. She glared at him as he strolled toward her. Aware that the workers had paused to watch again, she headed for the library.

"We'll talk in my workroom," she said, and pushed open the heavy oak door. He strolled into the room, and she hurled the door shut. As the sound reverberated around them, she faced him. "What the hell do you think you're doing?"

"What do you mean now?"

"You know damn well what I mean, Colby—"

"You used to call me Jake."

"Knock it off. I mean it." She fought for calm; even her fingers itched to scratch the sardonic smile off his face. "This is my home—"

"Your home was with me."

"Don't interrupt."

"Don't shout."

"I'm not shouting." With great effort she spoke in a lower tone. "I don't want you here. You're disturbing my life. And I like the way we live, in this house, in this town. My children will be getting an excellent education at—"

"At St. Maria Louisa School. You've already enrolled them for preschool." She gaped at him, and he grinned. "My lawyer called this morning. The detective agency I hired to find you finally sent in its written report."

"I hate that," she said with deceptive softness. "Didn't I go through enough of that when I lived in that awful barn of a house, being spied on . . ." She stopped when his neck and face reddened. "Never mind that. It's past. I want to talk about this house—"

"You weren't incarcerated in that 'awful barn of a house.' You had everything my wealth could provide." He was stung to the core that she could vilify what they'd had. They'd loved each other wildly. It should have been forever. "You had friends, and places to go. We traveled—"

"It was pure hell," Zane shot back, exaggerating in her anger. There had been problems—what marriage didn't have problems?—but there'd been moments of heaven too, long nights of loving and happy days of sharing, of being together. But she'd been brought down to earth with a crash. "I concede I was happy at first—"

"So was I," he said abruptly.

She frowned at him. "Then be honest. After the first few months it went downhill. The little nasties began, the offer of payoffs—"

"Nasties? Payoffs? Don't be ridiculous." He glared at her.

"You know what I mean. Those lovely little tales your uncle and cousin wove about me. The money they accused me of taking."

Jake stiffened. "That was straightened out. They apologized."

"Sure. So did you. But what did it matter? What were those apologies worth? You hadn't believed me—"

"At first it looked suspicious. But I didn't accept their word without questioning it. Look, we went all over that then. It's over. I told you I was sorry—"

"Is it over?" she interrupted. "I don't think so. As you said, I had it all. Money, prestige, position. Everything but trust and good will. And friends? Don't make me laugh. When I went to church and met Maureen McCarthy, I was warned to stay away from her. You'd never met her, and neither had your uncle and cousin. But because I met her in a small church in the wrong part of Chicago, she was suspect. 'She can't be your friend, Zane.' Isn't that what you said?"

He nodded. "I was worried about your being in such a rough part of town. You could've been endangered—"

She waved her arm as though to brush his words away. "Bull. Forget it. I've heard it all. So I'm telling you now, Jake Colby, this isn't your turf. You don't dictate policy or anything else here. I'm in charge, so pull off your dogs. And don't try riding roughshod over any of us, or attempt to take over Spanish Moss. This is mine. You didn't buy it." She saw pain flash across his face, though it was gone in a second. It jarred her. Jake was so inscrutable, so aloof. Wasn't he? Didn't she know him as well as she thought?

Jake stared at her, his fury rising to match hers. His guts twisted with an agony of knowing that because he'd wanted to protect her, she'd felt smothered. When he'd been a child, though his family hadn't had the wealth he had now, there'd been a kidnapping scare. From the time he'd been ten, it had been drummed into him that he should protect himself and all he had. He'd done so to the best of his ability. He'd never told Zane about his childhood, about how paranoid his parents had been, always, checking on his whereabouts, his friends, even providing a bodyguard for him when he'd been in college. They'd died when he was nineteen, and his uncle had been his guardian for two years. Though Uncle Lionel hadn't been as bad as his parents, he'd fussed often and volubly about personal protection. Jake realized now that he'd suffered from a paranoia of his own about Zane.

Zane noted his abstraction. "Well?"

"I'm not leaving. Those are my children. And you know that if I decide to fight you, I'll win." When he saw her face whiten, he felt an amalgam of black satisfaction and regret. Inhaling roughly, he held out his hands. "The house needs renovating . . ."

She stepped around him. "Stay out of my way," she said, throwing open the door. "I mean that, Colby."

4

Jake was everywhere, all around Spanish Moss and all around her. Less than a week after his arrival it was as though he were a fixture in the house. Continually off balance, Zane felt as if she were sparring with a titan. The children got along well with him though, and during their midafternoon snack on Jake's third day with them, she told them who Jake was.

"Our daddy?" Brill repeated. He frowned at his orange slice.

Zane nodded, not trusting herself to speak further.

The three sat in silence for a few minutes, until Bett looked up and said, "I still like him."

"Maybe I do too," Brill said doubtfully. "Where's he been?"

"Chicago," Zane said, then coughed to clear her throat. It helped to chew the slices of orange. It was something to do, and it soothed her frazzled nerves. "He's a very busy man."

"Oh. Now he isn't?"

"Well, yes . . . no. He's still busy . . . but now he'd like to visit for a while."

"Fathers in Chicago only visit?"

Zane stared helplessly at her son. "No . . . yes. They do, but they live in the same home . . . most of the time."

Brill nodded sagely. "I'll tell Jake to do that."

Zane sighed. Brill could simplify anything to his satisfaction. Bett smiled at her brother, pleased with his solution.

It jolted her that they took it in stride. It didn't change their feelings toward him, and they welcomed him immediately and completely into the family.

The children were happy. They played and pretended to help the indulgent workmen. The adults, on the other hand, walked on eggs. Melda talked to Zane and Jake, and they to her. They spoke to each other in monosyllables.

What bothered Zane the most was that she was getting used to seeing Jake around Spanish Moss. He spent many hours on the phone handling his business long-distance, but it all seemed under control, and he made no mention of leaving.

Soon, she thought morosely, she'd be down on her knees, begging him to stay. That fear more than anything had her nerves constantly jumping. Their lives were changing as rapidly as Spanish Moss. Eventually she would grow dependent on him. The children already had, as had Melda and the house itself. She couldn't allow that vulnerability into her life again. It had almost destroyed her when she left him. He'd become such a part of her, she'd felt unfocused, only half a person, without him. Life had been a bitch. Not again!

The renovation was the only thing that was proceeding smoothly and steadily. The main structure checks had revealed a need for replacing some of the major support beams, weakened from dry rot and worms. But the architect had rushed to reassure Zane that, for a house that had suffered such benign neglect, Spanish Moss was in better than fair shape and could be brought back to its real beauty. Eventually.

"Thanks," Zane muttered softly when the foreman finished telling her that they'd run into a few snags in the kitchen, that the heavy old stove that took up one short wall would have to be completely refurbished. The expense would be exorbitant. Might be better to order a new French ceramic stove. They were still made and could be ordered from a manufacturer outside Paris.

Dollar signs danced in front of Zane's eyes, but she was determined to pay back every cent, if it took the rest of her life.

Paying back the money was a minor problem anyhow, compared with the more immediate problem of having to move into the overseer's cottage that evening. The renovations on the kitchen would begin early the next morning.

Melda sought Zane out in her workroom to tell her that. Zane grimaced. How were they all going to fit in that small cottage? Perhaps Jake would consider moving into town. She was about to suggest that to Melda, when the older woman continued.

"I don't think I stay in the little house with you. I go to my sister's until it is finished. She can use my help for a few days anyway." She smiled widely, patting her large stomach. "I am too big for the small beds there."

Zane stared at her with horror and dawning comprehension. The unfamiliar irritability that Jake's presence engendered surfaced once more. "Surely we won't be out of the house that long. The cottage is pretty run-down."

"Is true, Miss Zane, the slave quarters are much broken. But the field boss's cottage is not bad."

"But . . . but . . . when will you go?"

Melda smiled benignly. "This afternoon. My sister is close by, and if you need me, I will come each day to cook and clean."

"Fine," Zane whispered hoarsely.

After Melda had left, Zane headed out to her garden to gather greens and the luscious tomatoes that grew there. When she had enough for the salad she wanted to serve with the gumbo she'd made, she continued on to her herb garden. She'd used all her dried sassafras in the gumbo. It was time to pick more and hang it in the summer kitchen to dry.

She never heard the footsteps in the soft earth of the garden, but she saw the shadow. Her head snapped up and she stared at Jake, silhouetted in the bright afternoon sun. He was a beautiful man, one she'd happily pledged her life to, and one who could very well destroy the life she'd made for the twins and herself. She'd have to fight his pull. His very presence on earth kept her from contemplating a liaison with anyone else. There must be a way to break that tie. She had no illusions about Jake's power, hadn't from the moment she'd met him. She'd gotten a job in the mailroom of Colby News Service. Her third day on the job she'd dashed out of the mailroom and smacked into him, dropping her bag and scattering envelopes, memos, folders, mail tubes, the lot. The instant she lifted her head and gazed into his dark gray eyes, he became her nucleus, her raison d'être. She was her own woman now, she reminded herself, mistress of her own fate. She'd kept it that way.

"Your garden?" he asked. At her nod his smile twisted. "One more talent I didn't know you had, Zane. How many more are there?"

His soft smile shook her. "None." Unnerved by his nearness, she struggled for balance. Part of her wanted to throw herself into his arms; the other part wanted to rail at him for all the pain he'd caused her, wittingly or not.

He glanced around at the organized plots of healthy

green plants. "Very neat. Unlike the way you used to carry the mail when you first started working."

Her eyes widened as she stared at him. He'd read her mind! How could he have known she'd just been thinking about that?

They gazed at each other, caught in a time warp of memories, shaken to the core by their past, by the togetherness that had been so sadly riven.

"When we bumped in the corridor," he went on after a moment, "I was as surprised as you. It took us twenty minutes to pick up the mail that day." His smile was ironic. "I couldn't concentrate on anything but your beautiful eyes."

Zane was captivated by his smile, by his soft, caressing voice. "I didn't know who you were," she said breathlessly.

"You said you had to hurry. You were delivering the executives' mail, and you were afraid some vice president would come by and scream about his mail being late."

"And you said you'd run interference for me."

His smile broadened as he remembered how he'd gone along with her, maneuvering it so that she ended up at his office. "You closed your eyes and groaned when I sat down at my desk."

"And you ..." She shook her head. She couldn't repeat how, when she'd immediately turned to leave, he'd rushed to the door and stood with his back to it, asking her to stay for a minute. "It's silly to travel down memory lane." More than silly, it was torturous.

"I took you out to dinner that night," he continued as if she hadn't spoken, "and asked you to marry me. You were horrified."

"No! I mean, I was surprised." She'd been delighted, wildly in love with him even as she'd argued with herself that she couldn't be.

Jake watched her closely. "We went out to dinner every night that week and the next. Finally you married me."

"It's past," Zane said hurriedly, trying to smother the swamping memories of laughter, of loving, of being entwined with the man she loved, of craving nothing more. "It collapsed as fast as it built." And she'd learned to live with the emptiness, with the hollow pit in her being that had come with her separation from Jake.

Ire and frustration kept him mute. He wanted to lash out at her, hurt her as she had hurt him. The recollection of their passion was still fresh in him. Where the hell did she get off shoving it all on the back shelf of her life?

She continued to stare up at him. "I—I really should get the greens washed for the salad," she said lamely.

Shrugging off his ire and the sharp pain of her words, he nodded, trying to smile. "The smells from the kitchen are mouth-watering," he said, going down on his haunches next to her.

"Thank you." Zane felt shy, as though someone had praised the "Mona Lisa" and called it her work.

"What are you picking?" She'd never cooked for him. He hadn't even known she could. Somehow he felt cheated of that special intimacy.

"Sassafras leaves. I used all I had to make the filé for the gumbo." She put more in her basket, then frowned down at the basket, wondering how she'd gathered such a harvest. Jake made her forget where she was, what she was doing.

He plucked some sassafras himself and sniffed it. "You told me about your grandmother, your family . . . what happened to them in New Orleans, but not about this place."

She looked at him again, puzzled by his comment.

Why hadn't she told him about Spanish Moss? She

must have felt that her life, before they met, was not important to him. He'd asked her little about her past. It would be silly to fight with him about that now. She should have made him see how she'd felt when they were living together. The niggling voice deep inside her that had been her companion for four years, constantly telling her that she should have talked to Jake before she left him, started in again. Guilt and anger warred within her. "I'd always meant to claim this place. It has ... memories. My roots are here." She put more sassafras in her basket. "My grandmother moved from here to New Orleans when my father moved to Chicago, before I was born, but she never sold Spanish Moss."

Jake leaned over and put some leaves in her basket. "You never lived here?"

"No. I visited, and I knew it was here. And it was mine. It seemed a good place to ..."

"To hide from me?" He sighed when she nodded reluctantly. "I'm sorry about that. I guess I buried my head in the sand about the divisions between us. I thought if I gave you everything—"

"You did. But you traveled a great deal. Sometimes we saw each other only on weekends. We didn't talk, we socialized with others." And when they were alone, they made love, not able to get enough of each other. The lovemaking was beautiful, but they should have taken more time to know each other, to talk, to reveal.

He nodded slowly. "I realized that, after you'd gone. Then I couldn't find you." He'd been wild with pain. Neither his uncle nor his cousin had been able to do anything with him. His work had suffered. He'd avoided any and every social event. He'd begun to hate the office, hate their home. He'd been lashed with guilt, with want, with love ... and he hadn't been able to find her. "After

a while," he said, "I decided I should get on with my life,
that I could live without you—"

"As I've lived without you," she said hollowly, not adding that she couldn't get through a single night without
thinking of him.

"Yes."

Silence stretched between them.

"Have you decided to marry again, Jake?" As she
asked the question, a thousand arrows seemed to pierce
her.

He shrugged. "No thought of that. I am married."

"Yes, but you could obtain a divorce easily. I deserted
you. Your lawyer could—"

"Don't construct a case for me, Zane," he said abruptly, and gestured to a plant. "What's this?"

"Sweet basil. I plant it everywhere. It keeps the flies
and bugs down, and I can make pesto sauce and mari-
nara sauce with it. It's good in many recipes really."
When his brows rose in surprise, she almost laughed.
"What did you think I did before I hired Melda? Live on
takeout? I'm too health-conscious for that."

"I remember. Isn't the sun too strong for your skin?"

"Yes. I wear block. Somehow the heat doesn't bother
me though. Everyone told me I'd be flattened by it. I
guess I'm too much like Grandmother Zoe."

"I'd like to have met her."

Stunned, she sat back on her heel. "You would?"

"Very much." He grimaced at her incredulity. "Listen
to me, Zane. What we had was quick, volatile, even out
of control. We didn't take the time . . . no, we didn't
make the time to find out about each other, to protect
and nurture what we—"

"I knew you and yours," she said bitingly. "It was a
humbling experience. If I'd stayed longer, my self-esteem
would've been in the subcellar."

"Zane, please. You never liked Cal, but—"

She held up her hand. "Wait a minute. Your cousin all but called me a streetwalker and a thief. Your uncle concurred."

"My uncle regretted that, deeply. So did Cal. And they admitted it. They apologized. And did it in front of me so—"

"And how about behind your back? Your uncle looked at me at times as though he'd scraped me off his shoe. And good old Cal. Was he so great when you weren't around?"

"Are you talking about the night you said he came on to you?"

Perspiration beaded his forehead. His lips had tightened as if he were in pain, but he didn't look away from her. Zane was sorry she'd said anything. "The night he did come on to me," she said tonelessly, sorry now that she had deliberately downplayed that encounter to Jake. She'd grown so diffident with him by then, however, she hadn't been able to break through her own reserve to tell him that Cal hadn't just made a pass at her, he'd practically assaulted her.

"He swore on a Bible he never did it. I told you that I talked to him, many times—"

"And you believed him over me."

Jake's jaw clenched. He shook his head. "I acted stupidly. I should've told you at once that I didn't doubt you. I assumed, like a fool, that you'd know that." He drew in a deep breath. "Then you were gone. You took so little, as if you were going for only a few days. Just some cash, no jewelry, a minimal amount of clothing. That's why I didn't worry, or institute a search, for a long time."

"I didn't think we could trust each other anymore. It seemed fruitless. And I had my credit cards. I used them in every ATM I passed while still in the city. Then I was almost wealthy. After that I left the area and headed like a rocket to Louisiana."

"You had to escape me because you couldn't trust me," he said slowly, as though the words hurt.

But I loved you so. "Yes," she answered and biting her lip when he winced.

"I hurt you so much."

She looked away. "I don't want to talk about this anymore." She glanced back at him, and her mouth dropped. His face was ashen, his hands were shaking, and his eyes glittered with a strange light. "Jake? Are you all right? Are you ill?" Shock had her heart thudding. She reached for his hand. It was hot and dry. "Jake? Relax. It's past."

As though he'd just realized she was holding his hand, he turned his palm up, gripping hers. "Tell me. Are you saying you've lost all faith in what we had?"

"We've been apart a long time," she reminded him gently. "Too long."

Her words poured through him like a poison. He felt nauseated, dizzy. The taste in his mouth was acrid, metallic with regret. "I don't agree," he said. "Where was my uncle when Cal made this pass at you?"

"He'd gone to his club. Meeting friends and staying overnight. He often did that, as you know. Jake . . . forget what I said. It's almost four years ago—"

He pushed to his feet and stalked away, his fists clenched.

5

Heat and rain. Rain and heat. Everything steamed. Zane felt as though she were melting herself. Her world had tipped, and everything was sliding. She couldn't find purchase in her world because of Jake. He'd gotten under skin ... inside her veins ... He'd become the beat of her heart.

They'd been in the overseer's cottage for three days. Seventy-two hours of tripping over one another, vainly trying to find some privacy, lining up for the one tiny bathroom with the temperamental plumbing. If the faucet in the kitchen was turned on, the shower could become icy cold or blistering hot. That wasn't too bad ... most of the time.

One morning though, Zane ran cold water in the sink to wash vegetables. She heard Jake's bellow and the stream of curses before Brill galloped into the tiny kitchen.

"Daddy's yelling. The water burned him."

Bett was right behind her, eyes wide, thumb in her mouth.

"Oh, dear. I forgot." She'd been managing the meals, having told Melda just to stay at her sister's. It was bad enough with four people crammed into five small rooms. The cottage was a constant mess, and all any of them seemed to do was pickup and put away. "Tell him it was an accident—"

"I figured that," Jake said, coming into the tiny kitchen. He remembered at the last instant to duck so he wouldn't hit his head on the low door frame. "This is ridiculous, Zane. We should just go to a hotel in New Orleans."

The children whooped. Zane shook her head.

"Not until I meet my deadline this week." She sent the twins a sorrowful smile when they groaned.

Jake nodded. "All right. I'll try to fix the pump, so it won't die when we run water."

"It's pretty old."

"I know." He turned around and smacked his hip on the small table, cursing under his breath.

Zane put her hand over her mouth to keep from laughing when he whirled to face her. "Sorry."

"Dammit, Zane. Don't laugh."

"Sain'cyr says dammit," Brill said brightly.

Flinching, Jake looked at Zane, mouthing that he was sorry. "Brill, why don't we have a talk."

Zane watched them leave the kitchen, Jake bending earnestly over the boy, Brill gazing up at his father.

"I like Daddy," Bett said softly.

Zane knelt in front of the little girl. "Do you?"

"Yes."

"Good." *So do I, dammit.*

That evening when the children were bedded down, later than usual because of the heat, Zane took a quick shower, then strolled outside. The light breeze wasn't enough to chase away the mosquitoes, but the air was fresh, and many degrees cooler than inside the uninsulated cabin.

"Hi."

She whirled around, seeing Jake's silhouette on the

tiny cottage porch. "Hi." She felt shy and awkward, yet glad to see him. With each day that passed she grew more accepting of his presence. She teetered constantly on the high wire between happiness and despair.

"Mind if I join you?" he asked.

"No. I just thought I'd walk down to the garden. It's cooler on the path."

"And if you're lucky, you might beat the varmints to the best vegetables."

She laughed. "I haven't yet."

Jake paused in front of her, his index finger touching her chin and lifting it gently. "Moonlight becomes you, Zane."

"I think that's a song lyric," she said huskily.

"Then it must have been written about you." He leaned down slowly, giving her ample time to pull back. When her eyes drooped closed, his heart thundered in his chest. "It's been so long," he whispered. Then his mouth slanted over hers.

Resisting him would have made sense. Instead she parted her lips, allowing him entry, as her arms encircled his waist.

His strong arms all but lifted her off her feet. Hearts thudding in rhythm, they took each other with their mouths, telegraphing their desire, their need. The world melted away, and there was only their aura, their slice of paradise.

They swayed together in a tornado of passion that swept them away from the questions, the rationales of any other life. No children, job, or home could surmount the storm where they dwelt, or pull their focus from each other.

Finally Jake lifted his mouth from hers, though he still held her close. He was out of breath, unable to speak, but was damn sure he'd never let her go.

"Jake, I—"

"Don't say anything yet, Zane. Please."

Slowly they descended from the lovers' plane.

She pushed back from him, flushed, unsteady, breathing raggedly. "We—we always had the power." She looked away from him.

Brushing damp strands of hair from her forehead, he smiled down at her. All he wanted to do was make love to her, yet he stepped back. "Yes, we always had that." Sensing her hesitancy, he lifted her hand to his mouth. "And we still do. I'm staying, Zane."

She could see only the glittering intent in his eyes. Darkness had all but obscured his features. "So you said."

"As long as you don't forget," he said, and turned back to the cottage.

She didn't know this new Jake. The old one would have seduced her . . . and she would have been a willing participant. She didn't know whether she liked or hated his restraint. Had she ever known him?

Their other life was a billion heartbeats behind them. And the past was dead to her. Hadn't she spent the last few years telling herself that? Hadn't it been a milestone when she'd stopped crying herself to sleep because of loneliness, because of overwork, because she missed Jake so much, her whole being ached?

Why had he reappeared in her life now? Unfair. How many times must she wrestle the nightmares to put them to rest? She touched her still throbbing lips with her fingers. It hadn't been just a kiss. It had been a wild and wonderful joining. In wry acceptance she knew there could be no other man for her in this lifetime. Sighing, she continued on to the garden.

As she neared the vegetables, she spotted a coon hurrying out at the far end. "Thief," she said softly. He wasn't the only one who'd stolen that night. Jake had taken back what she'd so generously given him on their marriage day. Herself. Did he know? Would she be hurt again? Somehow that seemed moot. Whatever the future held, without Jake it would be empty, a black void. How could she send him away?

It had been fun in the cottage, despite the "packed sardine" sensation. Delighted with their new parent, the children constantly laughed and played. She too, had been relaxed, happy. And when she looked at Jake, he was always watching her.

She was intrigued, yet cautious. His solicitude, his determination to renovate Spanish Moss in the best possible way, his gentleness with her and the children were real. But reason told her to be on her guard. The children loved him. She wanted him. She couldn't deny that. Could she protect herself by keeping him out of the inner circle of her life? And did she have the strength to do that?

It would be easier to hold back an avalanche than to keep Jake Colby in check once he decided on a course. Just the same, she'd try to go slowly.

Retrieving a few vegetables her night marauder hadn't found, she ambled back to the house, her mind going round and round. Sleep was long in coming that night. Her gaze strayed constantly to the wall that was the only barrier between her and Jake.

The next morning she rose from her narrow cot before sunup and hurried into the bathroom, hoping to get a good start on the day. The door didn't lock, nor did it fit well on its hinges, but it was understood that when the door was closed, someone was using the bathroom.

She stepped into the tub carefully. Its porcelain was as stained as the fixtures were rusted. Turning on the water, she winced as the pipes wheezed noisily.

She was rinsing her hair when she heard the rattle of the shower curtain. Opening her eyes was a mistake. Some of the soap ran into them. "Ouch. Bett?"

"No. Jake."

Neither moved or spoke for several heartbeats.

Taking a deep breath, she turned her face up to the water, her hands shaking as she tried to wash out her eyes. When she felt him step into the tub, his arms sliding around her waist, she stiffened.

"I've never held you like this before, Zane," he said softly, resting his cheek against her wet hair.

She could feel his heart pounding at her back. Or was it hers? Helpless, wanting, she remained immobile. "I—I should get to work."

Chuckling, he kissed the side of her neck. "Now you're thinking of work?"

"Yes." But she wasn't. She was remembering the many times they'd loved in the shower, passionately entwined, water sluicing over them.

"What would you think of a short vacation trip to New Orleans for the four of us?" he whispered in her ear.

She turned in his arms without thinking, then tried to pull back when her breasts brushed his chest, her nipples instantly hardening.

"No, don't move, love." He leaned down and let his mouth graze the globes, rosy from the shower. He looked up at her, his smile warm. "You're staring at me like I just asked you to sign over your house to me. It was a simple question." Despite his light tone, his hands were roaming restlessly over her wet, naked body. "I was a fool with you," he muttered. "Too casual, too uncaring."

She shook her head, but he pressed a finger to her lips, forestalling any words.

"Yes. I noticed your growing withdrawal from me, but I ignored it. Because I craved your body, mind, and spirit as a man dying of thirst craves water, I convinced myself all would be well."

Zane felt caught in his glinting gaze. "You're being very blunt," she said shakily.

He nodded. "As I should have always been with you. I thought you were only becoming moody. I never thought you'd leave me. I was a damn fool. I believed there'd be time later to settle our differences. Then you were gone." He kissed her lightly again. "I should have let you know how much you meant to me."

She saw the hurt behind his twisted smile. Guilt and regret swirled within her. "Jake, please believe—"

"Mommy, I have to go," Brill bellowed from the hallway.

Jake smiled crookedly and retreated from the tub, swishing a towel around his waist and handing one to her. "Okay, sport," he said as he opened the door. "The bathroom's yours."

Brill smiled at them, seeming not to notice anything strange about the two of them being in the bathroom together.

Out in the hall Jake stared down at her for a long moment, his hot gaze roving over her towel-clad figure. "We'll finish this another time."

When she nodded and turned away, entering the small bedroom she and Bett shared, he shook his head. Why hadn't he told her he loved her? He did. He wouldn't hide his feelings anymore. He loved her in all the ways a person could love another. He should have delegated his work more years ago, spent more private time with her. Too late he'd realized that she found their sophisticated life-style as empty as he did. He should have talked with her until he learned what she wanted, instead of hanging back until it was too late.

What had been between them had been so wonderfully hot, so perfect, they'd rushed into marriage, convinced it would last forever. Yet it had seemed to sour the moment they returned from their three-week honeymoon in Europe. He knew now, as he'd known since she'd left, that he should have asked her opinion about letting his uncle and cousin continue to live in his house. He hadn't. When there'd been friction between the three of them, he'd passed it off as nothing serious. He'd been stupid.

In his and Brill's bedroom he picked up one of Brill's toys, and set it on the table that stood against the wall separating him from Zane. On impulse, he flattened his hand on the wall, making a dull, thudding sound. He started when he heard a light answering knock.

A towel still wrapped around his waist, he strode from the room. He hesitated in front of her door, then thrust it open. Zane was alone.

Silence stretched between them.

"You didn't answer my question," he said huskily.

"Is that why you knocked."

"I just put my hand there."

"So did I."

He reached out and took her hand.

They stared into each other's eyes. Something was happening, crumbling, building, exploding, weaving . . .

Zane felt vulnerable. Birds sang and bees buzzed outside the rusted screen on the window. The earth vibrated its message, hot, throbbing.

Jake looked down at her hand, then lifted it slowly to his lips. In his whole life no moment had been so solemn. "It's been a long journey."

She knew he meant finding her and the children. Had they found each other? She forced words past the constriction in her throat. "I stopped looking over my shoulder."

He smiled, not releasing her hand. "By the time I reached Isabella, Louisiana, I'd convinced myself it was another wild-goose chase. Then, there you were on the road." And life had begun again.

"I couldn't believe it was you."

"Now, about that other question . . ." He squeezed her hand.

"It's a possibility. I'm catching up on my work and could probably be done by the end of the week. Maybe we could take a day trip somewhere."

Her happy smile, her breathless voice, sparked again his regret over mistakes he'd made. "I should have told my uncle and cousin to move out when we got married," he said abruptly. "We might have had a better chance."

She stared at him, mouth agape. "Where did that come from?"

"I needed to say it. I've thought it enough." He shrugged. "Timing's bad."

She chuckled. "Not bad, just a little odd. But I'm glad you said it."

Relieved, he smiled back. "Or maybe we should have moved into one of those high rises overlooking Lake Michigan."

"I liked the house," she admitted carefully.

He nodded, realizing they'd taken some giant steps in these short moments. He was more than willing to change the subject though.

"About taking a trip . . . The children have been good about the cramped space here. Why not take them into New Orleans for a few days and entertain them?" He studied her reaction, watching both doubt and excitement race over her features. He pressed harder. "Soon they'll be starting school, learning history. Wouldn't it be invaluable for them to see the places where the Battle of New Orleans took place?"

"They're not four yet," she said dryly.

"True. But they're old enough to learn. Right?"

"But—"

"I don't mind this cottage, but you'll have to admit it's a tight squeeze."

"Yes. So you should—"

"Fine. I'll make all the arrangements. Excuse me. I have to get dressed. The architect will be arriving early, and we have to confer."

Zane stared after him, feeling outmaneuvered. He'd tricked her into agreeing with him! Still she couldn't muster up the ire she would have felt just a few days ago.

Their time in the tiny cottage should have been torture. Instead it had been a time of discoveries, the biggest one being that neither she nor Jake had known each other very well.

But here, at Spanish Moss, it was different. Every day she learned something new, and she'd seen surprised awareness on his face more than once. Yet where was it all leading?

In a whirlwind of time it was the day they'd leave for New Orleans. Even as she dressed in the minuscule bathroom late that morning, Zane was still not totally sure it was a good idea. Hands sweaty and trembling, she dropped her earring twice and had to search under the claw-footed bathtub for it. She was as conscious of Jake as though he were dressing in the room with her.

She couldn't see much in the cracked bathroom mirror, and she hoped her orange batiste sundress looked all right. Since her skin had acquired a faint honey-color tan, she'd used little makeup, only a touch of blush and lip gloss. She'd pulled her hair back with alabaster combs that had belonged to her grandmother.

When she was ready, she grimaced at her reflection, then straightened the skirt of her dress, staring down at her low-heeled sandals. She should have been cool, but Jake's presence had stoked fire within her that she feared would never be quenched.

Taking a deep breath, she opened the door and stepped into the short hall. She rubbed her hands together, trying to dry them. She was so busy fussing, she didn't see Jake walk out of his bedroom.

"Hi," he said huskily, his gaze lingering on her. She was exquisite. An orange rose blooming in the tropical heat. Hot. Cool. Luscious.

Zane's head snapped up, and she stared at him. He was wearing dark brown Gucci sandals, cotton pants and a shirt in pale salmon, and a cotton jacket in the same brown hue as the sandals. Recognizing the casual elegance of a Japanese designer who did a great job on men's apparel, she knew the outfit had cost the earth. Jake looked so elegantly beautiful, emotion choked her. She stared at him mutely. She loved every inch of him.

"You're lovely, Zane," he said. "But you always were." He cleared his throat. "Shall we get the children? They're playing outside."

"Yes." She couldn't manage another word. They were going out together, and she was tongue-tied. This man had been her husband. She'd been parted from him for longer than they'd been together, yet there was a rightness to being with him that transcended all else.

"Zane?"

Realizing she hadn't moved, she jerked her gaze from him and started walking toward the door. Jake took her arm, and even that casual touch jolted his heart and made his body throb with renewed passion. She'd always generated too much emotion in him. With everything and everyone else he'd been in control. With Zane he had none. She'd always been fire and ice to him, and that hadn't changed. As she'd always done, she was blasting him into orbit, sending him down in flames ... and he welcomed it.

Outside she looked around. "Where's the van?"

"We're taking my car, Zane."

"Oh, we're going in style," she muttered. "And where will the children sit?"

Grimacing, he looked at the sleek Jaguar he'd rented. "Right. I guess it is your van."

She reached in her purse for the keys as the children ran up to them.

"We're going in Jake's car," Brill said firmly.

Bett nodded.

Jake had to explain why they couldn't.

Zane watched him as she got behind the wheel of her clumsy, old van. He was good with the children, gentle and patient. When he got into the passenger seat without comment, she turned to him. "I don't have air-conditioning," she said defensively.

Jake nodded, hiding a wince. Louisiana had been having true summer heat, a July hot spell. "Fine."

"I like air-conditioning," Brill piped up from the back.

Zane glanced at him over her shoulder, then turned her attention to the rutted driveway. It was something else that needed fixing. "How do you know? You've never been in a car that had it."

"I know I would," he said positively.

"Louisiana needs another hardhead," Zane muttered.

"Next you'll be telling me he's like me," Jake whispered, moving across the bench seat.

"You said it, I didn't," Zane said pointedly, firmly gripping the wheel. There was a slight shimmy in the left front wheel, and she needed to concentrate to keep the van from drifting.

"This thing is a menace," Jake said through his teeth. He glanced back at the children, satisfying himself that they were playing a game and not listening to Zane and him.

"It will have to do," Zane said, lifting her chin.

"I don't like my children riding in this rattletrap."

"Tough. There's a lot you don't like, but you don't dictate to this family."

"I'm part of this family."

"Maybe not for long." The words rolled out of her in a spurt of temper. She regretted them as quickly as they'd appeared.

"We'll see about that." Determination hardened within him. The first time he'd done things wrong. This time that would change. He'd make her see they were a family.

The silence in the front seat was the only thing cool in the hot van. The torrid breeze that blew in through the open windows brought disarray and dirt, not coolness.

The miles unfolded until they could see New Orleans ahead. Zane wasn't that familiar with it, but she did know some places to park in the Old Quarter and aimed for those. Jake had told her he'd reserved rooms in a hotel in that district.

They parked, then carried their few bags to the Marie Terese Hotel. Jake signed them in while Brill and Bett explored the lobby, Zane following them closely. Jake told the desk clerk to have the bags taken to their room; they were going sightseeing first.

"I have to make a phone call," he said to Zane when she and the children rejoined him. "Do you want to stay in here? It's cooler."

Zane itched to ask who he was calling. Would it be his uncle or cousin? She mentally shook her head. It was none of her business. "We'll wait outside," she said, noticing a shaded bench across the street.

"What's first?" Brill asked anxiously as they crossed the

street. He glanced back at the small hotel. "Is he coming soon?"

Zane smiled, love bubbling over at her son's eagerness. "Well, there's much to see. Shall I tell you about the great pirate who rescued New Orleans?" At their chorus of yeses she ushered them over to the bench on the narrow brick street.

When Jake left the hotel, he was smiling. A rental car would be delivered to the hotel that evening. They'd drive back in air-conditioned comfort. Even better, Zane's van would be towed to the garage and be given a complete overhaul.

His smile vanished when he saw no one standing in front of the hotel. He started sprinting back toward the van, then he heard Brill laugh. Skidding to a stop, he looked around. They were sitting on a bench totally engrossed in one another. The children's gazes were fixed on Zane as she told them what had to be an entrancing tale.

Heart pounding with relief, he crossed the street. He stopped a few feet from them, eavesdropping shamelessly, watching them avidly. He couldn't lose them now, not any of them. But he knew many changes would have to be made. His brief phone call to his uncle had provided him with some agonizing insight. What had happened between him and Zane had been wonderful. But he'd been blind to her hurt. And he'd paid for it by losing her. That couldn't happen again. Yet what he'd just done could certainly damage, badly, the tenuous relationship between them.

He sighed. Not now. First they'd play a bit. "Hi." The three faces that looked up at him were eager and laughing. His heart lurched painfully at the thought of losing that in his life. It would be a slow, torturous death.

"All set?" Zane asked.

"Yes. I've arranged for a rental car, and for yours to be overhauled. I feel I owe you that much, since I'm not paying rent." He smiled. "I know you wouldn't begrudge my need to feel useful."

"Save the baloney," Zane said from the side of her mouth as she sailed by him, the children hurrying after her. She had to fight not to smile when he laughed out loud. It was so wonderful to be with him again, she couldn't help enjoying herself. Playing! She hadn't done it in such a long time.

He caught up with her. "I guess from the story you just told them, we should go right to the place where Jean Lafitte crashed a dinner party and threatened the people of New Orleans because they would be enslaved by the British."

"You know about that?" She looked up at him admiringly. "He was quite a man, actually. I suppose it took Andrew Jackson to see that."

"And a few others. Come on, you two." Jake was eager to be the father, to show them historical landmarks in the Crescent City, to talk to them . . . to be with his wife, his family.

6

For the next three hours the Colby family trod through museum after museum, antebellum homes that had become landmarks and precious treasures of New Orleans. They studied the diorama of the Battle of New Orleans, which had been fought weeks after the War of 1812 had ended and remained a most colorful part of American history.

Finally the children's eyes began to droop. Yawns appeared.

Jake signaled for a taxi. Within a few minutes both children were asleep, cuddled against Zane.

"They look like you," Jake said softly. When she looked up at him, eyes wide, he smiled. "You look surprised."

"I am. I always thought they looked like you," she blurted out, then blushed when he gave her a sexy, torrid grin.

"I missed you," he said, his voice raw. "Badly." Admitting it eased some of the pain bottled inside him. "I needed you, to talk to, to discuss my day, my life." He touched her hair. "I know I never opened up to you the way I should have, but that's how I felt. How did you feel?"

"Jake, we can't—"

"I won't have my family separated," he interrupted. "I need them. I need you." He smiled ruefully. "Though if you'd told me I'd feel this strongly when I started for Louisiana, I would have argued the point."

Laughing shakily, Zane shook her head. "It didn't work before, Jake." Though her heart thudded painfully and the realization of how much she needed him had seeped through her long before this, she couldn't deny anymore that she'd ever be happy without him. Some of the painful tension that had been her companion for so long melted. The strange inner peace was fraught with astonishing, even revelations. She gazed at him anxiously. "How can it work between us, Jake? There are frightening, wide gullies of misunderstanding."

He nodded. "I know that. We'll take them one small step at a time. I want to try, Zane. How about you?"

Her world tilted, tipped. She was sliding. She turned away. "I need time."

"I've spoken to my uncle, and told him what you said about Cal, and that I believe you." Fury rose like a flood when he thought of it, not at Cal, but at himself. He'd been the fool who'd endangered her, not Cal, who deserved a damn good drubbing.

"You have?" Shock held her immobile. "What did he say?" Strangely, she didn't want to hurt Jake's uncle. She was more understanding now about the need to protect one's children, the sometimes irrational coming to their defense, since she had her own.

"He was pretty shaken. And he intends to talk to Cal." He paused, looking out at the congested traffic. Caught in the beginning of rush hour, their cab was moving at a snail's pace. "I'm talking to him too, laying on the line how I feel and what I expect for the future." He looked down at the sleeping children, then up again at his wife. "Uncle Lionel wants you to know how bitterly he regrets anything he might have done to make you leave. He said he should have tried harder, and he misses you."

He reached over and took her hand, stroking the back of it with his thumb. "Zane, please believe me when I say I want to try again with you." He smiled, trying to hide his own insecurities. "If you won't let me live with you as your husband, I'll stay as handyman."

"You?" She blinked in surprise. "But nothing tears you from the business, nothing is more important." She bit her lip when blood rushed up his face. "I'm not trying to insult you, Jake."

"But you are," he said quietly. "And I don't like thinking I deserve it. Zane, we had the wonderful ingredients for a great marriage, companionship, the most torrid passion—"

"For heaven's sake, Jake." She glanced down at the sleeping children, then at the back of the driver's head.

"You're blushing." That pleased him inordinately. Anything that hinted at emotion and attachment, rather than coolness and detachment, could make him happy. He touched her cheek. "We had it all ... and I was fool enough to lose it."

Hot, electrified, she tried to scowl. Were they making resolutions? Deciding their future as well as putting their past to rest? "Who wouldn't blush? Once you decide to open up, you're downright blunt."

"I should have tried it sooner. Maybe then I wouldn't have lost you, the only woman I ever had loved, ever could love."

The taxi wove through the traffic, stopping and starting, hesitating then jerking forward, as horns blew all around them in the congested center of the lovely city of New Orleans.

For all Zane noticed they could have been cruising at warp speed over the moon's surface. Her heart had jumped into her throat at his words, and she reeled with their power. When they'd been together, Jake had told her many times that he loved her, and had demonstrated it over and over. In that short year and a half she'd come to know the wondrous variations of love, and it had been a joy to have him as her teacher. But nothing had made her heart swell within her as it was doing now as she dwelt on his words.

Jake stared at her as she sat motionless, her lips parted, still as a statue. He was caught by the vision she made. Girlish. Womanly. Sophisticated. Wordly. Ingenuous. Delightful. "Zane? Darling, you must have known I loved you."

"Yes . . . yes . . . in the beginning. Then I thought you'd changed—"

"Never."

Blood hurtled through him as he tightly gripped her hand. "Zane. More and more I've come to realize that we didn't talk enough, about anything and everything, about our expectations, our hopes, and mostly about our feelings." He lifted his hand to her mouth, tracing her lips. "I'm not going to hold back this time." He started to say more, but the car jerked forward, careened around a corner, then halted in front of their hotel. Grinding his teeth in frustration, he stared at her for a moment. "This isn't the time, but we're going to talk." He shoved some bills at the driver, then got out. Reaching back in, he lifted the twins, jockeying one on each shoulder.

"I can carry—" Zane began.

"No need. I have them." He looked down at the sleeping faces. "They're beautiful," he murmured, stepping aside as the doorman opened the door, so she could precede him. "We have a suite on the third floor—"

"I'll get the key." She rushed to the desk and gave the clerk her name.

"Ah, yes, Mrs. Colby. Welcome to Marie Terese Hotel. You and your family have one of our best suites." The clerk beamed at her, seemingly impervious to her aghast expression as his and Jake's words sank in. "Suite." As in singular. As in one bedroom. She drew in a deep breath as she took the key, telling herself to remain calm. Maybe there were two bedrooms.

"Thank you," she said to the clerk, then turned and hurried to the elevator. Jake waited there, still carrying the sleeping children. His ready smile turned to wariness as she shot him a sharp look.

"Now what?" Sardonic amusement laced his voice.

"Later," she muttered, while inside she was crying, "I'm not ready!" True, she and Jake had laid to rest some of their past problems, but that didn't mean she was prepared to step forward into the future with him. And if he hoped to resume their intimate relationship tonight . . . How would she ever be able to refuse him?

Jake frowned inquisitively at her as the doors slid shut, then they began their shuddery, clanking ascent. "Tell me."

She glanced meaningfully at the other two passengers, then stared stonily at the doors.

On the third floor they walked along the wide, short corridor with its satin-finished wallpaper to the corner suite. A suite with two bedrooms.

They carefully undressed the twins, then settled them in one of the bedrooms.

Leaving the room, Jake quietly closed the door, then faced Zane.

"All right. You've been itching for a fight since you went to the desk for the key. Spit it out."

"How elegantly put," she said bitingly. Arms akimbo, she turned to him. "This suite cost the earth. We could have taken cheaper rooms. I want to pay my share."

"And this is the nettle under your skin?"

"The desk clerk assumed we were married." Fear, mistrust, and a desperate need for love roiled through her, obliterating reason.

"We are, dammit," Jake said.

"Don't you look down your aristocratic nose at me, Jake Colby."

"Oh? We're discussing my nose, not the desk clerk? Make up your mind."

"And I don't want any of your cheap cynicism."

"Stop blustering, Zane, and say what you mean."

"I don't want people thinking we're married."

"Your face is as red as a beet, and you're sputtering. Here, I'll get you some ice water."

"I don't need it. And I am not sharing a bed with you."

They hadn't really resolved anything, and she had to be sure. She'd melt if he touched her. How many nights had she spent dreaming of their lovemaking, imagining herself in his arms, only to wake up alone? She was in agony because he was near . . . and she'd die if she was parted from him again. Without thinking, she plucked a beautiful arrangement of dried flowers from a faux Ming vase and flung them at him. They fell short.

"Your own special flèches d'amour, darling?" Rather than being disturbed, he was intrigued by her anger. It was more emotion than she'd revealed to him since the day renovations began on Spanish Moss. What had set her off? That he'd reserved a two-bedroom suite? And why did she think he expected to share a bed with her? Not, of course, that he'd mind. He'd thought of little else since they'd kissed in the garden that night, then he'd held her naked body, wet and warm, against his the next morning. He'd been careful not to push her though. Now he was wondering if a little push was just what she needed.

"Don't call me darling," she said through clenched teeth.

"Why not?" Pride, stubbornness, all the barriers that had kept him from her fell in a heap at his feet. Taking a deep breath, he told her how he felt. "You are my one and only darling. My sweetheart, my love, my life. You're all things to me, and you always will be, no matter how much we argue, or disagree, or get angry." He laughed when she gaped at him, stunned. "I love you, Zane. That's not going to change. Don't you understand that yet?"

"I fell in love with you the moment I saw you. You were so flustered but so beautiful. So young . . ."

"I was twenty-two," she said wistfully. "Not so young."

She smiled uncertainly. "I admit I was pretty bowled over by you too."

His own smile died. "I wanted to be married to you then, and I do now." He held up his hand to forestall her when she opened her mouth. "Please let me finish. You have to know this, no matter what you decide, Zane. I admit to being stupid and pride-bound. That's what kept me from you all these years. At first I was angry, but I thought you'd return. Then when you'd been gone months and I had to accept that you wouldn't be coming back to me on your own, my anger grew. I stupidly thought to salve my pride by not looking for you." He smiled crookedly. "All I did was punish myself."

She sank down in a nearby chair as though her legs no longer had the power to hold her.

He moved to the one opposite her and sat down too, his hands clasped loosely between his knees. "When I arrived in Louisiana, I was still fooling myself. I thought I'd see you, arrange for a divorce, and get on with my life—"

"Did you find someone else?" she blurted out, then looked away. "I've no right to question you."

"Yes, you do. You're my wife." He inhaled and reached out one finger, stroking her hand. "I wanted to find someone. I even tried taking a couple of women to my bed." At her wince, he caught her hand. "It didn't work. Your face was there. I saw you in my dreams. When I worked, your smile was in front of me. When I was out with others, I heard your laugh. I tried to eradicate you from my life, but I couldn't. Finally I decided I'd find you and take care of the ghosts. Once I'd seen you, I figured I'd be over you. I was wrong. When I saw you in the rain that first day, I knew I'd never be able to get you out of my life. You and the children are my life."

He let out a silent sigh, feeling as though a great weight had been lifted from his soul. He felt light, sure, unfettered. Yet how did she feel?

Zane looked at his face, then down at his hand holding hers. She wanted to lie to him. She'd been lying to herself so long, it seemed the right thing to do. She still needed her fences, desperately. There had been a sense of unreality in his words. Maybe because she'd wanted to hear them so much, she'd misheard. She'd longed for him. Truth was so painful.

"I've ... I've missed you." The quiet words were bombs between them, exploding, fragmenting, ripping apart barriers that had been erected to keep out dangerous emotions and passions. The world she'd constructed to protect herself and the children was crumbling.

"Darling," Jake said huskily. "Will you let me court you? Please." Tears trembled in her eyes, then slipped down her face. "Darling, don't. You'll make me cry too."

When she saw the moistness in his eyes, she laughed through her tears. "I—I never thought ... to see that," she said, and hiccupped. She clapped her hand over her mouth to stop the irritating hiccups that plagued her whenever she became too excited. "Too fast," she mumbled.

"Yes." He clasped her hand more tightly. "We'll go slow ... and talk about our hurts and hopes."

"It was never slow between us," she said, forcing down the hiccups.

He nodded. "I know what you mean. That first night when I took you out to dinner, I knew then I couldn't lose you. It was so explosive, so damned sudden, I thought I'd been hit by a truck. But it was real too."

"There's so much we still have to settle. Your work and mine. Your uncle. Your cousin." Embarrassment and hurt flooded through her, flushing her face.

He swallowed hard. "I love my uncle, almost as much as I loved my father. But I'll let nothing come between us again. I swear to you, I'll never doubt you or give you cause to think that I do. I give you my word."

"I didn't lie," she whispered.

"I know," he said. "And if I could take away the pain I caused you with even a moment's distrust, I would. But, Zane, you have to promise me you'll tell me whenever anything hurts you. I'll do my damnedest to change, either myself or the situation."

"And I promise ... not to run." She sighed. "I wouldn't have the first time if I'd thought we could talk. Even when we argued, we held back."

"Now that's a change." He smiled ruefully. "We should have thrown things like we do now."

She gasped, then laughed. "We don't throw things."

"But sometimes we'd like to. Right?"

She nodded, then shuddered.

"What are you thinking?"

"About the house. All we did was walk on eggs with each other."

"We'll get another place, farther out of the city, if you want to return to Chicago. And of course we'll keep Spanish Moss." Surprised pleasure flashed in her eyes, and he felt a twinge of regret. "Did I never try to please you?"

"You always tried to please me ... with jewels, lovely trips, evenings out at the symphony, the opera."

"But I never asked where you wanted to live."

She shook her head vigorously. "I wanted to live with you. It was only after it seemed intolerable that I thought of Spanish Moss." She shrugged. "Now I've come to love it."

"I don't blame you. I like it too." On impulse he jerked on her hands, pulling her into his lap. He leaned back, cuddling her to him. "I want to kiss you," he whispered against her forehead.

"Will it be as good as before?" Chaotic emotions plummeted through her, making her body shake with want.

"Better," he said hoarsely. Her nervous giggle had his libido shooting through the roof. Letting his mouth slide down to hers, he played with her lips, touching, sucking, teasing. When her hand fastened behind his head, locking him to her, his heart thundered in his chest and passion streaked through him lightning fast. His mouth hardened on hers, and he kissed her fervently.

Their breaths mingled, their bodies straining to join. As always it was too fast, too meteoric.

Zane pulled back, her breath rasping from her throat. "Jake?"

"Yes, darling?"

"It was always so wild."

"And still is."

"Yes."

"I love you, Zane."

Tears filled her eyes again. "I never cry. It's so silly."

As shaken as she, he bent his head, taking her mouth in a fierce, stirring kiss, shaping and fitting the soft contours of her lips to his. He'd forgotten her power, her delicious wielding of the sexual weapons that unmanned him. Tenderness filled him when he felt her trembling hands cup his shoulders.

Flames of desire scorched them. Forcing down the fire, Jake made a conscious effort to go slower. He swept his lips across hers, coaxing her emotions to sweetly higher levels. Then his tongue edged between her lips, touching hers.

Electricity stunned them both at the contact.

Driven by the primeval force to be joined to her beloved, Zane wriggled around so that she was pressed more firmly against him.

The pressure of her bottom against him hardened him exquisitely. He held her hips to him, circling them over him, letting her feel what she was doing to him. When she pulled back, he grinned at her lopsidedly. "Sorry, darling," he whispered. "You do affect me."

"Yes," she said dreamily. "And you affect me."

"It's only fair." Her words vibrated through his being, making him tremble with crystal clear memories of their passionate marriage. Groaning his need, he bent over her again, his mouth open on hers, sucking in a surprised breath when her lips parted and their tongues met.

Without taking his mouth from hers, he feathered his hand down her arm to her rib cage, then upward to cup her breast. His heart beat out of rhythm as he recalled her soft, sweet curves, and he groaned, wanting her badly. He kissed her neck as he gently squeezed her breast. The feel of her exploded memories and passion within him. In a sudden movement he lifted her and set her on her feet. Before she could speak, he pulled her sundress off over her head. He tossed it aside, then slipped off her flimsy bra.

She gasped as he circled her nipples with his thumb.

Unable to catch his breath, he watched them harden to a nubby sheen. Not all his memories prepared him for the torrent of sensation that battered his control. She was exquisite, all the beauty on the planet. Did she know she had him? That she'd always had him?

At his first touch Zane knew she could refuse him nothing. Her tortured breathing matched his as her nipples puckered and pulled taut under his touch.

"Jake." His name was a mere exhalation of breath, but she knew it was a surrender, one she'd wanted, needed for so long. All her regrets, faded as the myriad love emotions built in her, escalating to a sweet agony. She desired him with an ache that only he could assuage, that encompassed her body and mind and spirit. She needed him, all of him. She always had.

Jake lifted her and carried her into the bedroom. Laying her down on the bed, he kissed her forehead, temple, her eyes, her cheeks. He nuzzled her neck, then chuckled when she wriggled under him, trying to kiss him back. He touched his tongue to the sensitive curve of her ear, then let it plunge inside. His body hardened, wanting desperately to imitate the action. Her groans skyrocketed his libido, pumping blood so fast, he was all but deafened by the roar. Her arms clung to him, her nails digging into his shoulders even through his shirt. His every sense strained to the woman who had dredged every exciting and loving emotion from his being, who had brought him a passion like no other. How could he have been foolish enough to live without her these past years? Regret at his own stupidity forced a harsh chuckle from him.

Through all the veils of sensation she heard it and pulled back. "Why are you laughing?"

"At what a fool I am, darling. Never again. No more separations. I'm yours. Keep me, Zane."

"Jake," she whispered, laughter shaking through the

tenderness. "I've never heard you commit yourself like that."

"Believe it, love. Take me."

"Oh, Jake." It was all the dreams she'd had when she'd been without him, it was all the heaven that her marriage had been . . . and more. Could she trust it? Could she afford not to?

Sliding downward, he pulled her swollen nipple into his mouth, sucking, laving with his tongue, as his hands intimately explored her body.

"Jake . . . Jake!" Her hoarse cries trembled on the air. "It's been so long."

Delight and relief shivered through him at her words. Would she believe he felt the same? No other woman had ever taken him, body, mind, and soul, as Zane had done, as she was doing now.

In her harsh keening he heard sexual surprise, and he would have smiled had he been capable of such effort. She was not the only one rocked by the torrid flood, though. She set him aflame, and he couldn't be impervious to the fiery need that matched hers. Never, never had he felt such wonderful heat, such flaming emotion. Not even the first time they'd made love had he felt so fully caught, so ultimately freed, as he did at that moment. She was all of life to him. He lifted his head, more in love than he'd ever been, more determined to be hers.

"I won't give you up. I love you, Zane."

He lowered his mouth to her breast, sucking in the same wonderful rhythm as before as his hand stroked lower, slipping her panties off her.

Giddy with desire and rampant pleasure, she gazed down at his head, her hands fluttering over his rich, thick hair. When he lifted his scorching gaze to hers, she tried to smile. Words fought past her dry throat. She loved him madly. She could never kid herself about that again. "Jake?"

"Yes, my darling, I'm here. Kiss me, Zane. Please."

It was all the invitation she needed. All the want and desire that had been tamped down on her, that had been the basis for her struggle for independence, crumbled like a dike in front of a flood. Now a torrent, her love cascaded from her. Rolling him onto his back, she stripped off his clothes, until he was as naked as she. Then she kissed him, openmouthed and with full ardor, nothing held back. She let her tongue slide along his lips, then into his mouth, swallowing his gasp of hot delight.

Caught up in the wonder of sexual love, aroused, arousing, she let her hands play over his body. "So long," she murmured.

"It's been hell."

She looked down at his chest, the arrowing of dark hair, and suddenly put her mouth there, her lips seeking and finding his nipples.

"Darling," he groaned. "I can't . . ."

But Zane wouldn't let him move. She was mesmerized by the wonder of it all. His skin was rough silk abrading her skin, sensitizing it, sending shivers through her. As she slid lower, she sensed the blood pounding through him, even as hers was doing.

Half groaning, half laughing, he hauled her up and flipped her on her back. "I want it, my love, but I really can't take it. Besides, it's my turn."

Trembling with anticipation, she watched his mouth move toward hers, her hands going up to clasp his head and hurry the process.

Kissing her had always been his joy. He loved her soft, strong mouth, her wonderful triangular face that was somehow softened by her firm chin. His mouth slid down her neck, laved each breast, then touched her stomach, where her muscles contracted reflexively.

Passion didn't build between them, it erupted. Molten, golden, it had been long denied, neither could contain it, only ride with its fearsome flood.

Hungrily kissing her again, Jake glided his hand over her velvety skin, closer and closer to the triangle of curling hair that covered her womanhood. When he flattened his hand over that sensual area, she stiffened. He pulled back instantly.

"What is it, darling?"

"I ... I don't know."

Balancing himself on his forearms and controlling his rampaging passion with great effort, he studied her. "Tell me," he said, his voice hoarse yet gentle. "Don't you want me?"

"Yes, I do," she said. Her hand tentatively traced his mouth, and she tried to smile. "It's just that the power we create is so fearsome. We could always hurt each other."

"Is that what we're doing?"

"No. We're making love ... but the aftermath ... the separation—"

"We won't be separated."

"We don't have to be in different states to be apart. It happened when I was still in the house with you—"

"Don't compare this to Chicago, Zane. Let it be a new beginning." Uncertainty flickered across her face, followed by hope. "Don't be afraid of me, darling, or of what we have." He laughed roughly. "So many live their whole lives without ever experiencing what we have. Wouldn't we be fools to throw it aside?"

"Yes," she said slowly. "We'd be crazy. But we did it once."

He digested that, watching her passion recede and her

fear build. "No. I won't let you pull back. I love you, and I want to keep you safe."

He caressed her, kissed her, carefully rekindling the flame. As the fire incinerated her fear, as her body began moving in the sinuous, reckless way he loved, he touched her again.

This time she reared up against him, and once more he fought for control. "Easy, darling."

He stared down at her, and her eyes fluttered open at his stillness. "I love you, Zane. I didn't know how much. And I'm going to do my damnedest to show you."

Zane smiled. Piece by shattered piece, he was putting her together again, his passions the glue that held her to him.

His mouth moved down her body.

Reflexively she stiffened, trembling with desire and anticipation, wanting him desperately, but fearing her own surrender. It had been so long.

She hadn't realized she'd spoken aloud until Jake lifted his head, gazing questioningly at her. She couldn't wait any longer. Gasping at the sudden force of her need, she clutched his shoulders and pressed her hips against his.

"Jake ... please ..."

Jake hesitated, on fire, barely in control, fearful of hurting her. Her words penetrated, melting his last resistance. Groaning, he plunged into her, taking her and giving himself. *Keep me, Zane, keep me!*

Selfless passion raged through him as he held tight rein on his riotous feelings and strove to give satisfaction to his wife. Rolling his hips, he penetrated deeper. When her body bowed in hot anticipation, he withdrew and plunged again, watching her eyes glaze, her breathing turn ragged and shallow.

"I'm with you, darling," he told her, his shoulders and arms taut with the strain of holding back. He quickened the tempo and felt her returning thrusts. His body tremored with throbbing passion.

In a wild kaleidoscope of giving, their souls seemed jarred loose of their bodies, carried away and joined forever in a lasting covenant. Love was the victor in their joining.

"Zane, darling!"

"Oh, Jake, Jake."

Long and sweet, passion held them suspended in its quivering grasp as moan after moan escaped them.

Bodies slick with lovemaking, they held each other as sanity returned, and they fell back to the planet.

Eyes closed, Zane gripped him, reality already penetrating her lingering rapture. Even if Jake stayed, a part of him would be separate from her, just like before. But she swore she'd never regret her decision. She loved him. There'd never be another man for her.

"Open your eyes, darling," Jake whispered. "That was beautiful beyond belief. I've missed you so." He brushed the damp strands of hair from her face. "Not just the loving. I've missed your being, your presence, your laughter, your mind. I need you. I won't be parted from you again."

She smiled, rejoicing in his words, but vowing to remain realistic. "Until Colby News Service needs you."

"Shouldn't be a problem. In the few weeks I've been here, I've started delegating more responsibilities to my vice presidents and managers, something I should have done the day we got engaged. And my main office will be wherever we choose to live. So if you want to stay at Spanish Moss, I'll move everything down here to New Orleans."

"What?" She was so surprised, she almost jerked out of his arms.

He smiled ruefully, tightening his hold. "Don't look so

shocked. I won't be separated from you and our children."

"But—but your family."

He shrugged. "They have their own lives and jobs. This is our private life. Why would you think they wouldn't be reasonable? It's my business. They work for me."

Zane smiled limply, shaking her head. She'd run from his family, not just from him. Pulling herself to a sitting position, she looked down at him. "Jake, I want us to be together, but—"

"No buts. I want it too." He gazed up at her, one arm draped across her middle. "Don't move away from me."

She smiled. "All right." Taking a deep breath, her hands threaded together to keep them from shaking, she plunged on. "It wasn't just that you weren't home all the time, or that we couldn't communicate." She looked away from him. "That evening Cal tried to ... force himself on me was the last straw. All the time we were married there were the constant innuendos from him, your uncle's disapproval, the stories I knew filtered back to you." Her smile was fleeting. "You already know most of this. I guess I need to emphasize what I see as important."

Jake sat up. "And I was dead wrong in the way I handled it. You need to know that. It won't happen again. And I'll handle Cal. I want you to know I wasn't a complete fool. I had warned him about cynical remarks to you, the double entendres he would make when he thought I wasn't paying attention. I should have realized how bad it was for you and rearranged his face."

She stroked his cheek, smoothing away his anger. "In some ways I was the fool. I should have told you everything up front, not just mentioned some scattered incidents." She shook her head. "I knew Cal was spoiled, self-indulgent. I should have decked him myself . . . and I might do that if I ever see him again."

"I wouldn't worry about that. I'm sure he's making every effort to avoid me . . . and you right now."

She was startled. "You've spoken to him?"

He shook his head. "I didn't have the restraint to do that. My uncle conveyed my message."

"That's your shark on the prowl look," she said quietly.

"And I could kill to keep you, Zane. I love you."

"I've come between you and your family."

"No." He paused. "I love my uncle. He did everything he could to be a surrogate parent to me, but he has blind spots about Cal. I told him that. And when we lived in Chicago, as I said, I warned Cal about upsetting you. I guess he didn't believe I'd do anything." He scowled. "I didn't for too damn long. Now I have. Once more I'll tell you, I made a mess of it. I should have told you then, as I'm doing now."

She saw regret wash over his features, and her heart swelled with her own regrets. "Yes. We should have told each other much more." Taking a deep breath, she let the last wall crumble. "I should have told you how I felt, how trapped and shut in my life had become. Instead I took your cash and ran. I owe you that."

He shook his head. "You owe me nothing, Zane. Deep down I guess I knew I'd betrayed you, by my aloofness, my assumptions that you'd know what I was thinking . . . Stupid."

She sighed. "We both were."

"Not anymore."

Trembling, she gazed at him. "Meaning?"

"I love and believe my wife. And I will eradicate anything or anyone that tries to come between us."

He saw uncertainty flicker in her eyes once more and smiled bitterly. "One day you'll trust me again."

She drew in a shaky breath. "I do now," she said, and pressing her body against his, she kissed him with all the hope and trust and love she felt for him.

7

The screeching of saws, the thudding of hammers, the constant billows of wood dust filled Spanish Moss through the rest of July, throughout the entire month of August, and into September. Zane considered it all part of the ritualistic aura surrounding the refurbishing of the grand old mansion. Every day except Sunday the workmen started early and finished late. Scratches, old varnish, peeling paint, sagging beams, spotted walls, and damaged floors disappeared.

Outside the house landscapers were like locusts as they rushed over the grounds, testing, feeding, seeding, planting. Slowly the lawns and gardens took shape. Beauty that had once only peeked out became blatant loveliness. Thatched and weed-choked gardens were transformed to havens of scented color. Bushes were trimmed, trees pared, vines eradicated—except for the Spanish moss, of course.

Zane was tearfully enchanted, and she was sure her grandmother Zoe would have been pleased too.

Zane was also glad Jake had insisted on air-conditioning, which had been installed in her workroom first. She was still able to work there, but soon that room's renovations would be started, and she'd move temporarily to the redone living room.

In the meantime she enjoyed the new coolness of her

workroom. With the doors and windows shut she barely heard the necessary disturbances that went on nonstop through the rest of Spanish Moss and its environs.

Most days Jake spent a good deal of time in her workroom, managing his own affairs. He'd set up a desk in the far corner, and was often on the phone or bent over the papers that were delivered by overnight mail every day. Eventually he'd have a large office adjoining hers, an addition to Spanish Moss that would blend well with the existing structure.

Despite the moments when she feared her beloved house was coming down around her ears, she was happy. Ecstatic. Jake had done that. It had been six weeks since their visit to New Orleans. Each day they'd become closer. The twins had come to depend on his presence. Melda and the others looked to him for direction. Zane looked to him for love.

When she heard the door to the workroom open, she didn't even look up, though her heart flipped. She couldn't stop her smile. "Miss me that much?"

"Actually, more than I thought I would," a man said. "Somehow I always thought you'd know that."

Zane's head snapped up, and she blinked as though the heavyset man in the doorway were a mirage. Jake's uncle had aged. His skin looked fluted, the hue metallic. His jawline had sagged, and his eyes had a weighted sadness. Despite his heaviness, his clothes seem to hang on him.

"Lionel." She exhaled, noting that she'd sprayed black ink on the new strip when her hand had trembled in reaction. "You're looking well," she said cautiously, lying as she fought for balance.

He smiled, as though he'd seen through her polite dissembling. "May I come in?"

"Yes." But she didn't want him there. He was the bête noire. Would he unravel the beautiful dreams that were being woven during the reconstruction of Spanish Moss, the reconstruction of Zane and Jake, the reconstruction of the Colby family?

"You hate me still," he said flatly.

She shook her head, mute, miserable.

"I didn't believe you," he went on. "I believed my son, because I couldn't accept he could be so dishonorable. Yet in my heart I knew your innocence. I was a fool." He drew in a shuddering breath. "Curse me if you will. I deserve it." He rubbed his hand down his face, then took another step into the room. "Cal has always been in Jake's shadow. He hates it, but he knows he doesn't have the talent or know-how to be anywhere but where he is. If he weren't related to Jake, he'd be a scrambling office manager at best. I know that. So does Jake. I suppose one reason why I love Jake so much is because he never let on to Cal he knew."

His smile was bitter. "I never thought you'd leave us. Then when you did leave, I was sure you'd come back soon." He shook his head. "I was stunned when you didn't return. And I felt guilty. I knew my part in it."

Silence stretched long and uncertain between them.

"Zane, you have children. I would love to see them. No, the truth is, I long to see them. But if you tell me to go, I will. I came down to Isabella to apologize for the many times my son and I made you unhappy. If you can't forgive, I understand." He smiled bleakly. "We hurt you, and we devastated Jake. When you left him, he missed you desperately. His pain was like an open wound. When he realized you weren't coming back, I thought he might die." He looked down at his hands. "Many times while you were still there I questioned Cal about things he said about you. But I wanted to believe him, and so I let things slide."

"I know how much you love your son," Zane finally said.

He looked up at her quickly, hope flaring. "I knew how intolerable it was getting for you. Jake didn't. I was there most of the time, while he wasn't. He assumed that if he warned Cal to stay away from you, you'd somehow know it and Cal would obey him." Lionel smiled fleetingly. "Jake's too bright in some ways. One of his faults is that he assumes too often that he's dealing with intellects that match his. Another is that he believes people will intuitively understand that he's often right."

Zane couldn't help smiling. She was well acquainted with Jake's assumptions.

"Cal's in London, Zane. He's going to remain there. The sales staff is large and varied, and that's one of his strong points. He can sell."

Cal. How stupid she'd been to blame him or his father. She'd nearly ruined her own life because she hadn't spoken up and told Cal to back off. "I should have punched him in the nose," she said, "and I should have told you what I thought of your son." She exhaled when he smiled slightly and nodded. "I would like you to meet my children . . . but I won't let anyone dictate my life or theirs, Lionel—"

"Neither will I," Jake drawled, strolling in through the open door. He smiled briefly at his uncle, then walked over to his wife and took her in his arms. "No one will have anything to say about our life, Lionel. As I told you in my letter . . ." He shrugged, smiling offhandedly when Zane looked at him inquiringly.

Lionel nodded. "I understand." He glanced at Zane. "Your husband made it clear you'll be living here, that the business will be run from Louisiana and that I'll be handling the Chicago office until my retirement." He paused. "I suppose I came down here because I was hoping to ensure I'd get an invitation to visit from time to time, get to know the children."

"I . . ." Zane began. She glanced at Jake. Encouraged by his smile, she went on. "That is, we want our children to know you. It's only right." When she saw the tears fill Lionel's eyes, she knew she'd made the right move for all of them. Her own eyes moistened.

Jake gathered her into his arms. "Don't ever wonder why I love you. Thank you for forgiving all of us."

"I can forgive you." She smiled wryly. "I don't know if I can forgive myself for not standing and delivering as good as I got, for not punching Cal out, for not opening up the can of worms and making you see what was happening. That was stupid. And I hate that."

Jake laughed.

"Shall we go and find the children?" she said, and reached out her hand to Lionel.

Later that night, after the workmen had left, after Lionel had returned to the hotel in town, after Melda and the twins had gone to bed, Zane waited in the overseer's cottage for Jake to come to her. She'd left a note on her pillow when he was taking a shower, saying she'd be waiting for him here. She hadn't necessarily intended to be mysterious, but somehow it seemed right that they share her good news here, in the first true home they had ever had together.

Gazing out the living room window, she saw him striding across the lawn, which was illuminated by the back porch light, toward the cottage. He had never looked better, she mused. Gone were the bitter lines about his eyes and mouth. He seemed to have dropped ten years, getting younger instead of older. And she knew for certain he was very happy.

He swung the door open, spotting her at once. "Hi.

Why are we here? You've got something hot and sexy planned?"

"Yep."

His eyebrows went up. "You're full of ginger this evening. Something you haven't told me about? A new contract maybe?"

"Nope." That would be nice news, she thought, but she wouldn't get greedy. Three weeks earlier her strip had been picked up by two more large newspapers.

He folded his arms across his chest. "You're being cryptic as hell. Okay, lady mine, tell me."

Not able to contain herself, she laughed out loud and threw herself into his arms. "I'm happy."

"So am I," Jake murmured, taken as always by her scent and the feel of her. He closed his eyes, tightening his hold. "Happier than I've ever been." When she pulled back, tugging on his hand, his eyes opened. "Am I going to be seduced?"

"I hope so." She pulled him after her into the refurbished cottage's sole bedroom. The two tiny bedrooms had been combined, creating one large, airy room that Zane liked almost better than the master bedroom in the house. "We're going to bed."

"I'm more than willing, darling," he murmured, his gaze flowing over her as she undressed. "And very ready after watching you."

"Good."

As always the love between them exploded like dynamite. They held and caressed each other, climbing the sensual mountain of pleasure, skillfully, caught so in the wonder of it that they laughed and cried at the climax.

"I keep thinking it can't get better," Jake said against her neck. "But it does."

"Are you relaxed?"

"Ummm, I am."

"Then I can tell you that you're going to be a father again in April. Great, huh?" She rolled onto her side to face him, and her smile faded. Jake was pale and slack-jawed, his eyes unfocused. "Jake? I'm happy. Aren't you?"

"Oh, honey." He gazed at her. "I love you. And of course I'm happy. I'm thrilled."

He hugged her, but not before she glimpsed the sheen of tears in his eyes. She held on to him tightly.

"I found you again," she murmured, "in the summer heat, and when it approaches once more, we'll be parents again. Now we have it all, a new beginning, a new home, wonderful children, and a brand-new baby as icing on the cake." She pressed her face into his neck. "I'm so happy."

"So am I." He kissed her deeply. "Summer will always be my favorite season." Jake murmured, enfolding her in his arms and pressing her to him.

And though an early breeze of autumn belled the curtains, the summer heat enclosed them for all time.

Summer Strangers

Patricia Potter

Author's Note

Two days after Bantam called about my writing a novella for the Southern Nights anthology, I attended a Fourth of July celebration on the Decatur courthouse grounds. It was a magical evening, a sultry Atlanta night haunted by a pending storm and full of electricity and excitement and music.

I had been thinking about a story set on a Southern island, but that night I knew that this was my story, that this evening represented Southern nights more accurately than any exotic location.

And then there was the band. Yes, there really is a Seed and Feed Abominable Marching Band, and who can resist that? Who can resist musicians who take such a delight in musical nonsense and yet produce such wonderful sounds?

During those hours on the courthouse square the story of Corey and Patrick evolved. They are people who could easily have wandered the lawn as I did that night. Although they reside only in my imagination, they are bits and pieces of people I know.

It was also a joy to set the stage in Atlanta, a city I dearly love. Because I have written historicals and did not particularly want to compete with Margaret Mitchell, I had always avoided Georgia as a setting. Now, with "Summer Strangers," I could indulge myself, and the pleasure in doing so inspired two upcoming LOVESWEPTS. I only hope I can convey to each of you the excitement and flavor of the city.

And the irresistible lure of Southern Nights.

1

Corey Adams didn't believe in looks across the crowded room, much less across a crowded square.

But still her eyes kept going to the most outlandishly dressed man she'd ever set eyes on. And his eyes kept returning to hers and holding them. As if some invisible force were at work.

Ridiculous. And entirely unlike her. Corey prided herself on common sense. Her one lapse in that area years before had resulted in unmitigated disaster.

So she forced her gaze away from the man in the band, his arms and hands fully occupied with a monster of brass, and made herself peruse the rest of the crowd picnicking in the courthouse square on this Fourth of July.

An hour earlier a storm had washed the air, and a fresh, light breeze brushed across the celebrants, breaking the hot, humid choke hold on the city. Clouds still bounced across the sky, though, like huge inflated beach balls, each one threatening to break and release great torrents of rainwater on the people below.

No one seemed to care, however, as the small but enthusiastic Seed and Feed Abominable Marching Band played everything from Sousa to the theme song from *Chariots of Fire*, as well as some very whimsical pieces. Enthusiasm ran high in the town square of Decatur, a small, tightly knit community lying on the outskirts of Atlanta. The Fourth was celebrated here in the old-fashioned way, with a parade consisting only of residents, who proudly pulled their offspring in decorated red wagons or led a variety of dogs from a haughty Great Dane to a scruffy mutt with a big red, white, and blue bow tied around its neck.

Corey, a very recent transplant from Detroit, had never seen anything quite like it. There was a gracious ease in the proceedings, a laid-back enjoyment of life that was entirely new to her.

Her eyes went back to the dark-haired man in the band, and her insides rocked as she saw him wink, as if he knew she was trying to avoid his glances. She felt a strange but compelling attraction that stretched across space and people and noise, touching her as intimately as a hand might.

She turned to one of her new friends who had almost literally dragged her here. As she had done for years, Corey had meant to read a book tonight. It wasn't that she didn't appreciate the feeling or purpose of the occasion, but the Fourth was usually one of the very rare days she had to herself, when the telephone didn't ring with yet another unsolvable problem or plea for help that wasn't available. All her life she had driven herself, and those few hours she took for herself she hoarded jealously, anticipating the sense of privacy and personal freedom they gave her.

But Ellen Saniford hadn't taken no for an answer, and now Corey had to admit that coming here was a very good idea. She couldn't help feeling the contagious excitement and pleasure and anticipation in the smiling, laughing crowd. This is what life should be like, she thought. This could make you forget the dark underside and Ray and kids like him. Like she had once been.

Corey shook her head. She wasn't going to think of that tonight, only of the sultry Southern night, the smell of fried chicken, the brush of a breeze through her long hair, the sight of the nearly one-hundred-year-old regal courthouse against the darkening sky, the sound of people enjoying themselves.

And the rhythmic, pervasive oompah-pah of the tuba.

The tuba being held and played by the man with the searching gaze . . .

The man wearing a red hat with horns on it . . . the man in a tuxedo jacket and swim shorts that showed off long strong legs when the band stood up and took a bow.

But while the others bowed to the public in general, he very obviously bowed to *her.* He and the tuba, which also inclined toward her and which had everyone following its direction. Right toward her.

Corey knew her face flamed. She was not used to attention, especially being the center of it. Her companions, three women and one man, all looked at her curiously, and she grabbed a chicken leg and gnawed nervously. The effect the man had on her was ridiculous. He was obviously an itinerant musician, probably irresponsible. Who else would wear such a costume and play the tuba, of all things?

And, she surmised, he probably was married and had nine children at home. That was her luck. That was why she always played it safe. She dated rarely, and when she did, she chose men like herself, serious men she could trust, men who cared about the same things she did. Nice, safe men.

Now that she thought about it, she'd dated only twice since she'd arrived in Atlanta two months ago. She had been too busy to meet anyone, even if she wanted to, and she hadn't, particularly. Ever since her breakup with Douglas Cavanaugh six years ago, she had steered away from any kind of romantic involvement except the most superficial kind. Maybe that was her problem. Wayward neglected hormones.

The band was wrapping up now, packing away instruments, vacating the courthouse steps for another group, a more conservatively dressed concert band. She lost sight of the man in the crowd as people shuffled and moved around during this break in entertainment. She sighed. Just as well. She would never see him again.

Yet his penetrating expression remained in her mind; that intensity of purpose seemed out of place on a face with the easy grin and eyes that crinkled mischievously at the corners. She hadn't been able to determine the color of his eyes, but she imagined they were blue.

Nonsense, she told herself. He was just flirting as other members of the band flirted with the crowd. It was part of their job. This particular band, she'd heard, enjoyed the absurd, and flirting and pranks were all part of the act.

Feeling suddenly restless and completely foolish over a momentary obsession—it was totally unlike her to have such an obsession—she told the others she thought she saw an acquaintance and would return shortly. She rose and moved toward the entrance of a rapid rail station on the edge of the courthouse. Her eyes swept over the crowd, which was growing increasingly expectant as the vivid, violent colors of the sunset flared across a raucous sky before being subdued by the softer hues of twilight and melding into a dozen shades of blue.

The new band was playing a song called "Music of the Night" from *Phantom of the Opera*. It was one of Corey's favorite melodies, beguiling and mysterious and lovely. She felt the pang of loneliness as she sometimes did, when she allowed it. Right now she didn't want to, yet it was there anyway. She hated the sudden feeling of not being in control. It was *him. He* was responsible, and the notion didn't endear him to her. He had no right to invade her this way with a look.

I'll never see him again, she scolded herself. *I don't want to see him again.*

"Beautiful, isn't it?" she heard a voice behind her say.

The soft, husky drawl exuding a sensuous intimacy would put the Phantom to shame. She knew who the owner was. Her heart quaked, and despite the hot muggy air, shivers ran down her spine.

Corey forced herself not to turn around. She had the strangest feeling that if she did, she would be lost in some way, that part of her would be stolen. Perhaps if she ignored him, he would go away. Her legs trembled, and her hand clasped the nearby railing.

The band finished the song, but the plaintive melody seemed to hover around her. An explosion sounded in the air. She looked up and saw a trail of blue and silver streak through the sky from the first volley of fireworks. Just then the band started the "1812 Overture."

The low notes filtered through the now hushed crowd as magic filled the evening. A seductive, sultry expectancy was building . . .

The music began its ascent to the triumphant climax just as the dark, brooding heavens were split by distant lightning, which joined the man-made fireworks jeweling the sky.

Corey felt her senses bombarded until she thought she would explode with the fullness of them. She had not turned to face him, but she knew he was still there. Somehow he had moved toward her, and she had leaned back into him, pressed by the crowd, she told herself, into enforced intimacy. His arm went around her waist to steady her, and one hand was suddenly rubbing her bare arm with a sensuality that seemed part of the night, part of the music, part of the enchanted web being woven around her.

Corey knew she should move away. He was a stranger. She knew nothing about him except that he wore a strange hat and played the tuba, but somehow her body melded into his. No words were necessary, only sharing, sharing of this particular moment of total absorption, of beauty made of both man and nature, of excitement as the giant cymbals in the band clashed together, and the horns blew in triumphant joy, and the bells started ringing. The sky exploded with wave after wave of silver, red, and blue, and the music came to its emotional, victorious conclusion.

The arm around Corey tightened, and she felt his warm, lean body against hers, his breath whispering against her cheek, his fingers pressing into her arm. Two strangers, she thought. Two strangers united in an interval of intense sensations, in a glorious celebration of beauty and country and life.

A hushed silence fell as the last note sounded and the final flash of light dropped from the sky. God wasn't quite through, however, for once more vivid lightning ripped through the sky, almost like a signal of approval.

People around them began to gather up belongings, and the movement startled Corey from the trance she was in. She felt the stranger's body next to hers, his hands still on her, and the naturalness of it astounded her. She'd never done this before, had never been so easy with a man whose name she didn't even know. Didn't want to know, she convinced herself.

She turned and looked up at him. He was one of the few men she'd ever looked up to. She was tall herself, but he was well over six feet, his body lanky but possessed of a hard strength she had felt when he'd held her. The funny hat was gone, and dark, almost black hair twisted in undisciplined clumps around a face that was far too striking to be called handsome.

His eyes weren't blue after all, but a dark emerald green, like pictures she'd seen of a Caribbean sea, and his smile was easy, much too easy. She'd known smiles like that before, much to her misfortune. Smiles like that came from people who had never known trouble.

Corey tried to move away, remembering another smile, but his hand caught her arm. "Don't run away," he said in that incredibly deep, sensuous voice of his. It soothed, like a tiger trainer's crooning to reluctant animals. And despite herself, it had that calming effect on her.

Something inside her quivered as her eyes met his, and something passed between them, quick but powerful, and undeniably compelling.

Come with me, his eyes were saying. *Come with me, and I'll take you on a wonderful journey.*

"No," she said aloud, but every other part of her was saying yes. Suddenly she felt herself being guided by him, moving with him away from the crowd.

"My name is Patrick," he said, his body leaning into hers.

"I ... I ... my friends ..." Corey started.

"Tell them I'll take you home."

Ordinarily such a command would have made her hackles rise, but the voice wasn't arrogant. Instead, like the Phantom's song, it was reaching out with an alluring invitation that promised ...

Promised what?

"I don't know you," she managed, her eyes unable to leave his, even as she wondered why on earth she was talking to him, why she wasn't running like hell.

"Yes, you do," he said, his forceful gaze demanding that she believe him. And she did. In some mysterious

way, she did know him, at least felt an incomprehensible
tie to him.

Because it's magic, she thought. It's the night and the
music and the emotion, nothing more. But she'd never
had magic before. "Yes," she said suddenly, thoroughly
surprised at her own response, but now irretrievably
committed.

She'd had experience with all types of people before,
had seen the truly evil as well as the weak, and she knew
instinctively that this man was neither. And for the first
time in a very long while, she felt like doing something
impulsive, something wild and foolish and completely irresponsible.

He grinned, an irrepressible smile that would have
made denial impossible in any event. Her eyes flicked
over him. The tuxedo jacket was gone now, replaced by
a green cotton pullover shirt and snug casual slacks. If it
hadn't been for the gleam of mischief in his eyes, he
would have resembled any up-and-coming yuppie.

"Your horns are gone," she observed drolly, wondering
at how comfortable she was with him, and finally attri-
buting it to the fact that this was only a moment of
whimsy, something to be enjoyed and then let go.

A corner of his mouth twitched. "I feared they would
give you the wrong idea."

"That you're a satyr?"

"Nothing could be further from the truth, fair
maiden."

"I expect that's what all satyrs say."

He chuckled. "Trickery one-oh-one in Satyr School."

Corey couldn't stop herself from smiling. His crooked
grin was irresistible. *He* was irresistible with his dark tousled hair and crinkling eyes. She had heard about crinkling eyes before, but she'd never seen them. A

description, she'd always thought, for books alone. But his crinkled. They really did, God help her.

Be careful, she warned herself. Be careful. It's the mood, that's all it is. She would soon find his warts. She was quite sure of it.

But when his hand suddenly caught hers, she felt warmth surge through her, and for the first time in her life she didn't care about tomorrow.

"Where are your friends?" he asked, his words a caress. They surprised her. Somehow he hadn't appeared to be the type of man who would worry about manners. He was more the type to carry a woman off to a hut in the woods, like a bandit.

Corey's face immediately flushed. She'd never been much of a romantic before, and now . . . dear God, she was acting like a thirteen-year-old with her first crush.

She looked around frantically for her group, and found them staring in her direction, Ellen's eyes wide in surprise. Corey hurried over, feeling Patrick's hand against the small of her back. Possessive. It made her tremble.

Corey introduced him to them, and only then did she realize that she knew just his first name, and that he didn't know her name at all. Somehow the thought appealed to her. At the moment she didn't want to know more; she didn't want to spoil the filigree of enchantment, of unreality, and no one seemed to expect more than what she gave. Ellen merely winked and looked pleased when Corey announced she would not be going home with them.

All the time, she felt as if she were someone else doing these things that were so out of character: allowing a stranger to take charge of her, agreeing to go with him, thumbing her nose at normal precautions. Excitement bubbled up inside her, excitement and fear and anticipation.

I do know something about him, she told herself. He plays in the band; he openly came to my friends. And he'd nodded his head at people they passed, accepting their greetings, as if he knew everyone. He couldn't be dangerous and do that.

But he *was* dangerous, she sensed, in an altogether different fashion, because he made her emotions sing in a way they never had before, not even with Douglas. This man was nothing like Douglas. Weak, obedient Douglas. But she hadn't known that then.

And then she was being guided away again by that hand, and the touch crawled along the nerve ends of her body and streaked inside to the core of her.

A musician, she thought. And from the grin, a man who took little seriously.

Tonight neither would she.

2

Patrick wondered what in the hell he was doing.

He had always been impulsive, but never this impulsive. He was practically kidnapping a stranger from the courthouse square.

But she had caught his gaze the moment his eyes had swept across the crowd, and he hadn't been able to keep them away for long.

She was pretty, and he liked the way her long, dark hair was allowed its freedom, the way it swung with her movements. He liked the slender body that moved with grace. He liked the way she listened so intently and seemed absorbed in music while others talked and laughed. He liked everything about her, even her too solemn expression, which challenged him to do something about it.

It was an idiotic compulsion, and he recognized it. The tuba had been another. And he knew well enough that once he got an obsession, he would see the damned thing through to the end, whatever that might be. This quixotic side to his nature was the bane of his family's tranquility, but there it was. He couldn't, wouldn't, do anything about it. He liked himself as he was.

Patrick's eccentricities, his folks always explained. But thank God they never tried to change him, although he'd always felt his father would have dearly liked a son who followed in his footsteps rather than one who made his own, which were, his father used to say, like impressions in sand, of no lasting value. But the words had never stung, because they were said with affection rather than anger. And lately they hadn't been uttered at all.

Patrick did not particularly hanker after lasting value. He enjoyed the immediate, and what he wanted right then was to pursue his fascination with *her*.

He'd wondered if she was married. When he'd searched for her after his band had stopped playing and found her leaning against a railing, he quickly noticed there was no ring on her slender fourth finger. Her head was turned so he could see her profile, and there was a wistfulness about her expression that struck straight through to his heart. Her hair seemed even darker in the deepening twilight, and her facial features were delicate except for a stubborn chin. He liked that. He liked determined people, and it seemed to him there were not many around.

Maybe his fascination had to do with the magnetic energy in the air tonight, the sense of joie de vivre that was so vibrant. And then he dismissed the thought. He couldn't remember being this fascinated with a face before. Although outwardly carefree, he was cautious in his relationships, willing to wait until he found someone he wanted to spend his life with, someone who understood his widely divergent interests and could share them with an unrestrained appreciation that matched his. But this evening there was no caution.

Especially not after the way he'd felt when she'd stepped back against him and her body fitted neatly against his. Fireworks of a different kind shot through him. His arm went around her, and she seemed to belong there, her head resting against his chin, her dark hair like silk against his skin, and the smell of roses drifting upward like some intoxicant.

She'd turned around, and her eyes were as beautiful as the rest of her, large and dark, like fine, rich coffee. As their gazes met and reached into each other, an unfamiliar tenderness rolled over him, tenderness and a sense of destiny, the strangest feeling of belonging. A tremor streaked down his back.

"My name is Patrick," he'd said, holding out his hand. He wanted her to give a name of her own. But she didn't, though her hand closed on his in wary consent. Still he received the impression of a wild animal ready to give flight. But then she was moving with him, and he knew he was not going to let her go until he knew more about her.

He went through the formalities of introductions, mouthing the right words, even though his thought processes were in turmoil. He only remembered from that brief encounter that one of her friends called her "Corey."

Corey. He'd never met anyone named Corey before. Hell, he'd never met anyone who made him feel confused and more impulsive than usual.

His hand still in hers, he guided her to his Jeep, the blue Jeep he loved because he could take it anyplace, particularly up to his beloved mountains. It wasn't the most respectable transportation for an assistant district attorney, but he had never cared about what others thought, not when he took up the tuba instead of football, or when he decided on the district attorney's office rather than his father's well-respected law firm, or when he moonlighted in the Abominable Marching Band rather than the Symphony Guild. He had never wanted to imitate his older brother, the perfect son and brother, who had died in Vietnam.

He looked down at his companion ... Corey ... and couldn't help a grin. She looked as completely baffled as he about the swirling energy carrying them along some unfamiliar path.

Patrick opened the door for her, his hand going to the small of her back, and again he felt an inexplicable warmth. The light from a nearby street lamp lit her face, the serious dark eyes, the stubborn chin, the fine cheekbones. Her face was full of hesitancy. Laughter sounded behind them, and music in front from a car radio.

Patrick went around the car, opening his own door and sliding inside. Before she had a chance to change her mind, he started the engine and inched his way through the parking lot to the road. Only then did he cast a glance at her.

"Corey," he said. "It's a pretty name."

The atmosphere within the Jeep was tense, electric, apprehensive. The magic was there, but Patrick also sensed a certain wariness. His right hand went over and covered hers, moving her closer to him.

"Don't be frightened," he said. "There's any number of people who would vouch for me. I was an Eagle Scout."

Her solemn expression lightened. "And now you wear horns and play a tuba." There was a wry, whimsical note in her voice, as if she really didn't know whether she approved of these things or not. "What a transformation!"

"Do you have something against tuba players?" He glanced toward the back to make sure his tuba was there. Before he'd changed from his band costume, he'd asked a friend to deposit Ole Joe there.

"I don't know. I've never met one before."

"Harry Smith is a tuba player."

"He's with *The Morning Show*?"

"Yep," he said with enormous satisfaction. "You would

be surprised at the ranks of tuba players." He gave her such a beguiling, mischievous grin that Corey couldn't help returning it.

"And you? How did you become a tuba player?"

"My father was a football player, all-state. My brother was a football player, all-state, and everyone wanted me to be a football player, all-state," he said with a strain of amusement. "Everyone but me. I like my teeth. To convince them of the futility of their hopes, I took up the tuba. And then I discovered I liked it. It's a great topic for conversation." He shrugged as if that explained everything when it really explained very little.

Corey couldn't help smiling back. He had so much self-deprecating charm, he could cajole a smile from the wariest of skeptics. She sat back in the Jeep, her body relaxing. She was amazed at herself. She knew too much about the world not to be wary, yet now, nothing in her life had ever seemed so natural as sitting next to ... Patrick.

"Where are we going?" The question popped suddenly from her lips as they moved onto a freeway.

"To the home of friends of mine ... a jam session. Is that all right?"

Corey didn't know. She wanted it to be all right, and she tried to rationalize her desire. He was obviously well known; he had been greeted by so many people. And his eyes, so warm and laughing ... There could be no harm in him.

He noted her hesitation. "What about something to eat first?"

Corey grabbed the suggestion like a lifeline and nodded, surprised at the sudden hunger the suggestion invoked. At least she hoped it was hunger for food. Ever since she first glimpsed him, her appetite had somehow disappeared, and now she realized she'd had little to eat since early this morning, despite the huge picnic spread in the square. For a moment she wondered about his last name, but then decided she didn't want to know it. Last names would take the magic away, and she didn't want to lose it.

Patrick turned on the radio. The station was being shamefully indulgent on this Fourth of July, and Corey felt shivers go up and down her spine at the selection of patriotic music—not the marching kind, but the wistfully sad music about leave-takings, and homecomings, and homecomings-that-weren't-to-be.

Her gaze went to Patrick's face. It was set now, some of the ease gone. His hand was tight against the steering wheel. Then, as if he sensed her searching gaze, he turned to look at her, and the smile was back on his face.

"How did you like our little celebration?"

"I thought it was wonderful," she said. "Especially the parade."

"Not the tuba?" he teased.

"It ranks right up there with the parade," she said. "But I'd heard a tuba before, and I'd never seen a parade like that."

"Never?"

"Never," she reaffirmed. "Where I grew up the Fourth of July only meant guns going off, with live ammunition."

"And where is that?" His deep voice was soft but probing.

"A little piece of land much like Lebanon, I suspect," she said. "Public housing." The words were bitten off, as if tossed out on a dare. How could she explain the vast difference between where she grew up and the all-American Norman Rockwell Fourth of July she'd just witnessed?

His hand went out to her again, warm and gentle, and she wondered about a musician with sensitivity. But then she had once thought that about another man, too, and he'd made her stop believing in fairy tales.

She waited for more questions, but they didn't come. Instead he grinned at her. "Do you like camping?"

"I don't know," she said, bewildered at the change of subject. "I've never been camping."

"What about Ferris wheels and merry-go-rounds?"

She had done that. Douglas Cavanaugh III had taken her. He had taken her and held her, and proposed to her, and she had been grandly happy. For a while.

She nodded.

"And what do *you* like best in the world?" he asked, his voice compellingly warm.

An ache started deep inside Corey, a gnawing, needy ache that she hadn't known before. She tried to think of an answer, but she didn't know what it was. She'd known when she had been a child: a normal family that lived in a house with a white picket fence, and a mother and father who loved each other and her too. But that time was long gone.

"A night like tonight," she said suddenly, taking herself by surprise. "The music and fireworks and ..." She stopped. How could she say *and all the wonderful sensations ... leaning against you ... the strange enchantment*. It didn't make any sense. It wasn't even real.

His right hand left the gearshift and closed around one of hers. She felt its strength and warmth, the restrained caress that was so much more sensual than demanding. His fingers played along hers, stroking, lighting little fires that streaked through her body.

"And you?" she forced herself to say past the lump that had settled in her throat. "What do you like best?"

"Usually whatever I'm doing at the time, and especially right now," he answered, the laughter gone from his voice. He meant it, she knew. He really meant it. His fingers squeezed hers, and she wondered how it would feel to accept everything so gladly. He's a musician, she reminded herself. He probably has no responsibilities, wants none.

So unlike her. Corey wondered whether that was the attraction. She had always taken everything so seriously, had shouldered responsibility for so many people. And now, for the first time in her life, she felt free. Like a bird that was suddenly flying after being caged.

She liked the feeling. She liked it so much, it terrified her.

His hand left hers and returned to the gearshift, and the car slowed, coming to a stop in front of the most disreputable shack she had ever seen. An old, tottering sign nearby proclaimed "B-B-Que," and a smoky, wonderful smell permeated the entire area. Patrick blew his horn, and almost instantly an elderly man emerged from the neat white-trimmed house behind the shack. He grinned as soon as he saw the Jeep, his eyes taking in Patrick, Corey, and the tuba in the back.

"You and Ole Joe wanderin' again?" he said to Patrick, his dark eyes creasing with affection.

"Always." Patrick grinned. "This is Corey, and Corey, this is Pete Brown, the best fiddler and cook this side of the Mississippi."

"Whole lot more demand for food than fiddlin'," Pete said to Corey.

"We were hoping you might have some barbecue left," Patrick told him.

"You know I always save some for scalawags like you," Pete replied. "Want to come in, or take it with you?"

Patrick looked over at Corey, then winked at Pete. "What do you think?"

"Gotcha, Pat." Pete winked back. "Mighty pretty young lady. I'll get it right quickly."

Corey looked at Patrick curiously.

"A very old friend," Patrick explained.

True to his word, the older man emerged quickly, a bag and two soft drinks in his hands. "You and the young miss come back and stay awhile," he said as Patrick paid him.

Patrick looked at her quickly, warmly, and nodded. "We will," he promised.

He started the Jeep again, and she knew she should ask where they were going, but she didn't care. The sky was still alive with clouds, distant lightning occasionally flashing, and the air was pregnant with the promise of something so wonderful that Corey no longer questioned it. She leaned back, for the first time in years allowing her tumbling emotions to overrule her pragmatic mind. She felt like Dorothy in the land of Oz, and she couldn't wait to see where the road was leading next.

3

After seeing Fourth of July crowds everywhere, Corey wondered how Patrick ever found a place of peace and silence. But he did: a small park that ran alongside a boisterously moving stream. It was near midnight, and Corey wasn't at all sure she wanted quite so much privacy. Not because of fear of her companion, but fear of herself.

She had never before felt the feelings invoked by the man beside her, and that made her wonder for a moment what her feelings really had been for Douglas. With Patrick she knew an odd sense of belonging, and yet a trembling excitement that reverberated inside like the beginning rumblings of an earthquake.

She started to get out of the car, but his hand restrained her, and then he was out himself and opening her door with a flourish. "M'lady," he said, holding his hand out to her.

Easily, so very easily, she took it. A rumbling noise penetrated her ears, but she wasn't sure whether it was her heart or distant thunder. A cool, moist breeze ruffled her hair, and she felt incredibly alive. She was aware of Patrick extracting the bag of food from the car and of being led down to the stream. It was very dark, with the sky still darkened by roiling clouds. No moon or stars shone, and she was surprised how readily her eyes adapted and how trustingly she followed Patrick to the base of a tree, where his hand guided her down.

The ground was cool but not wet, and in the odd devil-may-care mood that had wrapped itself around her tonight, Corey wasn't concerned about whether her shorts would get ruined or her legs dirty. Apparently neither was he as he joined her, leaned back against the tree and pulled her to him so her back rested comfortably against his chest.

The hold was more gentle than lustful, and yet she could feel a certain tension in his body and knew it must be responding in the same way as her own. The heat that seared her everywhere their bodies touched must also burn him. She kept waiting for the wariness to return, the fear of hurt and betrayal that had kept her distant when a man came too close, the memory of a harsh truth she wished to obliterate but never quite could.

She shivered suddenly, and his hands slid up and down her arms in reassurance. She found herself twisting around and trying to see his face. Part of it was hidden by the darkness, but not the generous mouth, quirking with a slightly baffled smile, and strong jaw, giving impressions of strength and integrity. She knew now that fear would not come, and her hand went up to touch his cheek in an impulsive, searching gesture.

His lips came down slowly to meet hers, skimming more than pressing, as if posing their own question. And she responded with an unknown passion rising from deep within her. Her mouth caressed his, assenting, no, more than assenting. Asking. Wanting. Demanding in some primitive way she didn't understand. Her mind warned, but her body responded as their lips explored and tasted, and liking the taste, ventured further.

Her mouth opened to him, and his tongue entered, slowly exploring the contours with sweet sensuousness that created a throbbing yearning within her, an exquisitely painful and delicious need.

Corey found herself responding to his every touch, her tongue meeting his, playing with it in an abandoned way that amazed her, even as she relished the sensations each touch created. Even her toes seemed to tingle with a wonderful, electric, warm tension.

His hands ran through her hair and tightened around her shoulders. She closed her eyes to the gentle assault on her every sense, every emotion, and once again she felt as if she were running toward some unknown destination.

Corey felt Patrick's arousal against her body, and something of the old wariness returned. She instinctively flinched. His mouth moved from hers, and his hand wandered down her face as if he were memorizing it.

"Corey ... it's all right," he soothed. He leaned down and kissed her lightly, shifting his body slowly as if to relieve the pressure on a particular part of his anatomy. He smiled wryly. "I'm sorry," he said. "I don't want to scare you off."

Corey sat up, feeling both relieved and disappointed. She wanted to cling to him, yet those warning voices made her move away, even as her hand reached for his.

She battled with herself. She wanted to know so much more about him, and yet she was afraid to know more, afraid that hard facts would tear the gossamer web of enchantment.

"You have lovely hair," he whispered, breaching the barricades she was trying to rebuild around her heart. His voice, a deep sound softened by the slight Southern drawl, was like a soothing cloth over heated skin.

"You have lovely horns," she retorted, trying to lighten the moment, trying to fight against her overwhelming attraction to him. She didn't want it. She didn't have time for it. Her heart couldn't afford it.

"And you won't forget them," he replied dryly.

"Never. First impressions are lasting."

He chuckled softly. "Then I'll always have one of you staring up at the sky with that wistful candy-store look."

"Candy-store look?"

"Like a waif looking into a candy store," he explained.

Corey felt herself stiffening. He saw and sensed entirely too much about her.

"I smell something very good," she said, desperately changing the subject.

"The best barbecue in the South, and that means the world," he asserted with no little smugness.

He must have felt her need to lighten the mood, lessen the sexual awareness between them, Corey thought, both grateful and resentful that he read her so well.

She took the proffered sandwich and bit into it, and it was more than he'd claimed. Or perhaps she thought that way because of the look of total joy on his face as he took his first bite. She'd never met anyone who exuded such complete delight at anything and everything. Now she was sure that was the reason for the attraction. He was a musician who lived for the moment. No responsibilities. No cares. Exactly her opposite, and everyone knew that opposites attract.

He popped open their soft drinks, and Corey, too, found herself thoroughly enraptured with the smoky taste of slowly cooked pork and the tangy sauce, which dribbled on her lips. She felt his eyes on her, but she didn't feel self-conscious. His lips were also painted with red pepper sauce, and she was fascinated with how much she wanted to taste it there. The thought was incredibly arousing, and hardly had it passed through her mind than he leaned down and his tongue caught her lips, tracing a beguiling invitation. *Come with me.* She remembered the same invitation in his eyes earlier. *Come with me, and I'll take you on a wonderful journey.*

And she wanted to go. How much she wanted to go. So much that everything else was momentarily forgotten.

"Come with me," he whispered, speaking aloud the invitation. But the sound of it startled her back into reality. Another voice came from somewhere else, accusing words, defensive words.

She jerked away and rose quickly, before her emotions were seduced again. She walked several feet away, hearing the silence of his surprise. And then she felt him rise and approach her. One of his hands touched her cheek. "Don't ever be afraid of me," he said in a low voice.

"I'm not," she said defensively.

"Good." But there was no belief in the one word. "Let's go to the jam session, Corey. Or would you rather I take you home?"

The thought of losing him was almost as excruciating as her fear. A few hours, she bargained with God. "The jam session," she said, and she heard him release a breath.

He took her hand and pulled her toward the Jeep, the exuberance back in him. His contagious sense of fun enveloped her, and all her worries seemed to evaporate. She was ready, like Dorothy, to move on to the next adventure.

She was like a will-o'-the-wisp, Patrick thought. He was almost afraid she would disappear into the night, like some summer sprite sent to enchant and bedevil him, and then leave him alone and bereft. He was determined that would not happen.

Something questionably more than attraction was between them. He'd never particularly believed in fate, but he did tonight. From the moment he'd seen her, he'd known that he wanted her, and the more he was with her, the greater that feeling grew. He ached when he touched her, his soul rejoiced when she smiled, his heart tumbled when she gave him that searching, wistful look that told him of deep hurts within her, hurts that kept her from him despite those instinctive responses.

She said, and asked, less than any woman he'd ever known, and that alone frightened him. Was she afraid of inadvertently revealing secrets?

He opened the Jeep door for her, and she moved gracefully inside. When he got in himself, he turned on the inside light and studied her before starting the engine. "Do you have a last name, Corey?"

His gaze met her eyes directly. They were so damned large, so expressive, yet they held so many emotions, he couldn't untangle them.

"Not tonight," she whispered, and he knew that she meant everything to end tonight, that she would indeed try to flee. Damn, but he wanted to know why.

And he would.

Corey liked his friends, especially Ringo, the guitar player. Everyone called him Ringo, it was explained, because he looked just like the former Beatle. They were all in assorted T-shirts, each one equally irreverent. Patrick was the most formally dressed, and he came in for his share of teasing because of it.

Though they were in an old, shabby Victorian house near downtown Atlanta, Corey felt warmed by the obvious affection between the members of the group. She recognized several faces from the Seed and Feed Abominable Marching Band, and was surprised at being able to do so. She had been so completely mesmerized by Patrick, she hadn't realized she'd noticed anyone else. But now she recalled the large man with the rakish mustache who played the drums, and the saxophone player who coaxed such plaintive sounds from his instrument.

The drummer grinned. "We wondered what happened to Pat tonight. He was sort of in a fog. Ole Joe just didn't oomph like usual."

"Yeah," the saxophone player said, looking at her with interest. "And we ain't never seen Pat move quite so fast."

"Ah, friends, your envy is showing," Patrick shot back. "Behave, or I might just take her away."

"No," everyone replied in a chorus, and Corey was overwhelmed by their acceptance. She had always felt the outsider before, never quite accepted, and now acceptance had come so easily. Because of Patrick. For a second she wondered if that feeling of being an outsider had been her fault, a belief instilled as a child and later enforced so strongly by Douglas.

A ring of introductions went around, and she tried to remember the names. In addition to seven men, there were three women, all apparently wives or dates of the musicians.

"Where's Joe?" Ringo asked.

"Minding the car." Patrick grinned.

Ringo raised one dark brow, his gaze gliding merrily from Patrick to Corey. "I think," he said to Corey, "Ole Joe might have a lawsuit . . . alienation of affection."

Corey's lips twitched. "I don't think I've ever competed with a ton of brass before."

"I must say you're better shaped," Mo, the saxophone player, said with an even bigger leer.

Corey looked at Patrick, thinking it would take little to be better shaped than the tuba. "Is that a compliment?"

"It's the best Mo can do," Patrick answered. "He's somewhat of a lackwit."

Mo threw a sheet of music at him. "Come on, lackwork. We have a gig next week."

Patrick groaned, but he left her with the bantering group and returned bearing Ole Joe.

Corey sat with the women, leaning back on a tattered overstuffed sofa, listening. The group played mostly jazz and blues, and some light rock. She wondered what time it was. Thank God, tomorrow was Saturday, although she did have some clients she planned to see, especially Ray. But she banished that dark, disturbing thought, that haunting sense of responsibility that she didn't want at the moment. She wanted instead to watch Patrick, the way he turned his eyes to her and grinned as if they shared a delicious secret; she even wanted to watch the way his cheeks puffed out like a blowfish's as he played the mammoth instrument.

It must be love.

Except she didn't believe in love.

Just as she didn't believe in looks across the crowded square.

She *didn't*.

A dream. It was all a dream.

Corey lazily turned over in her bed. She didn't want the dream to go away. But then her gaze found the clock beside her, and her mind registered the time. She sat upright, horrified.

She'd never slept till noon before. And she had so many things to do today. Ray's hearing was Monday, and she needed to talk to him before then. She had to convince him that his bravado and defensiveness wouldn't play in juvenile court ... unless he wanted to go to a youth detention facility for several years. No time now for dreaming about strangers.

Strangers. Despite all the hours she had spent with Patrick last night, he was still a stranger. She didn't know his last name, or he hers. Neither had he asked for her phone number.

He knew, of course, where she lived. They had left the white Victorian house at dawn, and she had told him to leave her at a bus stop. But he had refused, and she knew if she ever wished to gain her bed, she would have to direct him to her apartment. When they arrived at the complex, she asked him to leave her at the entrance, but again he refused. He would not leave until he saw her safely inside, he said.

But he'd said nothing about seeing her again, and she could only guess that he, too, had been momentarily caught in some sudden aberration that disappeared with daylight. She didn't quite understand the bitter disappointment she'd felt, however, nor the bittersweet weariness now enveloping her.

She dressed quickly, wishing she didn't have to wear a skirt and blouse—her standard uniform when dealing with clients. Corey had always felt that slacks, which some other caseworkers wore, didn't command the same respect. And she needed every edge she could get today.

She had to get through to Ray.

Corey ran a comb through her hair, sorting out her thoughts and trying to place them in mental files. She needed all her wits about her, and she wasn't so sure they were there. She kept thinking about the greenest eyes she'd ever seen, a lanky form and easygoing smile. She groaned. Patrick was something she didn't need right now.

Still, she found herself smiling as she thought of him,

the swimming trunks and tuxedo and horns and tuba and gorgeous smile.

Think of Ray. Ray Gordon, who seldom smiled, who had fought all his life just to survive. Much as she herself had. How well she understood the seemingly cocky thirteen-year-old who hid his hurt and vulnerability behind a veneer of indifference. She'd once done the same thing. She often still did.

Corey easily identified with him. Like Ray, she grew up in a housing project with an alcoholic mother and no father. Like Ray, she had been arrested—not for drugs, but for shoplifting when there was nothing to eat. She too knew the hopelessness of juvenile hall.

But she'd had help, a social worker who'd taken her under her wing. And now she was trying to do the same, but Ray's problems were greater than hers had been: one brother dead in a drug dispute, another serving time in jail. Ray had looked up to his brothers, unworthy as they were, and he had been lured into acting as a drug courier by his brothers' friends, whose names he refused to reveal. He might soon be in a youth detention center for a very long time if she couldn't accomplish a miracle. Confinement, she knew from experience, would probably ruin him forever.

She had been trying desperately to help him ever since she started working with the boy's mother, one of nearly one hundred cases she now handled for the Department of Family and Children's Services. Annalee Gordon had long ago been defeated by life. Abused and abandoned by her common-law husband, she did not have the self-esteem to control her three boys, nor did she have any affection to give them. But from the first moment Corey had seen Ray two months ago, she had sensed a strength and promise, a bright intelligence that shone through the hard brittleness constructed out of need, and she'd felt she was seeing herself as she had been years ago.

There was so little hope in her job, so much defeat. Too much poverty, too much crime, too much indifference, too few resources. Ray had become very important to her; if she could help him, she'd realize a measure of success. She would be able to give back something of what was given to her—a chance.

She closed her eyes and wished as hard as she could.

She wished for a miracle for Ray.

She also discovered she was wishing for something else, too, a green-eyed miracle for herself.

When Corey arrived back at her apartment complex from juvenile court, her spirits were somewhere between her shoes and the pavement, but then they rose almost immediately.

His Jeep was in the parking lot. She would have known it anywhere—not only because of its bright blue color, but because the backseat was occupied by a gigantic tuba case.

Yet she didn't see Patrick until she mounted the steps to her second-floor apartment and found him sprawled across the top one, his eyes consuming what appeared to be a camping magazine. At the sound of her footsteps his gaze immediately turned upward to her face, and she saw his eyes spark in a way that warmed her heart.

Corey was surprised at how loudly her heart thumped. This had been a terribly discouraging day, and now unaccountably the afternoon had suddenly brightened.

Patrick with no last name. Patrick with eyes that laughed. Patrick the musician. Patrick who apparently had few interests outside his own pleasures. The kind of man she'd never thought would attract her, much less hold any fascination for her.

But now she was captivated by him, by his presence, by the crazy things he made her feel inside, by the inexplicable happiness he suddenly brought just by being here.

Be careful, Corey.

But though the warning ran loud and clear through her mind, other parts of her weren't listening. A churning had started deep within her body, a physical yearning so strong, she felt consumed by it.

"Hi," she said, trying to keep the trembling from her voice. A longer greeting was beyond her at this moment.

He grinned at her, that open devil-may-care smile that denied any troubles in the world. He straightened up, and his eyes perused her, from the high heels all the way up to the blouse buttoned nearly to her neck and then to the briefcase in her hand.

He shook his head slowly, and Corey wondered whether it was censure about her working on a Saturday or disappointment with her, now that he was seeing her without benefit of the night that softened reality and cast its spell of enchantment.

Except she still felt *it*. Dear God, she still felt every single drop of it. He had the same effect on her today as last night. God help her, this was no dream.

He was all reality this Saturday afternoon. She had seen part of his legs last night, but now she had full view, and full impact. He was wearing white tennis shorts, revealing legs that were a dark, rich bronze and muscular. There was incredible strength there. She remembered his telling her about his not playing football, yet she had no doubt now that he was an athlete, natural born and more trained than he'd cared to admit.

Suddenly embarrassed by what must be a wide-eyed stare at his lower anatomy, she raised her eyes, not that the view lost any of its fascination. He was wearing a light blue knit shirt that contrasted with the bronze color of his arms and the black crinkly hairs revealed by the shirt's open neck. His dark hair was mussed, as if he'd combed it with his fingers, and a crooked smile played havoc with what little sense she had remaining.

"I didn't have your phone number," he explained, his head tipped slightly to one side as if inquiring whether he was welcome.

"I thought . . ." Her words trailed off. She thought *it* had started and ended last night and this morning. Corey realized that conclusion was another reason for her depression all day. That and Ray. Then she mentally berated herself for even putting the two reasons on a par. Ray's problems were monumental; his entire life was on the ropes.

How could she equate that with a fantasy?

But the fantasy was sitting in front of her, and it was no longer a fantasy but a tall, perfectly formed, irresistible reality, with a crooked, uncertain grin that made her heart bounce like a ball.

"You thought . . .?" he prompted her.

"That you might have been a mirage." She was aware that she was smiling, even more aware that her answer was unusually spontaneous, but then he had that effect on her.

He reached out a hand and took her briefcase, then held her fingers in a warm, possessive clasp. "No mirage," he said. "Believe me, I didn't think such a thing about you."

His look was heated and intense, and didn't seem to go along with everything else about him, with that easygoing personality.

"Are you going to invite me in?"

All the unreality of last night, the lovely gossamer web of magic, wrapped itself around her again, around the two of them. "It depends," she said gently but with searching eyes.

"On what?"

"Whether you are really real or not."

"Oh, I'm very real," he said, accepting the challenge as he leaned over and pressed his lips against hers.

He was so real that he made her body tremble. Summer storm. Summer lightning. Summer thunder. Corey felt all of them and more.

None of the special bewitchery had left with the night. It was even more alive, perhaps because it had survived the harsh test of full daylight. Even as his kiss made her dizzy, she could feel the beat of his heart, the pulsing of a vein in his throat. So real. Yet unreal.

The joy she felt at being with him was unexpected and painful, exquisitely painful, his touch even more so as his kiss deepened until she thought he was going to consume her.

For the first time in her life she wanted to be consumed. And that shocked her so much that her body stiffened. She felt him reluctantly step away from her, and felt an immediate loss.

He was wearing that crooked smile again, that incredibly charming small-boy look that begged forgiveness even as it said "I'd do it again, given the chance."

"I hope," he drawled, "that didn't change your mind about letting me in."

She took a deep swallow. "How did you know I was going to agree?"

"Those lovely eyes," he said. "They were saying yes, and now there's a doubt lurking there. So I humbly beg your pardon for acting so precipitously. But I've been wanting to do that all day. I guess I too wanted to make sure you weren't just a dream after all."

His eyes dancing, he added, "You're definitely no dream."

Corey found herself responding, just as she had last

night. It had been a long time since she'd trusted a man, and Patrick was everything she knew she should guard against. A musician who appeared to take little seriously. And yet there was a certain safety in that too. Douglas had seemed the epitome of integrity, then she'd learned he was anything but. She had come to distrust the wealthy establishment. She wanted no part of it again. Perhaps that was why Patrick's freewheeling personality was so appealing to her. Still . . . She looked at the magazine he'd laid down. Travel. New trails. A wanderer.

But even though her practical mind told her to be careful, she felt deep pleasure in his presence, at watching a smile meant just for her. The uncertainty she often felt with men was gone, and she wondered at the incredible ease she felt with him. Some of the terrible strain of the past hours faded slowly from her tense body.

She handed him her key without a word, watching his smile broaden as if he had just been given the map to an enormous treasure. He leaned over and kissed her again—this time there was a sweetness about the contact—before he straightened again and unlocked the door. He stood back and ushered her, treating her like a princess. Which was, at the moment, exactly how she felt.

He stepped into her apartment as if he belonged there. She knew his eyes were rapidly skimming the place, and she knew a certain pride at what he was seeing.

The furnishings were meager because she didn't have much money. But she had wanted a home for so long that she had taken great care with this one. She had worked hard to make it warm and cheerful. Plants supplemented her limited furniture, and the few pieces she did own were good ones. One side of the room was filled with a bookcase, made by her with bricks and boards she had stained, and filled with favorite volumes she'd found at used book sales. A huge cloth cat she'd found in a craft show watched them with beady button eyes from a corner, and gaily printed scatter pillows gave the room color.

She noted the glint of approval in his eyes, and again she felt warm rushes of pleasure course through her. She wondered where he lived, what he liked. She wondered so much about him, whereas last night she had consciously tried not to. Now, she realized, she didn't even know his last name.

"Have you been here long?" she finally said. He had looked so relaxed on those stairs.

"Yep," he replied.

Corey was astounded by his answer, but then she had been astounded by him since the moment she'd seen him. No other man she knew would have admitted to waiting a long time with such imperturbability.

"I was hoping we could drive up to the mountains," he added.

"Don't you have to play tonight?"

"Oh, we'll be back in time," he said. "An hour and half on the road, two hours there, an hour and half back. There's a great little inn where we can have dinner. It's two now, and I don't play until nine."

Corey felt her pulse race, even though she gave herself thirteen reasons why she shouldn't go. She needed to make phone calls, to wash her clothes for next week, to do written reports, to . . .

She nodded, unable to do anything else as her eyes caught his. She had never seen such gorgeous eyes, the green so deep, it would do an emerald proud. The laughter was gone from them. Instead his gaze was intense, so very intense, as if he were asking her for much more than to spend a few hours with him.

She didn't know how to answer that question. She didn't know whether her soul was still bound tightly with strictures that ordered her to run whenever anyone got close. Like a frightened child. She didn't particularly care for that cowardly aspect of her nature, but she recognized it.

He wasn't giving her a chance to reconsider. He cocked his head to one side, ordering, "Five minutes to change. Wear something comfortable." Five minutes! She gave him a wry smile in return. A challenge. She would make it in four. Suddenly filled with a kind of delight, she moved quickly. "There're some drinks in the fridge," she offered as she whirled into the bedroom, her hands moving rapidly as she shed clothes. Excitement hummed inside, a perverse joy at doing something so completely spontaneous that she delighted herself.

She had done everything she could for Ray that morning. Tomorrow she would make some phone calls, but today ... Today she was going to forget. Forget the memories, forget the ghosts. She was going to enjoy.

She quickly ransacked a bureau and found comfortable tan shorts and a dark brown knit shirt that made her coloring more dramatic. She ran a brush through her hair as her feet went into sandals. She didn't give herself time to think of everything she should be doing rather than going out with someone who was still a stranger.

No, not a stranger. As little as she knew about Patrick, she felt strangely safe and sheltered with him. In all her life she had never known that feeling, and now she knew it with him.

She looked in the mirror for a quick appraisal and was shocked. She had never seen herself glow like this; a pink flush colored her cheeks, her eyes shone, and eagerness softened the usually serious set of her mouth. Don't let anything ruin it, she pleaded with whoever might be listening. A little longer. Just a little longer.

She saw an answering anticipation in his face as she opened the door. He glanced at his watch.

"Four and a half minutes," he said. "I never would have believed it."

"I didn't think musicians cared about time," she said.

"Oh, we care about a lot of things," he answered with that beguiling smile of his. "Particularly beautiful young ladies."

He grabbed her hand. "There are so many things I want to show you."

Before she could reply, they were out the door, skipping, not walking, down the stairs, and she was being handed into the Jeep.

"Ole Joe's a chaperon?"

"The kind I like," Patrick said with a wicked smile. "Silent. I didn't know when we would get back and whether I would have time to get him. He needs an outing, anyway."

He started the Jeep, and she closed her eyes, trying to forget about her disastrous interview with Ray earlier. She felt one of Patrick's hands touch hers in a reassuring gesture, and she knew he'd sensed her sudden somberness.

"Something wrong?"

The concern in his voice startled her. He seemed created for lightheartedness, for laughter, yet for the first time she sensed something deeper in him. She wasn't sure she wanted to find depths to him. She was not going to fall in love again. Never. It was too painful. A few hours of magic was one thing . . .

"No," she said. "Not now."

She watched his face change at her words, the smile came back, although she thought she saw a flash of frustration and heard an almost inaudible sigh, before he took his hand away and used it to shift gears.

For the next hour she couldn't take her eyes away from him. She leaned against the door so she could face him, the green eyes that sparkled like gems, the easy smile, the frequent chuckle as he recounted some ridiculous story, like when someone tried to abscond with Ole Joe and apparently gave up halfway down the block and left him there. Ole Joe, he said, carried his own vengeance in his weight. The good thing about a tuba, he said, is that no one wants to steal it. Not for long, anyway.

He seemed so open that Corey found much of her natural shyness disappearing. "Are you from Atlanta?"

"One of the few natives," he replied.

She cocked her head, thinking back to last night. He had mentioned a father, a brother. "Your family?"

"Been here in Georgia several hundred years," he replied, and she felt her heart drop. Tradition. She'd run headlong into tradition before, and came out by far the worse.

"You said you had a brother . . ."

The laughter drained from his face, and she watched him tense all over. It was so different from any other emotion of his that she felt she had invaded something distinctly private. "He died in Vietnam."

"I'm sorry," she said, realizing once more how little she knew about him.

His face eased. "It was a long time ago."

But it was still a raw wound, she knew instinctively. "No other brothers or sisters?"

"Nope," he said, his voice cheerful again. "My folks swore off after a few months with me."

"Now why don't I believe that?" she asked.

"It's true," he said with no sign of repentance. "I think

they believed I was a changeling for a while. No true Kelly would play the tuba. But they adjusted."

"Kelly?"

He glanced over at her in surprise at her question. This time she smiled whimsically, as much at herself as at him. "Do you realize I didn't even know your name until now? Patrick Kelly. I like it. It fits you."

"Irish," he said with deep satisfaction.

"Black Irish," she agreed with another glance at that dark hair and green eyes, "and full of blarney."

"Not always," he chided her. "And whom am I addressing? In addition to Corey, I mean."

Corey hesitated. Part of her didn't want him to know. She was afraid the knowledge would somehow spoil the sense of enchantment, of unreality, that she felt protected her heart. But he already knew where she lived. He would be able to discover her name easily enough.

"Corey Adams."

"And what does Corey Adams do that made her look so world-weary this afternoon?"

Another intrusion into the magic.

"Did I look that bad?" she said, postponing an answer.

"Like the weight of the world was on you."

"Does it look heavier than a tuba?"

"Nothing is heavier than a tuba," he quipped, obviously getting the message loud and clear. She didn't want to talk about herself, or about what was bothering her.

"In minutes," he said, "you will have the best view in Georgia. It has great restorative powers."

Her eyes turned from him and to the narrow road they were climbing up into the northern Georgia mountains. She had wanted to come here before, but she'd been too busy. Now she looked at them with awe.

The trees were somehow muted, the color more mellow than the bright green below. Wildflowers grew alongside the road, and to her left the side of the road dropped steeply to reveal a valley. Beyond, rolling hills were glazed by the shimmering rays of a bright sun.

They turned onto a narrow road, went about a mile, and then stopped where several other cars had already parked.

"Tallulah Falls," he said. Once more he moved to her side of the car with effortless speed and held out his hand to her, and they walked to the edge of a cliff. Trails led off in different directions, and at the moment they were alone. Corey looked out over the gorge. Magnificent falls tumbled down a rocky cliff, and a half rainbow rose from the mist. Totally delighted, she turned to Patrick, who smiled at her uninhibited reaction.

"I knew you would like it," he said smugly, his hands going to her shoulders.

Corey felt the now familiar fire brand her where his hands touched, and she knew the magnetism was still there, alive and singing between them. Whispering, beckoning.

Promising.

I don't want this, she told herself.

But she did. Dear God, how she did.

He looked so incredibly captivating, his mouth sensuous, his eyes mesmerizing, unwilling to let go of the hold they had on her.

Without taking his gaze from her, he touched the small of her back, turning her and guiding her down one of the wooded paths that ran alongside the gorge. One hand steadied her along the steep trail, until they finally stopped at a small clearing with a dazzling view of the waterfall.

He turned her so she faced him directly, and his head bent. "God, how I've been wanting to do this," he whispered, just before their lips met and exploded in a maelstrom of pent-up need, of expectation building since he'd kissed her at the apartment.

The smell of pine, the sound of water falling, the harsh glare of a Southern sun wrapped around Corey, and she felt sensations bursting inside her, clawing at the boundaries of her body, wanting to be free. She had never wanted anything as much as Patrick at this moment, and the need astounded her. Even when she thought she had been in love before, she had never felt this physical yearning, this terribly sweet pain to join body with body. She hurt as she had never hurt before because she didn't understand it, didn't know how to deal with it. So many emotions juggled for dominance, but they all faded next to that one all-consuming physical need.

She felt his body tremble as it molded itself to hers. His tongue, which had been ravishing, now turned to sweet seduction as it explored the roof of her mouth, playfully teased her tongue, soundlessly urged her to join in the sensual game.

Corey felt his manhood harden and press against her, and even through their clothes it excited reactions that grew in strength. And she knew those reactions would build and build until every sense was involved in the inevitable path toward glorious fulfillment.

5

The sound of approaching footsteps crunching against rock and leaves separated them. But there was no question in Patrick's mind that he and Corey had unfinished business.

Very unfinished.

Patrick had only to glance down at his trousers to know how unfinished. Even if he hadn't felt it in other, very real ways.

His smile fading slightly, he moved his hands to her arms as four people came into view, then disappeared again. But the moment was gone.

Patrick looked down at Corey's glazed eyes. He knew much more about her than what she'd told him, but not nearly enough. After going sleepless that morning, he had gone to his office and used the computer to discover her last name and her occupation. It had been easy enough with the address. He was taken aback only a second when he discovered they both had the same general employer, the state of Georgia. But then, he thought, nothing would ever surprise him again after last night.

Those hours they'd spent together were different from any other encounter he'd ever had. He wanted this one to last. He wanted to see her eyes glow with their special golden light. He wanted to see her mouth curve more often into a smile. He wanted her in ways he didn't yet fully comprehend.

Perhaps it was that trust she had given him last night, a trust he instinctively knew didn't come easily. It was part and parcel of what he felt when he was with her: a sense of belonging together, an immediate empathy that combined sexual urgency with a profound sense of pleasure. Like knowing that after the midnight hurricane, there would be a glorious sunrise.

He had never felt that kind of contentment before, only a curious chafing inside, a kind of searching that had never stopped—until he met her.

He should tell her what he knew about her. but he was reluctant. He suspected she would feel it was an intrusion, and he wanted her to tell him everything there was about Corey Adams and what had dimmed the light that should be in her eyes. Whatever it was, though, it had not quenched the fire. He could feel the blaze when their bodies touched, their lips met, and their eyes caressed in such intimate ways.

Another rustling of brush and the scattering of stones interrupted his thoughts. His hands slid down her arms, and his fingers, flexing with a frustration that was echoed in her tense body, meshed with hers. "I'm starving, Miss Adams," he said, not adding that he was starving for her. He realized he didn't have to when he saw the same hunger in her face. An aching started deep in his body, and he felt his manhood stretch and tighten; at the same time he saw her breasts grow taut against her shirt.

He couldn't remember ever wanting a woman quite this badly.

Patrick shook his head and led her back up the trail to the Jeep. He helped her inside, allowing his hand to linger a moment, before touching her face. It took tremendous effort to drop his hand and move to his side of the car.

He fastened all his attention on driving. At least he tried to, even as he felt her hand on his leg, a gesture that told him she didn't want to relinquish that special closeness any more than he did.

The lodge was as Patrick remembered it. Rustic and sprawling, it was the centerpiece of a fishing and hunting camp with log cabins spread around in adjoining woods. A stream bubbled merrily alongside the lodge.

Patrick had not been here in more than eighteen months, although he used to come on a very frequent basis, not to stay, for he preferred camping, but to eat the food. The owners served the best mountain trout he'd ever tasted.

He saw Corey's surprised look as her eyes scanned an empty parking lot and then went to her watch. "Are they open?"

"Trust me," he said, and savored her expression as she obviously decided to do just that.

As they stepped inside from the screened porch, a stocky woman greeted them, her mouth spreading in a wide smile as she saw Patrick. It quickly included Corey in its warmth.

They were ushered to a small corner table covered with a brightly checked tablecloth on which was centered a thick homemade candle.

"This is Martha," Patrick said, introducing the woman who'd seated her. "And Martha, this is Corey. I've told her about your great trout."

Martha beamed. "You must be real special," she told Corey. "He's never brought anyone here before. We've been waitin'."

After Martha left, taking two orders for trout with her, Corey tipped her head. "Do you know everyone?"

"Everyone who's important," he replied flippantly.

"Who has to do with food," she guessed.

"One of the joys of life."

"And others?"

"Thou."

"And . . . ?"

"A jug of wine."

"And nothing more?"

"Oh, a great deal more," he said, quite seriously this time. "We'll have time to explore it all."

Corey suddenly went still. "Will we?"

His gaze heated her through and through. "Oh, yes." The answer was a promise, a fervently said pledge.

She felt the heat curl up inside her, sparking an urgency that made her other hunger fade. There were so many promises in his eyes, promises she wasn't sure she should believe. He was, after all, a musician, and she had heard a great deal about their fickleness and wayward ways. But then he couldn't be any more untrustworthy than Douglas, a publicly upstanding scion of a monied family.

She believed Patrick was exactly what he seemed. No subterfuge. Perhaps that had been part of what had given the past twenty-four hours such a sense of freedom, of fantasy. She could let down her guard.

But now that feeling was settling into something altogether different.

Patrick's eyes were suddenly serious. "You were worried about something earlier today."

Inexplicably Corey wanted to share her problem, the one that she had been trying to push away all afternoon but that still nagged at her consciousness. Patrick's eyes were so warm, so sympathetic, compelling her to answer.

"A boy," she said. "He's in juvenile detention and will go to a youth development center if I can't find another place for him. I . . . saw him today."

"It's important to you?"

"I'm with the Department of Family and Children Services, and his mother is one of my clients, one of the first when I arrived. Ray and I . . . we just seemed to understand each other, and when he was arrested three weeks ago, he called me. Not his mother." She hesitated a moment, not saying that she and Ray had empathy because they had similar pasts. She had told Ray a little bit about herself, hoping it would give him some faith that he too could make it.

"He's . . . a good kid," she continued, "but one of his brothers used him, and now his brother's friends are using him as a courier, and he thinks it's macho to keep silent."

"Drugs?"

She nodded.

"How old is he?"

"Thirteen."

Corey felt Patrick's eyes on her, and again she was aware of currents behind the bright emerald green. The magic she had felt deepened into something stronger, something more intense, something more real. She felt her hand tremble slightly on the table. She didn't know if she was ready for this, if she could allow herself to dream again.

"And where do you think he should go?"

"A boys' ranch. He loves animals. He keeps rescuing them from the street, though he's really the one who needs rescuing. I think he would love the country. He could thrive there with some encouragement. That's all he needs. He's incredibly bright. And he wants it, I think, though he's afraid now to hope. God knows there's none at home. His mother is an alcoholic, was just barely able to hang on to the kids, mostly because she needed the checks from the government."

"But you haven't had any success?"

"Every place is full. There are only two boys' ranches, and I've tried them both. No luck. And his hearing is Monday. If he's sent away . . ."

Patrick felt his gut tighten. There was something in her voice that said more. Something in those guarded eyes too. Something that revealed she knew the boy's situation only too well. He heard the pain, and he wanted to do something. And he knew he might be able to. But he couldn't say anything yet, not until he knew for sure.

"What's his name?"

"Ray. Ray Gordon."

Patrick started to say something, but Martha returned with a tray with water glasses, iced tea glasses, and delicious-looking salads full of bright red tomato slices.

"How's Fred?" he asked Martha as he helped her with the tray and chatted as if he were part of the family rather than a customer. All the seriousness was gone now, and Corey wondered if she had imagined his concern. He hadn't asked how or why she was involved with the boy. Perhaps he really didn't care. Which was, she thought with just a little relief, well enough. She wanted things as they were between them—uncomplicated.

And that was the way they were through the meal. The food was, as he had claimed, delicious. The trout was pan-fried, the meat flaky and fresh, and the vegetables melted in her mouth. She'd always heard of Southern cooking, but hadn't found the true article in Atlanta, not in the short time she had been there. Now she knew what it really meant.

Patrick kept the conversation light and bantering, although his eyes, when they met hers, held a certain intensity. But a devilish mischief often lit his face. He was so much the natural charmer, the free and easy minstrel.

A future with him seemed unlikely, but that was how Corey wanted it to be. She didn't care to think again of a future with anyone. Not yet. Perhaps not for a very long time.

The drive back to Atlanta was accomplished mostly in silence, Corey feeling the contented laziness of a hazy Southern afternoon and fine meal, combined with little sleep this morning. But even with that almost lethargic sense of well-being, a certain expectant tension hummed in the warm, sultry evening air.

The Jeep was not designed for proximity—the gearshift divided the seats—but Patrick continued to cast glances her way, each one as intimate as a caress. She could almost feel the contact, and the languidness in her dissipated under his warm gaze. At each opportunity, at each stop sign and stop light, his hand went to her bare leg, his fingers drawing patterns that turned into brands. By the time they reached the outskirts of Atlanta, Corey's insides felt like the core of a seething volcano.

The top of the Jeep was down, and the warm air brushed through her hair. The moon had appeared in the early evening sky; it looked very fragile and transparent against the waning rays of a sun about to set. Corey suddenly felt very fragile and transparent herself . . . as if she were caught in a place she shouldn't be.

She moved closer to Patrick, her hand reaching over to settle on his lap, to regain some of the sense of belonging she'd felt earlier but that now seemed lost.

Patrick's hand wrapped around hers. "I'm playing tonight," he said. "Will you come with me?"

She wanted to. How much she wanted to, but the dragon of responsibility was still too strong in her. She had so much work to do, so much that she'd planned to do today, and now must do tomorrow. And despite the exhilaration of being with him, she was bone-deep exhausted.

Now was the time to cut this off before she got in too deep. Heck, she was already in too deep. It took all her will to decline.

Patrick didn't press. If he had, Corey knew she would have folded.

"Next week then," he said. "A real camping trip?"

"Don't you have to play?"

He grinned suddenly, that lighthearted sprite of a smile. "They can survive without me. They often do."

That offhand dismissal punctured some of her delight at being with him. She had lived with responsibility all her life, with a terrible sense of guilt if she ever felt she'd failed someone. Patrick apparently felt no commitment to anything. How could she feel this way, then?

But wasn't that what so attracted her? That he was her opposite?

She wasn't sure anymore. His attraction for her was so complete, not just a fantasy of last night. This afternoon had proved that. In some way she had become bound to him in a way she'd never been to anyone, bound by the spontaneous joy of being in his company, as well as the fireworks of their mutual physical attraction.

Mutual physical attraction, she scoffed at herself, was synonymous with lust. Plain and simple.

It was difficult for her to admit that, but she couldn't deny the craving inside her. Nor could she wish away the irresistible need to see him again.

"Two sleeping bags," he tempted.

She nodded even while every responsible bone in her body was saying no, no, no. "Yes."

She could almost see him sigh with relief, and she wondered at it. He must have women falling at his feet with that smile and those eyes and that disheveled hair and . . .

Douglas had been handsome too, but not in Patrick's careless, devil-may-care way. Perhaps Douglas's concern with appearances should have warned her, but for now it was enough to know Patrick was nothing at all like Douglas. He didn't have that hard-driving ambition that made her and her background a liability to him and his family. He didn't have a disapproving wealthy family or a political career.

"Yes, you will go, or yes, I need two sleeping bags?" Patrick asked as he stopped in front of her complex.

"Both," she replied.

"Done," he said with a small grin. "I'll call you tomorrow. In the meantime"—Patrick leaned over, his hand taking her chin and drawing her face closer—"I'll miss you." His lips told her how much, and Corey knew her own were saying the same. She felt dizzy with the longing inside her, with the way he energized all her senses.

Just the touch of his mouth created waves of sensation in her, and as the kiss deepened and his tongue reached out greedily, she met each exploration with eagerness, her own tongue joining in an exquisitely sensuous dance that sent her reeling. The usual fear of commitment, of betrayal, was gone, only a distant shadow in the waves of longing that made her body so susceptible to Patrick's every touch.

It was Patrick who, with a slight groan, moved away, not she, and he looked at her with eyes so full of tenderness that she reached out to him. Her hand went to the tiny laugh lines at the corner of his eyes, and trailed down to his mouth, lingering there as his lips changed from a wry expression to one of his quick, breath-stopping smiles.

"You must be a sorcerer," she said.

And you a sleeping beauty, he wanted to say. But he didn't. Instead he moved his lips to catch the tips of her fingers and nuzzle them. He heard her soft sigh. He hated to go, but at least he knew he had the next weekend. Time to fully awaken her, time to share so much.

"I'll take you in," he said.

Suddenly aware once more of the setting sun, she realized he must be late. "No. You have a way of prolonging good-byes."

Patrick grinned and said, "It's the company I keep." But he didn't protest.

Before he could get out of the driver's seat, Corey had opened her door and stood quickly. "I had a wonderful time."

"I'll call you," he said again.

"You don't have my phone number . . ."

But the words were lost in the roar of the Jeep as it pulled away.

6

Corey slept well Saturday night, her head full of dreams about Patrick Kelly. When she woke, refreshed, she felt as if she could conquer the world.

And she must do exactly that in the next few days, because she was going away that weekend, camping for the first time in her life.

She had dreamed of it as a child. Had dreamed of having a father and brothers, had dreamed of a clear lake and fragrant woods and toasted marshmallows like she'd seen on their small television.

But this would be much better. Now she had Patrick. That was better than brothers any day.

She felt incredibly alive and expectant. He *would* call. She knew it.

She trusted him.

She hadn't trusted a man in a very long time.

Corey had just plugged in the coffee maker when the doorbell rang, and she knew, before she answered it, that it would be Patrick.

He stood in the doorway, looking absurdly handsome with his hair still damp and his face so obviously recently shaved. And although he had played last night, his eyes were as bright and inquisitive as always.

Patrick held out his hand, and Corey noted the sack in it. "Fresh, hot doughnuts," he offered. "I wanted to wish you a happy morning." There was a hesitancy about him as though he doubted his welcome.

Pleasure flooded Corey, and she forgot she stood before him clad in only the oversize T-shirt she wore to bed, her long hair mussed and her face bare of makeup.

"You look beautiful," he said, and she felt exactly that way.

As if to prove it, he leaned over and kissed her, starting with the side of her eyes and moving languidly to her mouth. Corey was only partially aware that the bag he was holding had dropped to the floor, that the coffeepot had ceased perking. The world had narrowed to only the two feet in which they were standing.

She didn't even question the fact that she felt no caution, not even the slightest trepidation at what she now knew was inevitable.

Her arms went around him, her fingers tangling in the dark, thick hair. He smelled uncommonly good, his aftershave subtle and masculine and appealing.

The touch of his hands, their exploration, created millions of little pinpricks of fierce desire throughout her. She unconsciously moved further into his arms, her body molding to his with elemental need.

His hands moved along the T-shirt, caressing and kneading the curves underneath. Corey kept waiting for the warning signals to ring again, but they didn't. She felt his mouth move to the nape of her neck, his tongue tasting and teasing, and she felt his body tense and become hard against hers.

I've known him less than two days, and yet . . .

She felt she had known him forever. Part of her mind was woolly, blurring with the desire growing within her, with the pressure building inside. She could feel her breasts tighten, and nothing in her life had seemed so natural, so fine as their coming together.

Corey found herself taking his hand and leading him to her bedroom. They stopped just inside the door, the pressure of his hand on hers halting her movement. "Are you sure?"

"No," she admitted honestly.

And yet her body was responding with a yes. Her eyes met his. "Yes," she corrected.

He leaned back against the doorjamb.

"I'm trying to decipher that," he said slowly, a wry grin on his face.

But her lips dispelled his doubts. She stood on tiptoes and kissed him. Not merely kissed, but promised, pleaded.

Patrick wanted her in a way he'd never really wanted anything before in his life. He no longer doubted that they were meant to be together. The length of time they'd spent with each other had nothing to do with it. The happiest marriage he'd seen was that of an aunt and uncle who married on the day they met because his uncle was on his way to war. That example had taught Patrick to believe in sudden magic. Or was it simply fate?

When he had finished the gig last night, he'd gone home, and once more had been unable to sleep. He ought to be a zombie, but he felt just the opposite, as if he were the flame of a candle, radiating a fierce brightness. And all because of her.

She had taken joy in the same things he did, had looked in awe at his canyon, had let her hair fly in the wind, had met and joked with his friends. She was everything he had been waiting for and had stopped believing he would find. Someone who liked him for who he was, not who his family was, nor the wealth that went with it. She didn't know, and she didn't care.

Her eyes had a depth and sensitivity he longed to explore; her laughter was tentative, but it carried very real promise, a promise he wanted to fulfill.

And now both her eyes and mouth were inviting him to do something he very much wanted to do. His hand went to the small of her back, his fingers running up and down her spine, and he felt her tremble, just as he did. "Ah, Corey," he whispered. "I don't know what's best for you."

That statement removed any doubt from her mind. He cared about her, about what was best for her. She couldn't remember anyone ever putting her first.

She knew she wanted him, wanted him in so many ways. In less than three days, he'd softened her world, made it glow, and she suddenly realized it wasn't enchantment, but him. Patrick Kelly. Sunday morning reality. It was just as fine and heady and wonderful as Friday night sorcery.

"You're best for me," she whispered back, and meant it. This might not last, but she had to embrace it. If she didn't, she was afraid she would close herself up forever. Never to know the singing in her heart, the flight of that part of her soul that craved love. Never to feel the oh, so pleasurable tingling of her body.

She had to trust him. She *did* trust him. He wasn't another Douglas. She felt her fingers tighten as she finally released the remaining hurt and anger of the past.

His mouth came down and, in both a gentle and a fierce way, told her how important she was to him, important and vital and ... something more. She found herself melting into him, her tongue mating with his. She was barely aware of their movement to the bed, of his hands unbuttoning his shirt even as his lips, his mouth, continued to court her.

And then his hands joined in the courtship, caressing and loving her body. She sensed the restraint in him, as if he were giving her every chance to say no, and that only served to spur her trust and her own growing need. She felt her shirt being pulled up and off, and she wondered why she didn't feel embarrassed and apprehensive about her nakedness. Instead she reveled in it as she saw the admiration in his eyes before he leaned down and kissed one hard nipple and then the other. His hands cupped her breast as his lips went to the sensitive nape of her neck and traced a ring of fire with his tongue. She clung to him then, feeling the heated texture of his naked chest, the feathery tickling of his hair against her skin. It was an incredibly sensuous, arousing sensation.

She was as eager as he now to explore and taste. Her mouth went to his neck, her tongue playing games on his skin, one of her hands twisting in the dark, tousled hair, the other tracing lines on his back. She ran her fingers along the shoulder muscles, the slight indentation that ran down next to his spine, and she felt him shudder in reaction.

"Darlin' Corey," he whispered, his voice almost a sigh. She felt his manhood swell and pulsate, and she experienced a similar pulsating in the innermost part of her. It was as if part of her were reaching, reaching in some desperate quest, some unquenchable need. A greedy fire needing fuel. A terrible thirst demanding relief.

His hands moved down to her most private place, and she flinched for the briefest of moments. She felt him hesitate, and then the shadows left her, and she knew they were gone forever. Her lips moved from his neck and up to his mouth, meeting it with an unmistakable invitation, and his hands continued their gentle kneading, a kneading whose rhythm grew stronger and more feverish.

Their kiss turned searing, full of need, full of promise. She knew an ache so deep in her body, she wondered how it could ever be relieved. Her body strained toward his, arching to him, and she felt a momentary loss as his fingers left her and busied themselves at something else. Then they were back, and she was needier than ever because of his very brief absence.

His body pressed against hers, his manhood reaching instinctively for that soft, welcoming part of her. His muscles tensed as he obviously leashed himself to move slowly, ever so slowly, teasing her at first, making her want him with a craving that astounded her. He entered slowly, moving in and out slowly, preparing and tantalizing until she thought she would go mad with wanting.

His lips rained kisses on her eyes, cheeks, the corner of her mouth, her earlobes, until the throbbing inside her body felt like a jungleful of native drums. So much of her reached out for him, not only her body but her soul too, and she felt him respond. The tempo of his movement quickened, filling her with sensations that brought rapturous rushes of pleasure.

She felt a sudden wantonness, a glorious freedom, and she started to move with him, a sensuous waltz of two bodies in instinctive harmony . . .

The pleasure increased a dozenfold and then a hundredfold, until Corey didn't know whether she could accept any more, whether she would explode from the physical and emotional joy. No one could feel this good and live. No one could . . .

When she thought her body would disintegrate with the white hot heat and exquisitely sweet waves of pleasure, their bodies arched together and seemed to burst into a fireball of sensations. Convulsive spasms rocked both of them as they held tightly together.

"Dear God," she heard him whisper, and her mind echoed the awestruck words.

His arms cradled her as they fell gently back to earth,

their bodies still rippling from the climax. He held her as if she were the most precious jewel ever found, as if she were a treasure to be cherished, and she reveled in the feeling, in the tender yet very possessive hold.

She didn't know how long they stayed like that, their bodies connected in the most intimate of ways as an occasional spasm continued to echo the wonder they'd just shared.

They finally ate the doughnuts he'd brought and drank the coffee she'd made. It was very strong now, and the doughnuts were no longer warm from the bakery oven, but neither cared. They lay on the bed, Corey still wearing her T-shirt and Patrick clad only in a pair of worn jeans. She thought his chest quite magnificent with the sprinkling of black curly hair on the broad tanned surface. She particularly liked tickling it.

Even more, she enjoyed licking it after accidentally dropping some doughnut crumbs on it. She didn't even wonder at the newfound freedom she felt in doing it.

She wanted to talk about what had just happened, the storm that had rocked her universe, but she didn't know how. And she was afraid of saying things that might be premature. She was in love with him. She knew it, even though she'd spent only a few days with him, but she was terrified of saying it.

So she sighed instead.

Patrick introduced the subject. He moved slightly from his lazy position beside her and kissed her . . . a long, lingering "I don't ever want to leave" kiss. His hand then followed his mouth, moving over her facial features as if to memorize them.

And then he cocked his head slightly. "Have you ever been in love, Corey?"

Corey hesitated. She'd thought she had before. Once.

Long ago. A lifetime ago. But it had never been like this, powerful and fierce and tender. She wondered again at her own feelings toward Douglas Cavanaugh. She had been so young, so trusting. She had allowed him to make love to her, because she had thought herself in love, because he had said he loved her, and because she'd needed love so badly. And then she'd discovered it had all been a sham, that he'd used the carrot of love to get her into bed.

Several weeks later she'd realized she had never known her so-called fiancé at all. And she had been afraid to trust again. Until now.

"I thought so," she said slowly. "Once."

His hand moved to hers. "What happened?" he asked softly.

Corey had no immediate answer. How could she tell him about her past, and that terrible day when Douglas's father had seen them together in a restaurant? It was then that she realized Douglas was ashamed of her, had had no intentions of ever introducing her to his parents, much less marrying her.

Patrick's patient waiting prompted words she thought locked inside forever. "I was engaged . . . but his family disapproved. Douglas was to go into politics, and I . . . was termed a liability. A kid from the slums." With a juvenile record, but she couldn't say that. Perhaps she still didn't trust completely. Perhaps Patrick would leave too, if he knew that. She couldn't quite keep the bitterness from her voice. She'd had so many hopes once, had thought someone cared. A fairy tale that turned into a nightmare.

"And Douglas?" His voice was quiet.

"He . . . apparently agreed. I discovered what he really wanted had nothing to do with love . . . or marriage."

She closed her eyes against the memory of that last

evening with Douglas, when he'd explained the engagement was off, but that he still wanted to see her. He couldn't marry her, but he had some money of his own, a trust fund, and he could take care of her in another way.

She'd slapped him then, as hard as she could, and he'd glared at her, saying his father was right, she was just a guttersnipe. The words had hurt immensely. She was in her second year of college, on a scholarship, and she was working two jobs to support herself. She had been so proud of herself, and Douglas's comment had struck to the core of her.

Not long after, she changed her major from business to sociology because she felt a burning need to help those who were powerless, as she had once been powerless. So many times she still felt powerless, unable to stop the misery that she so often encountered. But sometimes, just sometimes, she made a difference, and that had been enough.

"What are you thinking?" Patrick's voice broke through the thoughts he'd triggered.

"How content I am with you," she said, throwing off the past and stretching lazily. She was surprised at how much she meant the words. She wanted to linger only in the present, to enjoy this man who apparently had none of the wealth and ambition that had once crushed a nineteen-year-old girl.

"Mmmmmm good," he said as he brought her against his chest and held her tightly as if intent on protecting her always.

Patrick left in early afternoon, saying merely he had some matters to attend to. She reluctantly agreed after a very long kiss and murmured promises about the next weekend. He would call before then, he said, and perhaps they could go out for dinner.

She simply nodded, knowing how delinquent she herself had been. She had an incredible amount of paperwork ahead of her, and she had to be in court tomorrow morning for Ray. Ray. Dear God. He had been in the back of her mind for the past few days, but she'd shoved him aside, and she didn't feel proud of herself for having done so. Even if she knew she had done everything she could.

So Corey tried again. She made some calls, but no one was available on Sunday. It was useless anyway, she told herself. She had already tried every contact, every possibility. At this point she could only urge the court to send him back home, which was anything but ideal. It would be only a matter of time before he got in trouble again, but perhaps in the meantime she could find some solution.

She wished she had more resources, but she was still new in Atlanta, where she'd moved not long after running into Douglas at the courthouse in Detroit. She'd needed a new start, and Ellen, who had moved south last year, helped arrange the job. Corey was still learning names and faces, still trying to find her way through the labyrinth of power and contacts here.

After a futile last effort she tried to concentrate on reports on home visits made last week, but she couldn't.

Concentrate, she told herself. Concentrate. But the only thing she could envision was a tall, black-haired man with laughing eyes.

Looks across a crowded room, across a crowded square. It *did* happen. It really did.

Patrick also spent the afternoon on the telephone . . . with more success.

He contacted a juvenile court clerk at home for the name of the assistant district attorney handling the Ray Gordon case. As luck would have it, the man was a personal friend, and Patrick soon learned that he intended to ask that, in lieu of another plan, the Gordon boy be sent to a state facility.

After two more calls he had arranged an interview for the boy at a boys' ranch in the state. There was no room, but the director would make room if the boy qualified—as a special favor to Patrick, who had roomed with the man's brother at law school.

When he was through, Patrick thought about calling Corey and telling her the good news, but he hesitated. It wasn't certain yet; the boy would still have to undergo testing and interviews first. And Patrick was very, very tired. He'd gone the last three days with only a couple of catnaps.

Besides, he thought sleepily, it would be a fine surprise for Corey tomorrow. Just as he closed his eyes, he suddenly realized it might be even more of a surprise than he'd thought.

He had not mentioned he worked in the DA's office. In the beginning it had been intentional. He had liked being accepted for what she thought he was, not because of his position or who and what his family was, just for Patrick Kelly, something he had been striving for so many years. And then, later, the subject never came up. There had never been a time to say, "Oh, by the way, I work for the district attorney."

They still had a lot to learn about each other, and it would be a magnificent adventure to do so. He drifted off to sleep, thinking quite contentedly about how pleased Corey would be on the morrow.

7

The first thing Corey saw when she entered the juvenile courtroom was the man she'd spent the night dreaming about.

He wasn't in a tux jacket and swim shorts, or casual slacks or tight jeans. He was dressed quite conservatively in a dark blue suit. And he looked just as at home here as he had playing the tuba on the courthouse steps and standing on a path at the Tallulah Falls Gorge. In fact, he looked suspiciously at home, as if he belonged here.

A terrible constriction balled in Corey's chest. She paused, unable to move as she stared blindly in his direction. Then the court bailiff entered, and she had no choice but to walk to a table beside Ray and his public defender, Sally Edenfield.

He was already seated next to the assistant district attorney handling the case. He winked at her and looked smug, as if he had accomplished some truly outstanding feat, but all Corey felt was a terrible sinking feeling in her stomach. He was an enemy sitting at the enemy's table. The feeling of betrayal settled like a boulder inside her, so painful she could barely stand it. She turned away and tried to focus all her attention on Ray, her hand moving to give him a reassuring pat. He looked scared as hell.

As she was, she thought. She looked at her hands and saw them tremble, but for a different reason.

Judge Caylor entered, and the case number and offense were read off.

Corey listened numbly. This was a sentencing hearing only; Ray, on the advice of his public defender, had already pleaded guilty. There had been no defense; Ray had been caught with several bags of crack.

Sally Edenfield put Ray on the stand to tell about his background. Ray's words were hesitant, and Corey understood why. She knew how hard it was to admit you were different from other kids, that there was no one who really cared for you.

"What are the names of the young men you worked for?" The sharp question came from the judge.

It brought no reply. Ray had only one thing left: pride. To give up his comrades, no matter how much trouble they had brought him, was something he would not do.

The judge continued asking questions: about Ray's home, his school, and ambitions. He received only stiff monosyllabic answers and an occasional mumbled "don' know."

Then Corey was called to the witness stand. Her eyes caught Patrick's, and he smiled, but now the smile hid things, and her stomach felt like lead. Why was he here, seated at the table with the assistant DA? She turned her gaze away from him and focused on Sally.

She presented the court with Ray's grades, superior ones until last year, when his brother was arrested and sent to prison. And that school record was earned, she testified, despite a very bad home environment.

"Your Honor," she concluded, "he only needs a chance, an environment where he can grow and live up to his potential. He has a great deal to offer. He just needs a special kind of help right now."

After she came out of the witness box, Judge Caylor looked over the reports in his hand, then at the boy, whose desperate eyes belied the bravado he tried to show. And finally he looked over at Patrick.

"We don't see you much in juvenile court, Mr. Kelly," he drawled. "I take it there's a reason you're here today."

Patrick bestowed that charming grin on him, and Corey's stomach tightened even more. "I've talked to Miss Adams about Ray," he said easily. "And I think I might have found a solution . . ."

Ten minutes later a stunned Corey listened while the juvenile court judge ordered interviews for Ray at the boys' ranch in a small southern Georgia town. It was one of the best, she knew, a place where hard work was expected, but where there was also counseling and caring. She had tried for weeks to arrange just this, and Patrick had apparently arranged it in a matter of hours.

Who was he?

Gratitude warred with distrust. He was obviously not just a musician. She leaned over behind Ray and whispered to Sally, "Who is he?"

The woman looked at her in surprise. "He's an assistant DA. His family's one of the oldest and most powerful in the county."

"But he . . ."

The woman's face clouded with confusion. "He what?"

"I thought he was a musician."

"Oh, that." Sally laughed. "I've seen him with that tuba. I think he plays just for fun."

As he played with her. Just for fun.

Piece by piece Corey's heart cracked as the knowledge seeped into her brain. She had thought she knew him, and she didn't know him at all. He'd held so much back. She'd thought they had shared the world during those three days, those three mystical days, but they had shared hers, not his.

A terrible sense of déjà vu fell over her. An assistant district attorney. A wealthy and powerful family. Everything she had learned to detest, to fear.

The enchantment had been a lie, the bright and shining Christmas present turning to coal. The Wizard of Oz was indeed a charlatan.

Corey knew she should feel grateful for the help he had given Ray, but she felt only a betrayal deeper than any she had ever felt. Because, she suddenly realized, her heart had been even more at risk.

The hearing was over, and Ray had turned to her, his eyes holding a glimmer of hope. "Thank you, Miss Adams," he said.

"You haven't gotten rid of me yet," she said. "I intend to keep track of you." She glanced around and noticed that Sally had approached Patrick and was talking to him.

Corey turned and fled.

Patrick saw her leave the courtroom, her back stiff, her chin held high.

He had also noted the shock and suspicion on her face when he had revealed his secret undertaking—and the deep hurt. He should have told her what he had been trying to do. And he had planned to before the court was in session, but she'd entered only moments before Ray's case had been called.

His elation at pulling off the impossible faded, and by the time he politely disengaged himself from Sally and went to look for Corey, she was gone.

Damn. He had an appointment with an attorney in an hour and a bail hearing this afternoon. He would have to wait until this evening to see her.

He knew her face would haunt him. He had wanted to

make her happy, had wanted so much to see that slow smile appear deep in her eyes and spread across her face. Instead he saw a profound disillusionment he didn't understand.

His surprise, his intended gift, had somehow gone very wrong.

Corey buried herself in work. She had four home visits that day, and she tried to concentrate on showing one young mother how to budget her food stamp coupons and prepare inexpensive but nutritious meals for her two young children. She arranged for an elderly client to get Meals on Wheels and took another to a grocery store to pick up staples for an empty cupboard.

But nothing could keep her thoughts from what had transpired that morning. Something real had been accomplished for Ray. Something worthwhile.

Because of Patrick.

But he had lied.

Or had he? Corey tried to recall every one of their conversations. She had always assumed that he was simply a musician and had never inquired further. There had been so many other things to talk about.

Emotions, turbulent and unbridled, rocketed around inside her. She had been so full of joy, so swept away by feelings she'd never thought she'd have, that the sudden splash of reality, the terrible possibility of history repeating itself, was devastating.

She hadn't been good enough for Douglas Cavanaugh III. And Patrick Kelly came from the same background, the same type of family. The rejection she had felt years ago, added to so much rejection she'd felt as a child, had nearly destroyed her then; she didn't know if she could survive it again.

She didn't return to her office but called in, and was

given a number of messages from Patrick. Her mind was still too divided, her emotions too raw, the sense of betrayal too strong for her to return them.

Corey knew that he would be waiting for her, sitting on the step just as he had before, and she also knew she wasn't ready to see him. She had to get her mind, her heart, in order first. She was much too vulnerable.

How could one man so quickly become an integral part of her soul, especially as guarded as hers had been?

A district attorney! How could she not have known that? But it really was not strange, she realized, given the brief time she had been here. She was still trying to put names and faces together in her own department. And Ray's case was the first one that had brought her in contact with the DA's office.

She tried to fit the two images of Patrick together: the musician she'd thought he was, the prosecutor she now knew him to be. She wasn't particularly fond of prosecutors; too often they were rigid, their vision tunneled in one direction. Her personal experiences had not endeared them to her.

Her laughing, green-eyed Patrick. Patrick, who knew the best barbecue and the best waterfall and the most splendid magic.

Her eyes filling with tears, Corey headed toward a movie theater. She didn't care what was showing. She just wanted to hide for a while.

Maybe even forever.

Corey watched the flickering images on the screen, absorbing none of them.

She had never believed herself a coward before, not been allowed that luxury. She had been a fighter all her life. At least she thought she had been.

Now she wondered.

Had she been running ever since Douglas? Running from involvement?

Had she been filling her own life, instead, with other people's problems? It was so much easier to advise someone else what to do, rather than risk yourself.

She wasn't sure how long she stayed in the theater before she left. She knew only that she had to confront her own devils.

She owed him.

She owed herself.

Corey drove slowly to her apartment, and saw his Jeep in the parking lot. Her stomach tightened again.

He was on the top step. A magazine was beside him, but he wasn't reading. The usual smile was gone, and he turned his eyes on her. When she hesitated halfway up, he unfolded himself and held out a hand to her.

Corey wanted it more than she'd ever wanted anything in her life. But was it real?

He slowly dropped his hand and gave her a lopsided grin, so full of uncertainty that she moved into his arms. As if she had no choice. As if she were a piece of metal pulled to a magnet.

His hands buried themselves in her long hair; his mouth kissed hers with an urgency she remembered only too well. But there was a certain desperation about it, too, as if he were afraid she would run away.

"Oh, Corey," he whispered. "What went wrong?"

She closed her eyes and simply felt the comfort of being back in his arms, the joy, the rightness of it. Then his lips were pressed against hers once more. Corey felt a tremor rock his body as his tongue plunged into her mouth, seeking possession. She stiffened, remembering the last, humiliating kiss Douglas had given her, and only slowly did she relax as she realized this one was different.

This kiss had a sweetness despite the roughness of need. This kiss was asking, not demanding.

She opened her mouth wide to him, her fear fading as her eyes opened and locked with his. Emotions passed between them as if they were words.

I thought I'd lost you.

I'm afraid.

Why?

She didn't have an answer for that. Not yet.

He slowly released her lips and took her hand in his. "I think we'd better go inside before we're both arrested on morals charges."

That made her grin. "You're a district attorney. Surely you could talk yourself out of the charges."

"I would rather talk you into something," he said, his eyes searching, asking.

"I should thank you," she said after a pause. "For Ray."

"Not necessary," he replied. "But I would like to know why you ran away."

She started to say she hadn't. But just as she'd never thought herself a coward, neither had she believed herself a liar.

"I suddenly felt I didn't know you at all," she explained.

"I haven't changed."

"But you never told me . . ." She hesitated, and he used that opportunity to take her keys and usher her inside.

"I didn't realize until Sunday night that I hadn't told you about my work," he said. "It just never came up . . . with everything else going on."

"But why didn't you tell me what you were doing for Ray?"

"I didn't know whether I could help him or not," he

replied. "I didn't want to get your hopes up. I could tell how important it was to you."

"How did you manage it?"

He shrugged. "A college friend."

"The good old boy network," she said, suddenly bitter. She pulled away from him, remembering everything Sally Edenfield had told her. A wealthy family. Connections. Ambitions. She felt like crying. She wanted Patrick the musician back.

"Corey?" His voice held puzzlement.

She didn't look at him, couldn't look at him. She was afraid she would fly back in his arms if she did. And she wouldn't do that. She wouldn't set herself up for a fall again. This one would be too far.

Looks across a crowded room. She had been right not to believe in them. She felt the tears welling up behind her eyes, and she angrily pushed them back, forcing herself to move to the kitchen. "A drink?" she asked brightly. Too brightly.

"What's wrong, Corey?" His voice was soft, but the tone of desperation was back. "Talk to me, dammit."

Everything was wrong. They were strangers. They had always been strangers. They would always *be* strangers. She the product of the slums, a place he couldn't even imagine, and he the scion of a wealthy Southern family. She had never really trusted the law, and he made it his career. He laughed at life because it had always been so good to him, and she took it so seriously because even survival had been difficult.

"Talk to me, Corey," he commanded again, and all the laughter had gone from his voice.

She lifted her eyes to his, making sure they were guarded. She couldn't let the enchantment cloud her mind. "I am talking to you," she said, but she knew she wasn't. She'd uttered only words, meaningless words. She saw from the tightening of his lips that he understood.

"Don't do this, Corey," he said, moving toward her. She flinched and stepped away. "Why?"

"Everything," she said, "has gone too fast. And we're just . . . too . . . different."

"How?"

"Sally Edenfield said your family was wealthy."

He shrugged, not understanding. "Not particularly so."

"I grew up poor, in a housing project. I never knew who my father was, and my mother was an alcoholic," she said tightly, with shame and defiance. "I grew up just like Ray," she said, as if that explained everything. "I had to struggle to survive, just like him. I even stole sometimes."

Patrick reached out to hold her, his eyes clouding with some of the pain he felt in her, but once again she pulled away, leaving him empty-handed, and growing more and more empty-hearted.

Her "confession" was just what he had suspected, and it made him care even more about her. Her innate strength, that hard core of courage, set her apart and attracted him as no other woman ever had.

His hand reached out to touch her long hair, and she stepped back. "You're a prosecutor."

"And that's so very bad? Why?" he said. "Why is that so bad?"

"I went out with a musician," she said stubbornly.

"A man with horns on his hat and swimming trunks," he replied slowly. "Is that what you want? Because if you do, I'll wear them every day."

Her eyes suddenly filled with tears. "I fell in love with *him*," she said, unable to hold back the words.

"But not the one in the courtroom today?"

"He's a stranger," she replied.

"And you won't give him a chance?"

"There is no chance for us," she told him bitterly. "Your family . . ."

"My family? What do they have to do—" And then he remembered. The engagement. *His family disapproved . . . I was termed a liability.*

He moved toward her, and unexpectedly her guard fell and she came into his arms, her head leaning against his heart, his head against the dark silkiness of her hair. He held her tightly against him, afraid even to move a muscle. She felt so good there. Dear God, she belonged there. He closed his eyes, wanting to prolong the moment, to lock her to him. How could someone steal his heart in such a short time? But she had. He moved his head slightly, his lips touching her forehead.

She broke away, her eyes huge and wet and hurting. "Please go," she whispered. "If you care for me at all, please go."

"Will that prove I care?" he asked after a long pause. "Is that what I have to do?"

She stood as still as a statue. Unbending. That strength again. But now he hated it. He leaned down and kissed her lightly, his lips moving over hers carefully, with a restraint that practically killed him. "Then I will," he said, and he turned around and left, closing the door gently behind him.

Corey stared at it, aghast at the terrible emptiness that flooded her. This was what she wanted.

Wasn't it?

8

Patrick suffered through the next few days. He had, in effect, been hoisted with his own sword.

He had wished to be wanted for himself, not for his family, and now he was being judged in exactly the opposite way.

He had been sensitive about his family ever since his brother died. Thirteen years older, Derek junior had been the perfect son. A football hero. An excellent student who joined ROTC in college because a buddy did, and then went to Vietnam for the same reason.

Teachers and coaches remembered Derek as a bright and shining light and expected the same from Patrick. Patrick, who had nearly worshiped his brother, felt he could never compete, be that good, be that perfect, so he went in other directions, tried to develop altogether different talents.

All the time he'd felt deep inside that he was letting people down, that he was disappointing his father, though his father had, in fact, been supportive of most of his endeavors. But Patrick had made a cross of his insecurity and disguised it with a devil-may-care attitude.

He had long ago stopped fighting the image of his brother, but he hadn't known until now that remnants of his insecurity still existed.

And so he understood Corey, far better than she could ever know.

Suddenly a plan took hold. His father was out of town on a business trip, but would be back Friday. Patrick called his mother and said he would be over there for dinner Friday night, that he needed their help.

Ray had a new hero.

Corey discovered that when she visited the boy five days after the sentencing hearing, one week before he would be going to the boys' ranch.

Ray couldn't stop talking about Patrick Kelly, who had come by several times to see him. If Ray did well, Mr. Kelly had promised, he would send him to college.

College. Ray said the word with awe. He had never thought such a thing possible. Neither had Corey when she had been his age. It had taken a helping hand to steer her toward a goal.

She was grateful to Patrick, but it didn't change anything. It didn't narrow the gulf between them.

Not that it apparently mattered to Patrick. He had not called, had not tried to see her again. Every time she went home, she half expected to see the Jeep and Ole Joe, but she never did. And each time she saw the empty place where he usually parked, her heart sank lower, even as she tried to tell herself it was for the best. She should be grateful to him. He was doing what she'd asked.

She hated him for it.

Five whole days had passed since that disastrous Monday, and as she drove home, she thought about the weekend with dread. She had an enormous amount of work to do, but she hadn't been able to concentrate in days, staring aimlessly at pieces of paper, her usually decisive mind incredibly indecisive. How could she advise or guide other people on how to run their lives when she was so abysmally managing her own?

She pulled into her parking lot and noticed a Mercedes. It stood out in a parking lot usually filled with compact cars. A neighbor must have visitors, she thought abstractedly, not really caring, since the Jeep wasn't there.

Corey made her way up the stairs. A man was seated on the third step from the top, a magazine in hand. *The Lawyer*, it said. Her eyes hesitated to make direct contact with the face.

Her heartbeat speeded until her mind registered the impeccably tailored gray suit, so unlike the clothes usually worn by Patrick. The body was different too, stouter.

Her eyes moved upward to the face. It was an older version of Patrick's. The same wry smile appeared on it as the man slowly straightened up and stood.

Corey's eyes continued to move upward to the top step. A woman, dressed in a tailored pants suit with a dark brown scarf around her neck, sat there. Her dark auburn hair was cut short and feathered around a pleasing face. Her most distinctive feature, vivid green eyes, fastened on Corey with warmth and curiosity.

Standing above her was Patrick with a small uncertain twist to his lips that was part smile, part question. There was also a heart-wrenching wariness in his eyes, as well as determination. Corey's heartbeat accelerated again.

The older man grinned at her and stuck out his hand. Corey automatically shook it.

"I'm Derek Kelly, and this is my wife, Leslie. Our son says we must meet your approval," he rumbled in a deep voice. "Since we've been waiting for this day for a very long time, we hope we stand up to inspection."

There was a warmth and amusement in his tone that startled her. She looked at the woman, and saw the vivid green eyes twinkle just as Patrick's did. She couldn't help liking her immediately.

Befuddled, she looked up at Patrick. His grin seemed to say, "Behold the ogres." She wanted to hit him. She wanted to kiss him. She wanted to ... She suddenly realized Derek Kelly was speaking to her, and she focused her attention on him.

". . . hoping you would go to dinner with us," he finished saying.

She looked down at her work clothes, and thought about her apartment. It was a disaster. Housekeeping had not been a priority during the past few days.

"Please," the woman said, her voice vibrant and warm and completely impossible to say no to. Corey looked accusingly up at Patrick, but saw absolutely no shame there.

She nodded slowly. "I ... need to change."

The woman's eyes softened at the hesitancy in Corey's voice. "Of course. We'll wait downstairs. But don't go to much trouble." She looked down at her own informal clothes.

Corey smiled suddenly, happiness filling her. "A moment ... or maybe five," she amended.

She moved quickly up the stairs, barely hearing the beginning of an exchange.

"She means it, Dad."

"Five?" she heard the older Kelly say skeptically as she opened the door and dashed for the bedroom.

As she changed to a fresh skirt and blouse, she felt the old fear, the old uncertainty, the vulnerability. She had done the right thing in sending Patrick away. Hadn't she?

Except he wouldn't stay away. And she was so glad he wouldn't.

She dabbed on some lipstick, wondering why she was doing this.

Because she didn't want to be rude, to embarrass Patrick in front of his parents.

An excuse!

Because I want to. Dear God, how much I want it. She was shaking inside, she wanted it so much.

What if history repeated itself? They didn't know anything about her. Yet.

Corey tried to pull on the mask she had perfected long ago, that kept her from being hurt, but it didn't work. Her eyes looked scared, scared and hopeful. *Be careful, Corey.* Don't set yourself up for a fall, she warned herself as she gave her hair one last stroke with a brush.

She went out the door and found Patrick waiting alone. She saw some of her own uncertainty in the stiff way he was standing. He leaned over, his lips brushing her forehead. "Thank you for coming."

"You didn't give me much choice," she said, but the words lost their sting in the breathless way she said them.

He agreed. "I was afraid you would say no. You could have said no." His hand caught hers, and her blood thrummed through her, warm and pulsing. "You're beautiful."

She caught her lip between her teeth. She was so ridiculously happy to see him. It was as if she had been living in the dark for the last week, and now the light was back.

"God, I missed you," he said. "I tried to stay away, but I couldn't, so I decided to dismiss your main objection."

"What if they don't—"

"They can't help liking you. And you'll like them, even if they are a little stuffy at times," he said with twinkling eyes, as if being stuffy were a charming idiosyncrasy.

Corey thought about them sitting on the steps, about his father's smile, and didn't consider them stuffy at all. But then they didn't know anything about her, either.

Before she could lose her courage, Patrick was pulling her down the stairs and settling her in the Mercedes.

Twenty minutes later she was feeling like Dorothy in Oz again. She and the Kellys were seated at a table in a charming French restaurant located in a suburban bank building. They had been greeted like family. At least that was familiar. Everyplace she went with Patrick, he seemed to belong immediately.

The warmth of the candlelight, a glass of good wine, and Patrick's smile made her glow inside. She was surprised at how at ease she felt. When Patrick's hand reached over and covered hers, she saw Leslie Kelly smile. She wondered whether that smile would last when they knew everything about her.

She quickly found out.

After they ordered, Derek Kelly cleared his throat as if he were about to make an opening argument. "I don't like to beat around the bush," he said. Corey felt her sense of well-being fade.

"My son says he loves you, and that you're afraid for some damn fool reason we won't approve. If you love him, I don't know why it matters whether we approve or not. We've been waiting a long time for him to get serious about a woman. In fact, we've damned well despaired of it." He glowered at Patrick, who merely shrugged helplessly at her.

His father turned his attention back to Corey, his blue eyes probing hers. "But I do know my son, and when he sets his mind on something, the angels in heaven couldn't change it." There was a very wry twist to his mouth. "Believe me, young lady."

Corey almost giggled at the frustrated expression on his face and the amused one on his wife's. She bit her lip instead.

"Now, he wants you, and from the way you look at

him, you want him, and that's good enough for Leslie and me."

"But—" Corey started.

He raised his eyebrows exactly the way Patrick did. "But?"

"We've only known each other a few days, and—"

"Poppycock. I knew Leslie one week before I asked her to marry me, my brother knew his wife one day before he married her. We Kellys know what we want. I was a tad slow. My son seems to be a bit slower." Again he glared at Patrick.

The words made Corey's head swim. She tried to make sense of them. "But . . . you don't know anything about me," she tried again.

"Patrick told us a little. You've got grit. Good for the bloodline. Got tolerance too if you put up with that damnable tuba."

"The bane of Dad's existence," Patrick quipped.

"Damn right. Probably why he does it," the elder Kelly said. "*You* try to write a brief on a bank merger with the blasted oomph, oomph, oomph in the background, and that was after he learned to play the infernal thing."

"Joe," Patrick corrected gently.

His father looked at him balefully.

Leslie was shaking her head, her eyes alight with humor. "They do this all the time. Do you think you could stand it?"

Then all three pairs of eyes were on her, waiting for an answer.

Corey was suffused with warmth, with a wonderful sense of belonging. She wasn't an outsider here; she was included in what was apparently a family joke. She remembered the cold, brittle face of Douglas Cavanaugh's father, the icy politeness that was more devastating than insults. She swallowed, looking for insincerity on the faces around her—and saw none.

She turned her gaze to Patrick's eyes and watched them shine with his love for her.

He loved her. He loved her enough to arrange this, knowing she might refuse to go, that it might all backfire. He loved her enough to understand her insecurity and make it right in some way. Who else in the world would show up with his family on her stairs?

Corey swallowed. He understood her better than she understood herself.

"Yes," she finally answered.

"Good. That's settled," his father said with much satisfaction. He took a long sip of wine. "Qualifying to be a grandfather is damned trying business." He winked at Patrick, who grinned back.

The rest of dinner was a blur to Corey. She was barely aware of what she ate and didn't know whether it was good or not. She was aware only of Patrick, whose laughing green eyes seemed to glaze with something other than amusement, and she was astounded that she was not embarrassed.

A folksinger came to their table, almost as if on cue, and Corey didn't doubt that Patrick's father had planned it. She now knew where Patrick got his single-minded determination, as well as his charm. Patrick requested "Black Is the Color of My True Love's Hair," and he held her hand tightly as the singer strummed the poignant strains on the guitar and sang the words in a sweet, bell clear voice.

The enchantment was back, but now there was reality too, Corey thought as she pressed Patrick's fingers. He was real. His touch was real. His promise was real.

She looked at him and smiled, and for the first time she felt free.

Free to love, free to soar with him, for he would teach her how.

"Somehow I think we're superfluous here," she heard a deep voice drawl beside her. Chairs were scraped back and farewells said, and then there was just the two of them.

In the whole world there was just the two of them.

Corey would never know how or when they arrived home that night. She was too lost in dazed happiness.

They entered the apartment locked in each other's arms and went straight to the bedroom.

"God, I missed you," he said.

"I kept looking for you on the stairs," she admitted.

"I wanted to wait until I could bring Mom and Dad," he said. "Unfortunately he's been in Washington on a case."

She giggled. "It was a shock seeing an older version of you."

Patrick chuckled and nibbled on her ear. "I was afraid you might run for your life, confronted with two of us."

"Mmmm," she purred as his lips slipped down to her neck. "You led me to believe he didn't approve of you," she accused gently as she started unbuttoning his shirt.

"He didn't for a while. I was wandering, not knowing exactly what I wanted. And he didn't have a lot of patience with that." He was quiet for several minutes. "We had a long talk last night. For the first time. Part of me had always thought I should be like my brother, for my father's sake. He was rather horrified I ever believed that, and even guilty that he hadn't understood it." His hand tightened on hers. "He told me he was 'damned proud' that I had gone with the DA's office, that I was doing something I thought important. It was a talk long overdue, and we had it all because of you, my love. One more thing to thank you for." His voice was rough with emotion.

"I like him and your mother."

"They like you."

"Because I bring grit to the bloodline," she said with a wince.

Patrick chuckled again. Corey loved the sound of it and the way it made the hair on his now bare chest ruffle as if a breeze had suddenly touched it. "That might be *his* reason."

"And yours?" she whispered next to his ear just before she started nibbling on it.

"Ah," he mumbled. "I think this is show instead of tell time."

He stopped licking her neck, she stopped nibbling his ear, and their lips finally met after too long an absence. The chore of reacquainting one another, Corey thought, was exquisitely delightful.

They moved apart only to undress each other, then he pulled her close to him, and their lips met and melded once more. She suddenly found herself on top of him on the bed, her body fitting perfectly with his as she felt his manhood harden and grow beneath her.

Waves of hunger, of raw desire, rocked her. She parted her legs, allowing him to swell in the cup of her femininity. All the time her mouth loved him, their tongues caught in a wild sensuous courtship of their own. The pressure built in her, as she knew it was building in him and felt it in the tautness of his muscles. She instinctively knew each place to touch, each seductive movement. Never in her wildest dreams would she have believed herself capable of this, never would she have thought that making love could be a beautiful and giving thing.

But that was what it was now. She wanted to give him pleasure, she wanted to give him herself, fully and completely, to share her soul, with nothing held back. She moved slowly on top of him, the friction between them so incredibly sweet, so incredibly painful, until she thought she would burst from it. And then he slid inside her, and his hands guided her upward and his manhood drove deep into her. They moved together in such accord and understanding and raw pleasure that Corey wondered how she could tolerate such blinding, dazzling rapture.

She looked down at him, at the face that had become a part of her, and he smiled with such breathtaking wonder, his expression so clearly full of love for her, that the pleasure inside her multiplied and spread to every part of her. She leaned down and kissed him, her tenderness a counterpoint to the urgent movement of their bodies. Each sensation intensified, until the final magnificent combustion that sent spasms rampaging through their bodies.

Corey collapsed on his damp body, and his arms went around her. "I love you," he whispered, his voice raspy with emotion.

She knew that he did. The knowledge was now strong inside her. And she wasn't afraid anymore. She didn't think she would ever be afraid again.

9

Corey woke Sunday morning feeling a lazy, hazy contentment. A masculine arm lay possessively across her own,
and she kept still, relishing the feel of it.

She remembered last night, every minute of it, every
exploratory delight, every tender touch, and she felt as if
the sun had come out in her soul and sprayed her whole
body with its bright, life-giving rays. She was radiant with
them.

Her hand reached out and touched his face, gently so
as not to wake him. His jaw was feathered with newborn
whiskers, and long, dark lashes shielded eyes that had
been misted with passion last night.

She was in love. So impossibly, happily, uncontrollably
in love. She couldn't resist moving her hand, tracing the
lines of his chest muscles, catching little tufts of hair, not
realizing he was awake until his body started tensing in
what was now a familiar way.

"You're awake," she accused.

"Umm," he rumbled, his hand catching her wandering
one. "I was just lying here, thinking how wonderful you
feel."

"I was thinking the same thing," she agreed lazily,
amazed at her ease in saying so, but he always had that
effect on her.

He brought her hand to his mouth and started nibbling on her fingers one at a time. "You taste good too."

She started nibbling on his chest. "You do too."

His body went rigid, and he clasped her to him. Once more they began that exquisite climb to ecstasy.

The sun was already high up in the sky before Corey moved away from the warmth of his body. "Coffee?" she asked.

He found her hand and held it, not wanting to lose her closeness. "I'll go with you."

"No. You stay here," she ordered. There was such a flare of delight in her face, he couldn't refuse.

Patrick moved lazily in the bed, stretching. He felt utterly content, although he knew there were things that must be discussed, ghosts that must be confronted before things could be truly right between them.

He dozed, waking when he heard the soft padding of her feet. Corey appeared, holding a tray laden with coffee cups, glasses of orange juice, toast covered with raspberry jam, and an orange.

"Breakfast in bed," she announced gleefully, and Patrick had to smile. She sounded like a child finally accomplishing a lifelong dream. She handed the tray to Patrick, then joined him on the bed.

He attacked the toast, suddenly realizing how hungry he was. He'd eaten little last night, and he didn't think she had done much better. He watched as Corey cut the orange into wedges and then plop one into his mouth.

She licked the juice from his lips, and their gazes met, love passing between them so strongly that they didn't need words. He put the tray down on the floor, and sitting halfway up in bed, took her back in his arms, positioning her so she looked up at him.

"We have to talk, Corey," he said.

She knew he was right. There were questions to be answered, information to be shared. They had both learned how damaging silence could be. They had reached a place last night where there was no going back, and she knew there were things he deserved to know about her. And she wanted to know everything about him.

Patrick held her tight, his fingers running along her arms. "After that first night," he said slowly, "I felt as if I had known you forever, that somehow destiny had placed you in that crowd for me, just for me."

He put his fingers over her mouth as she started to speak. "I think it was because of that that I didn't tell you much about myself. I just felt you *knew*, like I felt I knew you." He smiled. "Presumptuous of me, wasn't it?"

The smile slowly disappeared. "It wasn't until Monday that I realized how little we did know about each other. I knew the important things about you—the way you care about people, the way you react to things, the way you make me feel—but I didn't know the twists and turns that touched you, and I should have learned before . . . before assuming so much."

He stopped and kissed her forehead. "You . . . didn't like my being a district attorney. Why?"

Corey clutched his hand as if it were a lifeline. And it was a lifeline of trust and love and understanding he was holding out to her. "I told you about Douglas. I didn't tell you . . . I had a juvenile record that he knew about. I suppose he made me feel no one would want a wife with a . . . a record, especially someone . . . with your background."

He was silent for a moment, then he said, "Bastard. You were just a kid."

"When I was first arrested, I was so scared, so darned scared. I was twelve, not much younger than Ray, and my mother had disappeared for four days. I was hungry. I didn't know what else to do. She always told me that if I said anything about her disappearances, I would be sent to jail. When I was arrested, I was so ashamed, and no one seemed to care. Not the police, not the prosecutor. He made me feel so ... worthless." Her eyes went to him then.

"What happened?"

"I was lucky. I got a probation officer who cared, and there weren't many of them. She took me under her wing and was someone I could call when my mom disappeared. She even tutored me and helped me get a scholarship."

"Where is she now?"

"She was killed last year in one of the projects. It was one of the reasons I wanted to leave Detroit."

"Your mother?"

"She died a couple of years ago. At least officially. I think she really died long before that."

"There are others who care, you know," he said.

She knew he was right. She remembered how Ray's eyes had lit when he spoke of Patrick. In a world where there were so few who cared, fate was kind enough to give her a man who did.

"I love you," she said.

His green eyes gleamed with satisfaction. "I thought you would never admit it."

"Admit it?"

"Darlin' Corey, we've been in love since we first saw each other."

"Being in love and loving are two different things," she said primly, but laughter was in her eyes.

"Speak for yourself," he said as he started nuzzling her again.

Corey wanted to participate, but there was still too much to know, to understand.

"Why did you become a prosecutor? It seems so ..."

"Stuffy?"

"No. It just doesn't seem ... to go along with being a musician and ..."

"We all have our demons, Corey, although I suspect mine, unlike yours, have been of my own making."

He talked about his brother for a while, then fell silent for a moment. "I thought everyone expected me to take his place in some way. It took me years to discover it was a load I put on myself. But I believed it then, and I fought against it. I didn't want to be a substitute. I loved my brother, but I wasn't him, and I never could be. So I did everything I could think of to make the difference obvious. I joined the band instead of playing football, and I rejected law school. I majored in music instead. I thought my father was disappointed, but he was more disappointed in my lack of commitment than in anything else. You met him, and thank God he's the kind of man who believes in letting go. He could hope, but he didn't push.

"The crazy thing is," he continued, "that though I enjoyed music, it really wasn't what I wanted to do for a lifetime. I loved it because it was fun and it relieved my frustrations." He hesitated. "But for some damn reason, I could never really escape the idea of becoming a lawyer. I liked the mental gymnastics, the challenge, and I liked the idea of being able to make a difference. But I didn't like corporate law, which is my father's specialty. I like people, I wanted to work with people." He shrugged. "I was offered a job with the DA's office and was given some domestic violence cases. It became a specialty, and it puts me in a position where sometimes I can prevent tragedies. But I need the music, too, especially when ..."

His voice trailed off, but she knew him well enough to guess what he didn't say. *When something goes wrong.*

She thought it probably rarely did. Patrick attacked everything in life with an enthusiasm that defied failure. She was a prime example, she thought, so darn grateful for that unflagging determination of his.

There was still so much she didn't know, and yet she'd always sensed the essence of Patrick Kelly, just as he had said he'd grasped the important things about her right from the start.

They had never really been strangers, she realized now. The moment their glances had met on the courthouse grounds, they had become irrevocably connected.

Destiny, Patrick had called it.

Perhaps, but she would always think of it as magic. She suspected it would always feel like magic.

Especially if every moment was like this one.

Her hand went up to his face, feeling the scratchiness of his beard, and she thought how much she would like to awake to it every morning.

As though he read her mind, he grinned and said, "Will you marry me?"

"Does Ole Joe come along with you?"

"Depends," he said cautiously.

"Unless he does, the answer is no." She giggled, watching the anxiety and confusion on his face change to delight and understanding.

"Second fiddle to a tuba," he exclaimed ruefully. "In that case—"

"I love you," Corey said, smothering him with kisses. They may not be strangers any longer, but there still was a lot of uncharted territory.

And she knew that she was going to relish every exploratory moment.

FANFARE

On Sale in June

RAVISHED

☐ 29316-8 $4.99/5.99 in Canada
by Amanda Quick
<u>New York Times</u> bestselling author

*Sweeping from a cozy seaside village to glittering London, this enthralling
tale of a thoroughly mismatched couple poised to discover the rapture of
love is Amanda Quick at her finest.*

THE PRINCESS

☐ 29836-4 $5.99
by Celia Brayfield

*He is His Royal Highness, the Prince Richard, and wayward son of the
House of Windsor. He has known many women, but only three understand him, and only one holds the key to unlock the mysteries of his heart.*

SOMETHING BLUE

☐ 29814-3 $5.99/6.99 in Canada
by Ann Hood

Author of SOMEWHERE OFF THE COAST OF MAINE
*"An engaging, warmly old-fashioned story of the perils and endurance of
romance, work, and friendship."* -- <u>The Washington Post</u>

SOUTHERN NIGHTS

☐ 29815-1 $4.99/5.99 in Canada
**by Sandra Chastain,
Helen Mittermeyer, and Patricia Potter**

*Sultry, caressing, magnolia-scented breezes. . .sudden, fierce thunder-
storms. . .nights of beauty and enchantment. In three original novellas,
favorite LOVESWEPT authors present the many faces of summer and
unexpected love.*

%   %   %

Look for these books at your bookstore or use this page to order.

☐ Please send me the books I have checked above. I am enclosing $_____ (add $2.50 to cover
postage and handling). Send check or money order, no cash or C. O. D.'s please.

Mr./ Ms. _____

Address _____

City/ State/ Zip _____

Send order to: Bantam Books, Dept. FN, 2451 S. Wolf Rd., Des Plaines, IL 60018
Allow four to six weeks for delivery.

Prices and availability subject to change without notice.   FN 52 7/92

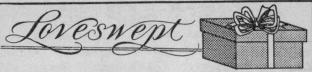

THE LATEST IN BOOKS AND AUDIO CASSETTES